PRAISE FOR

Cake on a Hot Tin Roof

"A fast-paced delightful amateur-sleuth tale starring a feisty independent pastry chef . . . *Cake on a Hot Tin Roof* is an interesting whodunit."   —*The Mystery Gazette*

"The setting and atmosphere in *Cake on a Hot Tin Roof* are very appealing . . . Rita is a very appealing character with loads of energy and a lot to deal with . . . All done with aplomb."   —*The Mystery Reader*

A Sheetcake Named Desire

"A tasty treat for mystery lovers, combining all the right ingredients in a perfectly prepared story that's sure to satisfy."
—B. B. Haywood, national bestselling author
of *Town in a Wild Moose Chase*

"A decadent new series with a Big Easy attitude."
—Paige Shelton, national bestselling author of *A Killer Maize*

"A mouthwatering new series! Brady's writing is smooth as fondant, rich as buttercream—the pastry shop's delectable confections are just icing on the cake for the appealing characters and intriguing mystery."
—Sheila Connolly, national bestselling author of *Sour Apples*

"Jacklyn Brady whips up a delectable mystery layered with great characters and sprinkled with clever plot twists."
—Hannah Reed, author of the Queen Bee Mysteries

Berkley Prime Crime titles by Jacklyn Brady

A SHEETCAKE NAMED DESIRE
CAKE ON A HOT TIN ROOF
ARSENIC AND OLD CAKE

Arsenic and Old Cake

Jacklyn Brady

BERKLEY PRIME CRIME, NEW YORK

MYS
F
BRA

THE BERKLEY PUBLISHING GROUP
Published by the Penguin Group
Penguin Group (USA) Inc.
375 Hudson Street, New York, New York 10014, USA

Penguin Group (Canada), 90 Eglinton Avenue East, Suite 700, Toronto, Ontario M4P 2Y3, Canada
(a division of Pearson Penguin Canada Inc.) • Penguin Books Ltd., 80 Strand, London WC2R 0RL,
England • Penguin Group Ireland, 25 St. Stephen's Green, Dublin 2, Ireland (a division of Penguin
Books Ltd.) • Penguin Group (Australia), 250 Camberwell Road, Camberwell, Victoria 3124, Australia
(a division of Pearson Australia Group Pty. Ltd.) • Penguin Books India Pvt. Ltd., 11 Community
Centre, Panchsheel Park, New Delhi—110 017, India • Penguin Group (NZ), 67 Apollo Drive,
Rosedale, Auckland 0632, New Zealand (a division of Pearson New Zealand Ltd.) • Penguin Books
(South Africa) (Pty.) Ltd., 24 Sturdee Avenue, Rosebank, Johannesburg 2196, South Africa

Penguin Books Ltd., Registered Offices: 80 Strand, London WC2R 0RL, England

This is a work of fiction. Names, characters, places, and incidents either are the product of the author's
imagination or are used fictitiously, and any resemblance to actual persons, living or dead, business
establishments, events, or locales is entirely coincidental. The publisher does not have any control over
and does not assume any responsibility for author or third-party websites or their content.

PUBLISHER'S NOTE: The recipes contained in this book are to be followed exactly as
written. The publisher is not responsible for your specific health or allergy needs that
may require medical supervision. The publisher is not responsible for any adverse
reactions to the recipes contained in this book.

ARSENIC AND OLD CAKE

A Berkley Prime Crime Book / published by arrangement with the author

PUBLISHING HISTORY
Berkley Prime Crime mass-market edition / November 2012

Copyright © 2012 by Penguin Group (USA) Inc.
Cover illustration by Chris Lyons.
Cover design by Diana Kolsky.
Interior text design by Laura K. Corless.

ISBN: 978-0-425-25172-0

BERKLEY® PRIME CRIME
Berkley Prime Crime Books are published by The Berkley Publishing Group,
a division of Penguin Group (USA) Inc.,
375 Hudson Street, New York, New York 10014.
BERKLEY® PRIME CRIME and the PRIME CRIME logo are trademarks of
Penguin Group (USA) Inc.

PRINTED IN THE UNITED STATES OF AMERICA

10 9 8 7 6 5 4 3 2 1

ALWAYS LEARNING   **PEARSON**

One

⚜

"Try to be reasonable, Rita. We *can't* keep everyone working full-time right now." Edie Bryce, office manager at Zydeco Cakes, pushed an ominous-looking stack of documents across the desk toward me. We were sitting in my office, a spacious room on the first floor of the renovated antebellum mansion near New Orleans' Garden District that houses the bakery. A pleasant May breeze blew through the open windows, a treat I allow myself when the New Orleans humidity drops below *stifling* on my personal weather scale.

Edie's almond-shaped eyes, inherited from her Chinese grandmother, were narrowed to mere slits in her round face, and she nudged the pile of papers closer, daring me to disagree with her. "Business is slower than ever," she warned, "and especially now that we lost the Alexander-Mott wedding, we're going to have to find a way to tighten the belt."

The sudden cancellation of the large upscale wedding that had been scheduled for the following week had dealt us a blow; even I couldn't deny that. We would retain a modest deposit, but it would barely cover the cost of materials and labor we'd put in so far. The profit I'd been counting on had evaporated. Not that I wished the couple any ill will, but I was grateful they'd canceled because they were splitting up, not because they'd changed their minds about hiring Zydeco to make their cakes.

And that's what I tried explaining to Edie. "I know this isn't an ideal situation—"

That's as far as I got before she cut me off. "Ideal?" She laughed and tapped a finger on one of the pages in front of me. "It's not even in the same time zone as *ideal*. It's all right there in black and white," she said. "I'm worried, Rita. And you should be, too. If we had enough business to keep everyone busy, I wouldn't even suggest a payroll cut. You know how much I care about everyone here."

And then she sat back in her chair, arms folded, waiting for my reaction.

My name is Rita Lucero. I'm a trained pastry chef and cake artist, half owner (along with Miss Frankie Renier, my former mother-in-law) of Zydeco Cakes, home of the finest specialty cakes in New Orleans. Since taking over the day-to-day operations last year, I'd been trying to maintain Zydeco's reputation and make up for the dip in sales we'd experienced when Philippe, Miss Frankie's son (who happened to be my almost-ex-husband), died. Not only did I have to show the cake-buying public that the quality of Zydeco's cakes wouldn't suffer on my watch, but I also had to convince his wildly creative and emotional staff to trust me. And even though I'd already known about half of them from pastry school, Philippe had won custody of their friendships when we separated, and the transition hadn't been seamless.

Edie and I hadn't exactly been friends in pastry school, but we'd grown closer since Philippe died. I'd known her long enough not to underestimate her when she was in a mood.

And she was definitely in a mood today. Her dark eyes glittered, and every few seconds she tucked a lock of sleek brown hair behind her ear—an unmistakable sign of agitation.

I tried not to look worried, but it wasn't easy. Though we'd had a few ups and downs, the staff had quickly become like family to me. I hated the idea of cutting hours and creating financial hardship for any of them. Even more frightening was the idea of losing one of them entirely. Business at Zydeco had taken a hit last year, and while it had started climbing slowly again a few months ago, the tanking economy had caused people to cut back on luxury items. The extreme cakes that we're known for at Zydeco were apparently one of the first things to go. We had done well during Mardi Gras season and still had a modest stream of wedding clients, but orders for other occasions like baby showers and birthday parties had dropped dramatically in the past few months. Every bakery of our caliber had been hit, but I worried that one of our rivals might actually be able to pay my staff what they were worth.

I looked over the bank statement Edie had placed on top of the stack and moved quickly on to the bakery's balance sheet. Our bottom line might seem impressive to an outsider, but it costs a small fortune to fund Zydeco's day-to-day operations. We had enough money in the bank to stay afloat for the next month or two, but if business didn't pick up soon, we'd be in trouble.

In spite of the evidence and Edie's warning, I refused to believe that cutting staff work hours was inevitable. I still hoped we could find a way to keep everyone working full-time *and* meet our expenses. "I think we should wait a bit longer. Things are tight, but we're not at the do-or-die stage yet."

Edie pursed her porcelain-doll mouth in disapproval. "Close enough for me," she said and pushed a color-coded calendar toward me. "That's what we have on schedule for the next two weeks. There's not enough work there to keep everyone busy, and we can't afford to pay people to sit around and shoot the breeze just because we like them."

The calendar was emptier than I'd realized. This was my first May wedding season at Zydeco, but even I could see that we didn't have the numbers we needed to call it a success. My spirits drooped, and for one brief moment I considered staging a reconciliation between the Alexander-Mott couple to patch up their failed relationship. The cake they'd ordered before Jamal found Celia in his best friend's bed would have kept the entire staff busy for two weeks, and the hefty price tag would have given our balance sheet a shot in the arm.

As if she'd materialized on my shoulder, I heard my aunt Yolanda whisper, "Careful, *mija*. The love of money is the root of all evil."

My aunt and uncle had raised me after my parents died when I was twelve. In the years since I went to live with her, Aunt Yolanda's deep faith had underscored more life lessons than I could count, but I would have argued with her on this one. I didn't want the money for myself. I just wanted to provide for those who depended on me.

"I know we can't pay the staff if there's no work," I said, grudgingly shaking off the urge to play Cupid. "But I'm sure things will pick up soon. They have to."

"Yeah. Maybe." Edie's voice was filled with skepticism. "Look, Rita, I'm not saying you need to lay somebody off. I'm just suggesting that we trim a few hours from everyone's schedule for a while, including mine. We'll make a push to find some new clients and maybe hit the wedding-show circuit a little harder in the fall. If we can weather through this now, hopefully we'll be back to normal next year."

"Why wait until fall?" I asked. "How many wedding shows are scheduled in this area over the next few months?"

Edie shook her head and crossed her legs. "None. Most of the shows are in the fall and winter."

"Maybe we could branch out and expand our radius," I suggested. "There might be something scheduled in other states."

"Even if there were, we'd just spend money we don't have on travel and lodging," Edie pointed out. "We're in a bad spot, Rita. We didn't get the wedding orders we needed from last year's shows, and we're paying for it now."

I looked at the schedule again, then sighed and propped my chin in my hand. "We might have to cut hours," I conceded reluctantly. "But you know I can't make a decision like that without talking it over with Miss Frankie."

Miss Frankie and I have a good working relationship and a surprisingly close personal one, especially considering that, had things turned out differently last year, Philippe would have signed the divorce papers and our marriage would have been over. I'd have gone back to my low-grade sous chef job at Uncle Nestor's restaurant in New Mexico, and Miss Frankie and I might never have seen each other again.

Instead, Philippe had been murdered before the papers could be signed, leaving me, technically, his widow. I'd inherited his house, his car, and his personal bank account—which, though a big deal to me, wasn't enough to give Zydeco the shot in the arm it needed.

Miss Frankie had become sole owner of Zydeco. But she wasn't a baker and she knew nothing about cake decorating, so she'd begged me to stay and help her, offering me a partnership to sweeten the deal. How could I say no? She needed me.

Okay, my motives weren't entirely unselfish. Zydeco was my dream bakery, and the staff Philippe had put together was top-notch. Plus, I'd been dissatisfied with the entry-level job at Uncle Nestor's restaurant. It had required only a moderate amount of arm-twisting on Miss Frankie's part to convince me to say yes.

Now I run the day-to-day business on-site, and Miss Frankie stays home and writes checks when we need them. Up until recently, anyway. We could have used one of Miss Frankie's checks right about now, but the falling stock market had dealt a few blows to her bank balance along with everyone else's. Six months ago, I wouldn't have hesitated to ask for a cash infusion. Now, I wasn't sure I should

Edie gave me a verbal nudge. "You can't think about this forever, Rita. I have to post the schedule this afternoon."

"Then post it," I said. "Keep everyone full-time for now, at least until I talk to Miss Frankie. We can cut back next week if she agrees that's the best solution."

Clearly, that wasn't the answer Edie wanted. She sat back in her chair and tucked that lock of hair behind her ear again. "Why don't you just call her now?"

I resented being pushed to make a decision, especially one I didn't want to make at all. Besides, I'd spoken with Miss Frankie earlier that morning and I knew she was having brunch with her best friend and neighbor, Bernice. Neither of them carried a cell phone, and I hadn't asked where they were eating. I couldn't have reached Miss Frankie if I'd tried.

Which I had no intention of doing.

"I'll talk to her later," I said decisively. "We'll figure something out, I promise. And in the meantime, please don't mention your concerns to anyone else. I don't want the staff to worry."

And by *worry*, I meant *panic*. I love my staff, but it's full of artistic, emotional, temperamental people. *Logic* and *restraint* aren't words that show up often in their vocabularies.

Edie's gaze flickered away for a moment, making me wonder whether my warning was too late.

"Have you talked to anyone else about this?" I asked.

She shook her head quickly. "Not yet."

"Good. If we do have to make adjustments, I think Miss Frankie and I should be the ones to explain what we're doing and why."

Edie stood but made no move to leave.

I smiled up at her. "Is there anything else?"

She started to say something, but just then we heard the tinkle of the bell above the front door, signaling a new arrival—unusual, since we don't handle walk-in clients.

Edie scowled over her shoulder, annoyed by the interruption.

I, however, tried not to look overly grateful for it. Maybe it was a prospective client. If so, I'd think twice before turning them away. Besides, our conversation had run its course. Even with the decrease in business, I still had plenty to do that afternoon, starting with calculating payroll so the staff could get paid at all.

Muttering, "We'll finish this later," Edie hurried from my office.

I had no doubt we would. Edie isn't known for letting things go. I tried to forget the warning and focused on getting the payroll figures logged into the computer. It would be easier to finish *this* without a head full of distractions. The air outside was growing warmer, so I shut the window and got down to work.

I'd just opened the first file when Edie reappeared in the doorway. She looked uncharacteristically tentative as she slipped inside my office again and shut the door behind her. "You'll never believe who's here," she said, her voice low. And then, before I could take a guess, she told me. "It's Gabriel Broussard. You know . . . from the Dizzy Duke? And he's got Old Dog Leg with him."

The Dizzy Duke is a bar a few blocks away from Zydeco. It's been the staff's after-hours hangout since the bakery opened. Philippe was a regular. Me? Not so much, but I do try to join them a couple of times every week.

Gabriel is one of the bartenders, six feet of sexy, dark Cajun handsomeness. He and I indulge in a little low-key flirting from time to time, and we've gone out a couple of times. He's spontaneous and exciting, but so far there's nothing serious between us. Partly because he's not the only guy on my personal horizon, and partly because I'm not sure I'm ready for serious. But hearing his name in the middle of the workday set off a pleasant internal buzz and I didn't fight it.

Old Dog Leg is a seventy-eight-year-old blind trumpet player who occasionally sits in with the house band at the Dizzy Duke. He's a sweet old guy and one of my favorites among the regulars at the bar. Still, for either of them to show up at Zydeco was unusual, but both of them walking through the door together? Unheard of. It sparked my curiosity in a big way.

I glanced toward the door and back at Edie. "What do they want?" I whispered.

Edie shrugged. "To see you. That's all they'd say. Do you want me to send them in or tell them you're busy?"

I still had way too much to do, but I hesitated for less than a second before closing my laptop and moving it out of the way. I really had no choice. If I sent them away, curiosity would eat me alive and I wouldn't get anything done. It was simple self-preservation that made me say, "Send them in, of course."

Two

Edie showed Gabriel and Old Dog Leg into my office and disappeared, promising to return with sweet tea, the signature drink of the South. I greeted both men warmly, although I may have put a little more sugar into the greeting I offered Gabriel. He wore a white shirt and jeans with a black leather jacket that would have made Young Elvis proud. It was hard not to smile at that. In return, he treated me to one of those lopsided grins of his that tend to do strange things to my insides, especially after a margarita or two.

Old Dog Leg used his white cane to maneuver around the furniture and, with a little guidance from Gabriel, settled into a chair facing mine. He was a little less stylin' than Gabriel, in baggy trousers, a plaid shirt, and the sunglasses he never removed, but he could've easily passed for twenty years younger than seventy-eight. I only knew his age because he'd told me; nobody would guess it just by looking at him. When I saw the worry lines creasing his usually smooth skin, however, the warm fuzzies I'd been feeling toward Gabriel fizzled out. Old Dog Leg had something on his mind.

I rounded the desk to give the old man a quick hug and sent Gabriel a "what's up?" look on my way back.

He answered with an "I don't know" shrug before claiming the chair next to Dog Leg's.

"This is a surprise," I said. "Are you two here for business, or is this a social call?"

The old man smiled at me as I sat. "I got somet'ing on my mind, lovely Rita. Gotta ask for some help."

That surprised me. Despite his blindness, or maybe because of it, Old Dog Leg was fiercely independent.

"Whatever you need," I assured him. "What's wrong?"

He tilted his head so that his round face turned toward the ceiling. "Got me a letter in de mail yesterday," he said in a singsong accent that was pure Louisiana. "From someone claimin' to be my brother."

I shot a surprised glance at Gabriel, but he was focused on Dog Leg and his expression didn't reveal anything. "I didn't know you had a brother," I said. "You've never mentioned him to me before, have you?"

Old Dog Leg let out a heavy sigh. "Don't talk about him much. He disappeared a long time ago."

From where I sat, this was getting more interesting by the minute. I leaned forward, eager to hear more. "Disappeared? How?"

Dog Leg gave me a patient smile. "Never knew de answer to dat question. He just up and vanished."

"And now he's back?"

"So it says in de letter. But dat's de trouble. Mebbe it him. Mebbe it not. I don' know." He jerked his head in my direction. "Show her, Gabriel."

Gabriel pulled the letter from his shirt pocket and handed

it to me as he explained, "Dog Leg brings his mail to the Duke and I read it to him. Take a look."

The small white envelope bore the logo of a Victorian-style house, the words *Love Nest Bed & Breakfast* in bold script, and a return address I placed on the West Bank here in New Orleans. I lifted an eyebrow at Gabriel. "The Love Nest?"

"It's a new one to me," he said. "But I looked it up on the Internet. Apparently, it's a deluxe romantic getaway for honeymooners."

My gaze swiveled back to Dog Leg. "Your brother's here on his honeymoon?"

"Don' know. He didn' say. G'wan. See for yourself."

I unfolded a single sheet of Love Nest stationery and found a short note in carefully printed letters:

Hey, D, it's me. Monroe.

Sorry I run off the way I done, but I'm back for a spell. Sure would like to see you if you can forgive me for what I done. I'll be at this address for a week. Come on by if you've a mind to.

Your brother,
Monroe

I turned the page over, looking futilely for more, but the back of the sheet was empty. I'm an only child, but I grew up with four cousins. If one of them ever disappeared, I'd want more than a *come on by* when he resurfaced. "That's it?" I asked.

Gabriel nodded. "So it would seem."

"Monroe never was much for writin'," Dog Leg said with a half smile.

"So it would seem," I commented, echoing Gabriel. "How long has he been gone?"

The old man let out another sigh, this one so deep I could feel it from where I sat. "Last time I seen my baby brother it was de first of May, forty years ago."

I gasped. "Forty years?" That's longer than I've been alive. No wonder he was uncertain.

"He just vanished?" Gabriel asked. "You have no idea what happened to him?"

Dog Leg shook his head. "Notta clue. Figured he run off, though. Least at first. After a while . . ." He lifted one round shoulder. "Well, you gots to wonder."

"You never heard a word?" I asked. "Monroe didn't give you any clue that he was thinking of leaving? Never sent a birthday or Christmas card in all the years since?"

"Nothin'. I tol' you, he wasn't much for writing."

Gabriel gave that some thought. "Did anything unusual happen before he left? Was he in trouble of some kind?"

"I axed myself dat a t'ousand times, but I don't know." Dog Leg's shoulders slumped and his frown deepened. "Him and me, we played together at de Cott'n Bott'm. You heard of it?"

"I have," Gabriel said, and then explained for my sake, "The Cotton Bottom was a popular club back then."

"Dat's right. It was *de* place to go for a while, and we had us a mighty sweet gig. Money was good. Plenty of women. And we was buildin' a name for ourselves. Den one day Monroe just didn't show up. It was a Saturday night, biggest night of de week. Got worried, y'know? So me and a coupla guys went to check on him. His room? Cleaned out. His stuff gone."

I tried to imagine how Dog Leg had felt, not knowing where his brother was for four decades. Losing my parents the summer I'd turned twelve had devastated me, but at least I'd been certain about what happened to them. Dog Leg must have gone through hell wondering whether his brother was alive or dead. But I didn't want to dwell on the pain of the past.

"How did he even know where to find you?" I asked.

"I'm livin' in de house our folks owned. Been dere all my life."

"Then why didn't he call instead? I mean—" I broke off, uncertain how to phrase my question without sounding rude. After a couple more fumbled attempts to get it out, Gabriel stepped in.

"What are you trying to get at, slick?"

"Well . . . doesn't it seem odd that Monroe would send a letter when he knows his brother can't read it himself?"

"Not so strange," Dog Leg said. "I wasn't like dis when Monroe knew me. Didn't get de glaucoma until I was in my sixties. Far as Monroe knows, I can see just fine."

Edie came back carrying a tray and sweet tea. We all fell silent while she passed around glasses and napkins. I used the interruption to try to wrap my mind around what Old Dog Leg had told us and to guess what he wanted from me.

"So what are you going to do?" Gabriel asked when Edie left the room again.

Old Dog Leg lifted one shoulder. "Only one t'ing *to* do. I gotta figger out whether he's Monroe or he ain't."

"And how are you going to do that?" I asked.

The old man's mouth curved slightly. "Well, dat's where de two of you come in. Somebody gotta get a look at him. A real good look. I want de two of you to do it."

It was a logical request, I suppose. Old Dog Leg couldn't do it himself. I put my glass on the napkin and asked, "What exactly do you want us to do?"

The air conditioner clicked on, and a blast of cold air poured out of the overhead vents. It felt good to me, but Old Dog Leg shivered a little. "I know dis is a lot to ask. I wouldn't botter you if I had *any* other way."

Gabriel put a reassuring hand on the old man's shoulder. "You're not bothering us. Just tell us what your plan is."

Dog Leg sent him a feeble smile and then turned it on me. "Well, we know where he's stayin'. Got hisself a room at dat place on de West Bank."

"The Love Nest," Gabriel said. "Do you need us to drive you over there so you can talk with him?"

"Not exactly." Dog Leg lifted a hand to his forehead, and I noticed that his fingers were trembling slightly.

Poor old guy. I hated knowing that he was worried and confused. "Then what?" I asked. "It's okay. We'd both be happy to help."

At that, Dog Leg smiled hopefully. "I'm sure glad to hear dat, lovely Rita. You're a good friend. Both of you. So here's my idea. I was thinkin' mebbe de two of you could check in dere for a coupla days. Get to know dis fella. Figure out whether he's tellin' de truth or not."

My mouth fell open. I wasn't sure what I'd been expecting him to say, but it wasn't *that*. I looked to Gabriel for backup, but he was busy making sympathetic noises, and his expression told me he was about to say yes. I spoke up before he could do something we'd both regret. "You want us to *what*?"

Dog Leg's hopeful smile faded. "I know it sounds crazy, Rita. Believe me, I do. I just don't know what else to do."

"I don't think it's crazy," I said, which was not entirely true. "But it does seem a little . . . over-the-top. Why not just talk to him and hear what he has to say?"

Dog Leg shook his head firmly. "Not until I know for sure dat it's Monroe."

"But how are we supposed to know that?" I asked. "Neither of us has ever met him."

"Easy. My brother had a birthmark on his right shoulder." Dog Leg held up one hand, the thumb and forefinger roughly three inches apart. "'Bout dis long and light pink. If it's dere, you won't be able to miss it."

"Okay," I said, "I get it. You want to be sure it's Monroe. So one of us will go over there and check him out. It won't take two people to get this guy talking."

Old Dog Leg gave his head another determined shake. "Can't just one of you go. Dat's a place for folks on their honeymoons. One of you show up alone, it's gonna raise questions."

I started to launch another argument, but Gabriel beat me to it. "He has a point. Nobody will think twice about a husband and wife checking in for a few days."

And that brought up another issue: that of me alone in a hotel room with Gabriel. I knew I should refuse for at least a dozen reasons, starting with the trouble I knew I'd have saying no once we got there.

It's not that I object to the two of us getting closer. It's just . . . complicated.

Gabriel's not the only guy in my life. I've also been seeing Liam Sullivan, a hunky homicide detective with the NOPD. Neither one is a serious relationship, and thanks to Aunt Yolanda's strict upbringing (and Uncle Nestor's frequent threats of bodily harm to any man who dared touch me), I'm not into the casual scene. And since I haven't decided which of them I like more, I'm keeping my options open and my knees closed. In fact, it had been three years since I'd been with any man and the idea of spending an entire weekend in such close proximity made me a little nervous.

I almost had the word *no* fully formed when Dog Leg rubbed his chin and sighed again as if he carried the weight of the world on his shoulders. "Dis man could be my baby brother," he reminded me. "Den again, he could be a crook. Either way, I gotta know. And I don't wanna spook him. What if he *is* Monroe? He starts thinkin' I don't trust him, he could run again. I don't want dat."

"But surely he'd understand why you're being cautious," I reasoned. "If he is Monroe, I mean. He's been gone for forty years. He has to expect that you'll have questions."

Dog Leg shook his head firmly. "You don' know my brother." He snorted softly and said, "Den again, neither do I. Dat's the problem. When I knowed him, he was young and foolish. Did what he wanted and never thought much about de consequences. I tried to warn him dat's de way to trouble, but he never listened. If he's de same as he was den, he's not thinkin' far ahead."

"But still—"

"Rita, I need your help. I promised my mama on her death-bed I'd take care of Monroe, and I failed. Mebbe dis is my chance to make it up to her—and to him."

"But you didn't fail," I assured him. "You're not responsible for what Monroe did. He's the one who ran off."

Old Dog Leg lifted a shoulder. "Mebbe. Mebbe not. But what if I still got me some family? I got nothin' else to go on. I don' have no other way of proving whether he's my brother or he ain't. If he *is* Monroe, den I'm gonna kill him for takin' off and scaring me de way he did. If he's not, I wanna know why he's lyin'."

Gabriel nodded as if Old Dog Leg's arguments actually made sense. Apparently, I was the sole voice of reason in that room.

"I understand how you feel," I assured both men, "but why not call the police?"

Gabriel rolled his coffee-colored eyes as if I'd suggested something ridiculous. Because going undercover and spying on some old man made so much more sense than contacting the authorities.

"Think about it, *chérie*," Gabriel said. "What are the police going to do?"

I knew I was fighting a losing battle anytime Gabriel rolled out the Cajun, but I wasn't going down without a fight. "I don't know, maybe run a background check on this guy or something."

"On a man who has done nothing wrong?" He shook his head. "The police have more important things to worry about." He bored a hole through me with his eyes. "Unless you have connections Dog Leg and I don't."

I knew he was talking about Sullivan, but I didn't let his suggestion bother me. I haven't kept either relationship secret, but neither do I flaunt them. Both men know what they're getting with me.

I briefly considered Gabriel's suggestion, but there was no way Sullivan could help out with an unofficial background check. A recent triple homicide had claimed most of his attention for the past two weeks. Even if he was willing to help, it might be days before he could run a check, and by then Monroe might have disappeared again.

"No," I said. "I guess not."

Old Dog Leg made a noise in his throat, which I did my best to ignore. I tried not to notice the big brown eyes Gabriel was using on me, but that was almost impossible. So I made one more effort to inject common sense into the conversation.

"I'm sure I'd feel the same way in your shoes," I told Dog Leg, "but neither of us is equipped to do what you're asking. We're not private investigators. I'm a pastry chef and he's a bartender."

"But you're de only two can help me."

I laughed skeptically. "The *only* two?"

"Who else am I gonna ask? One of de waitresses at de Duke? One of de guys from de band? I need somebody smart. Somebody wid a level head. Somebody who ain't gonna start drinkin' or worse and blow de whole t'ing 'fore I find out de truth. I know a lotta people, Rita, but not many I trust." He put both hands on the desk and shot another volley at me. "You know I'd do de same for you if you needed help."

Every logical cell in my body was shouting at me to turn him down, but Old Dog Leg's last argument had stirred up my sentimental cells, which are much more powerful than their sensible counterparts. The way Dog Leg had lost his brother was different from the way I'd lost my parents, but all great loss shares the same emotional aftereffect: the longing for one more chance. If someone showed up at my door claiming to be one of my parents, I'd do whatever it took to find out the truth and I'd probably be worried about scaring them off, just as Old Dog Leg was.

Still . . . I sipped my sweet tea and thought it over. "Don't you think it's kind of devious to spy on him like that?"

Old Dog Leg nodded. "Sure it is. But dere's only one way I know of to be sure and dat's to get a look at dis fella with his shirt off."

"So all we have to do is get a stranger to take off his shirt?" I laughed through my nose. "That ought to be a piece of cake."

"I'd try to get a look myself, but . . ." Dog Leg gave a little smile and a shrug.

And there it was. My last solid defense. Gone in a rush of affection for the old man. Though I still wasn't sold on the idea of checking into the Love Nest under false pretenses. The niggling sense that something was sure to go wrong just wouldn't leave me alone.

"You're being awfully quiet, Gabriel," I said. "How about suggesting some other way we can help Old Dog Leg without getting ourselves into trouble of some kind?"

He shook his head slowly. "Like I said before, I think Dog Leg's argument makes sense." He aimed one of his sexy, lopsided smiles at me and added, "Besides, I think it sounds like fun."

My heart did a little flip-flop in response, but I ignored it. "Don't get any big ideas."

He waggled his eyebrows, all Sexy Cajun-like. "Ah, *chérie*, I've already got ideas."

Flip. Flop. "Funny. But you know what I mean. If I agree to do this, it's about helping Old Dog Leg, not about . . . you know."

"Nothin' wrong wid a little romance," Dog Leg said. "It's a sad t'ing to go through life alone."

I shook my finger at him, even though I knew he couldn't see it. "Don't encourage him. If you want my help, you'll keep opinions like that to yourself."

Old Dog Leg chuckled.

I pretended not to hear him. "I mean it, Gabriel. No funny business."

Okay. I was tempted. Who wouldn't have been? But I'd lived thirty-seven years of life according to someone else's rules. First my parents', then Uncle Nestor and Aunt Yolanda's. I'd found freedom in Chicago when I went to pastry school, but I hadn't been there long before Philippe swept me off my feet. And I'd gone right back to Uncle Nestor's world when my marriage ended. I was now living on my own for the first time in my life, and I was determined to make future decisions on my own terms.

Gabriel held up both hands and looked at me with wide-eyed innocence. "As you wish. We'll keep the whole thing strictly platonic."

"Good." I sat down in my chair and got back to business. "What about work? It's going to be pretty hard to look like we're on our honeymoon if you're working at the Duke until the wee hours every night."

"I'll switch shifts with someone. No big deal."

"And what if this guy *isn't* Dog Leg's brother?"

"Den he's up to no good," Dog Leg said. "And if he's up to no good wid me, den he's been up to no good before. If he's goin' around lyin' to people, we gotta find out so de police can stop him."

Hmm. I guess there was *that*. Maybe it wouldn't hurt to check the guy out. If Gabriel and I could find evidence that Monroe was a phony, the police would be far more likely to run a background check.

Dog Leg must have sensed my resolve weakening because he leaned forward eagerly. "Will you do it?"

When I didn't immediately say yes, Gabriel locked eyes with me. "Come on, Rita. Do you really want to leave our friend in the lurch?"

I chewed my bottom lip and tried once more to think of another way to make everyone happy. But that was easier said than done. Old Dog Leg needed my help. Once I finished today's payroll, it would be easy for me to take a little time away from the bakery. With me gone, there would be more work for everyone else. Win-win.

With a little sigh of resignation, I pushed my chair away from the desk and stood. "Okay, I'll do it. But I'm going on record as saying that I think this is a bad idea."

"Relax," Gabriel said as he leaned up to kiss my cheek. "It's going to be just fine. Mark my words."

That nagging sensation of impending doom skittered up my spine, but the smile on Old Dog Leg's face made it easy to shrug it off and tell myself that Gabriel was right.

I really should have known better.

Three

After Gabriel and I made plans to meet at eleven the following morning, he and Old Dog Leg beat a hasty retreat. Hoping an infusion of caffeine would help my concentration, I grabbed a mug of coffee from the employee break room and spent the next few hours calculating payroll and running expense figures. Cutting my hours over the next few days would help a little, but it wasn't a long-term fix. No matter how hard I tried, I couldn't make the numbers going forward look any less bleak. Even if we landed a big job in the next few days, we really would have to scale back on the work schedule. We simply couldn't keep everyone working full-time and hope to make ends meet for long.

I shut down my laptop and called Miss Frankie to ask if I could drop by on my way home, then shelved my financial concerns until later. I come from a long line of worriers, but I knew that fretting about money would eat me alive if I let it.

By the time I left my office, Edie had already gone home for the day. I carried my empty cup back to the break room, rinsed it, and left it on the rack to dry, then wandered into the design area to see how what little work we did have was going.

Besides my office, the design area—a massive room with brightly painted walls and huge windows overlooking the garden—is easily my favorite room in the building. The gold, fuchsia, teal, and lime green walls might seem overpowering in a smaller room, but they work well in this large space. It is the design room of my dreams, with a dozen metal tables creating individual work spaces, each one surrounded by shelves crammed full of cake-making equipment.

I'd sketched this room more times than I could count when Philippe and I were married, and I'd been both elated and angry to find it in his bakery when I arrived in New Orleans. It had been one of the biggest carrots Miss Frankie had dangled in front of me when she'd asked me to stay. Some days I still pinch myself when I realize it's mine, but today all I felt was a cloying sense of panic that I could lose it to the crumbling economy.

Most of the staff had cleared out for the evening, but Ox, my second in command, was still there with Isabeau Pope, a cake artist who also happens to be Ox's significant other. The two of them have been dating for almost a year now. As long as their relationship doesn't spill over into the workplace, I've got no issue with it.

Ox, another friend from pastry school, is closing in on forty, and he's one of the most talented pastry chefs I know. He's tall and in tremendous shape, a dead ringer for an African American Mr. Clean. He was scowling at a sketch on the table in front of him, jotting down measurements and notes about ingredients.

Isabeau's at least fifteen years his junior. She's petite, blond, and cheerleader perky. She sat at a nearby workstation sorting through one of the bins where odd tools and pieces of small equipment get routinely tossed when we're busy.

Ox gave me a chin-jerk in greeting as I walked in. Isabeau treated me to a little finger wave.

I waved back and dragged a stool to Ox's station so I could talk to him while he worked. "Sorry I didn't get back here earlier. I've been working on payroll."

Ox glanced up quickly. "Get it done?"

I nodded. "Yeah. How did it go back here today?"

He shrugged, made a note on his design, and tossed the pen onto the table. "The retirement party cake is finished and ready for delivery first thing tomorrow. Dwight finished the twin baby-shower cakes, so I put him to work sorting supplies and making sure everyone's workstation is completely outfitted. I had to put Sparkle to work cleaning some of the equipment. With these two cakes finished, we're running out of things to do. You know I hate assigning busywork. It's a complete waste of time."

My stomach knotted as I listened to him talk. "Not a complete waste," I said, channeling my inner Pollyanna. "Those are all things that need to be done."

Ox rolled his eyes at me. "In what universe?"

His dour mood on top of Edie's dire predictions and my own worry pushed a hot button for me. I couldn't give in to fear or I'd never find a solution. "Oh please. This isn't going to last forever. And it's important that you and I don't act like it's the end of the world. If the two of us give off a doomsday vibe, it will undermine the whole staff."

Isabeau's blue eyes clouded as she sorted a handful of decorating tips into piles. "But it's bad, Rita. I spent the afternoon reorganizing the flavor extracts, and Estelle said she's going to check the expiration dates on the food coloring tomorrow. This is stuff almost anyone could do. We need real work."

Ox frowned at her affectionately and then admitted, "Okay, so maybe it's not that bad . . . yet. We still have that order for the EMS dinner on Tuesday and that will keep most of us busy for a few days. But I'm really starting to worry, and so is everyone else. People are speculating that you'll have to start laying people off."

So much for keeping my financial concerns from the staff. I thought about glossing over things, but I knew that would be a mistake. Ox had expected to take over at Zydeco after Philippe died, and he'd been hurt by Miss Frankie's decision to make me her partner. As a result, he and I had butted heads a few times over which direction to take the bakery. But he's also an old friend, and I'm lucky he stayed on to work for me. He's my right arm at Zydeco, and I wouldn't feel good about lying to him. "I know business is really slow," I said. "But I'm going to do everything I can to keep the staff working. I'll take money out of my own pocket before I let them take a hit."

Isabeau flashed me a grateful smile.

Ox frowned. "That's no solution."

"It'll buy some time until we get a few more contracts on the books."

"*If* we get a few more contracts on the books." He linked his hands behind his head and swayed gently on his swivel chair. "What we need is a new game plan."

Ox's specialty is coming up with new game plans, but since they usually mean more work for me, I tend to be cautious when he starts thinking. "Such as?"

"Nobody knows how long it's going to take the economy to rebound, right?"

I nodded slowly. "Right."

"So I think it's a mistake to just sit here and wait for people to feel safe spending money. I think we need to diversify."

The last difference of opinion between Ox and me had been over the bakery's King Cake recipe. Ox, the traditionalist, had insisted it was wrong to mess with our winning recipe. I'd argued for diversity, suggesting that adding filling to some of the cakes would appeal to a broader audience. Hearing him argue for diversity now surprised me.

I squeaked out an uncertain laugh. "And do what?"

"Exactly what we've been doing, only on a smaller scale. I think we should add a new line of moderately priced cakes so we can appeal to a larger demographic."

My jaw dropped. "Are you serious?"

"It's a good idea," Isabeau put in from her table. "I mean, it's not as if people have stopped getting married or having babies or birthdays. They still want to make those occasions special. Maybe they can't afford an expensive specialty cake, but maybe they'd order something less . . . unique."

She said *less unique*. I heard *ordinary*, and my defenses went up. It didn't help that the two of them had obviously discussed this before, which made me feel like I'd been ambushed. "But that's not what Zydeco does."

"Well, maybe it should," Ox said. "Listen, Rita, I don't know what our bank account looks like, but I know we can't go on this way indefinitely. The staff isn't just getting worried, they're bored. A few more weeks like the one we just had and they'll be at each others' throats."

"It's not as if we're completely out of work," I pointed out. "We just need to drum up more business. We can put people to work taking flyers to the upscale wedding shops around town and set up meetings with high-end wedding and event planners. Maybe even work out special deals for their customers. When you think about it, that's something we should be doing already. The new website you've created is great, but it's no substitute for face-to-face contact."

"I agree," Ox said. "Let's not ignore any possibility. But we'd be making a mistake to stick with top-of-the-line exclusively. We should do whatever it takes to keep Zydeco afloat, right?"

I nodded slowly, considering his idea but still running into a huge wall of internal resistance. But was I against the idea because it was wrong for Zydeco, or because I hadn't thought of it first, or because, once again, Ox was trying to steamroll me? "You're suggesting a huge change," I said. "I'm not convinced that it would be for the better. Would we be lowering our standards? Would our current clientele go somewhere else?"

"Not if we do it right," Ox argued. "I'm not talking about lowering quality, just about adding a line of cakes that people with moderate incomes can afford. At least let me pitch it to Miss Frankie and see how she feels about it."

He looked so earnest, I felt my resistance slip a little, but I couldn't make such a big decision out of sentiment. Nor could I make it on my own. I added it to my mental list of Things to Talk About with Miss Frankie. I was pretty sure how Miss Frankie would react, but there was a chance I was wrong. She had surprised me in the past. And no matter what she thought of Ox's idea, it was only fair that I let him throw his Hail Mary pass in person.

"Okay. Fine. I'll set up a meeting."

Ox beamed. "How about tomorrow after I deliver the retirement cake?"

"I'll see what I can do, but I can't promise anything. And that brings up the other thing I wanted to talk to you about. I'm going to be gone quite a bit for the next few days taking care of a personal matter. I'll need you to cover for me when I'm not here."

I knew Ox was disappointed at having to wait for his meeting, but he hid it well. "Anything wrong?"

"Not really. I promised to help a friend with something. Since we're running out of work for everyone this seemed like a good time for me to clear out for a bit. One less person to keep busy, right?"

Ox reached for his pencil again. "Yeah. Sure. Whatever. Just let me know when we can get together with Miss Frankie."

I promised I would and went back to my office to gather my things. Twenty minutes later, I tossed my bag into the Mercedes I'd inherited from Philippe and pulled out of the parking lot into evening traffic. It was a beautiful evening, cool enough to drive with the windows down and still very low humidity, which made my hair and my dry-air-loving lungs happy. But beneath that feeling of contentment lurked a whisper of apprehension, and I wasn't sure where it was coming from.

Four

✦

When I first came to New Orleans, driving into Miss Frankie's upscale neighborhood with its huge houses and manicured lawns had resurrected a whole slew of childhood insecurities. Having a little money of my own now had chipped away some of their rough edges, but they weren't completely gone yet. I might have been driving a Mercedes, but deep down I was still that insecure Latina from the wrong side of town.

As usual, Miss Frankie greeted me with a warm smile and an enthusiastic hug. She's several inches taller than me and thinner, too. No matter what she eats, she never seems to gain an ounce. I'm not sure how old she is, but I'm guessing somewhere in her early sixties. It's hard to tell. Her skin is flawless, and her stylist makes sure no untidy root growth would ever reveal her true hair color.

Tonight, she was wearing a pair of loose-fitting black slacks and a flowing black top covered with birds of paradise that exactly matched the tint of her auburn hair. Her finger- and toenails had recently been mani- and pedicured and polished with the same color. "Come on in," she urged as she tugged me through the front door. "Have you had supper yet? I was just about to sit down when you called, so I waited. There's more than plenty for both of us."

Miss Frankie is an excellent cook, and I hadn't eaten since noon. I didn't put up a fight as she propelled me down the hall and into the kitchen.

"Bernice was going to join me, but her nephew called at the last minute and asked her to watch the kids. Between you and me, I think she ought to say no from time to time, but you know how she is with those babies."

I laughed and dropped my bag on the table by the back stairs as we passed. "You talk tough, but you'd be the same way, and you know it."

The minute the words left my mouth, I knew I'd made a mistake, but it was too late to call them back. Miss Frankie's eyes dulled a little, and her smile grew brittle. Philippe had been her only child, and I knew her heart ached for the grand-children she'd never have.

Kicking myself for making such a thoughtless mistake, I slipped an arm around her waist and changed the subject. "Something smells good. What have you been cooking?"

She closed her eyes briefly. When she opened them, they were smiling again. "Now don't you think badly of me when you see what we're having. Promise?"

"Cross my heart." We stepped into the kitchen where a large red and white striped container filled with take-out chicken sat in the middle of the table surrounded by plastic tubs of mashed potatoes, gravy, coleslaw, and baked beans.

My feet stopped moving, and I turned a surprised look on my mother-in-law. Millions of families eat fast food every day, but it's an unusual choice for Miss Frankie. Her tastes are usually more refined. I, on the other hand, have fond memories of chicken buckets from childhood. Money was tight in Uncle Nestor's house, and takeout of any kind was a very big deal. My cousins had been all about burgers and fries, but chicken had always been my favorite.

I inhaled deeply and reached for a biscuit. "You surprise me, Miss Frankie. I didn't realize you liked the colonel's finest. Is this something new, or a guilty pleasure you've kept secret from me until now?"

She left me at the table while she gathered plates and silverware and carried them over. "It's not my preference. I'm partial to my mama's recipe. But Bernice was in quite a mood this afternoon and she requested it." She made a face at the bucket. "I didn't have the heart to say no. Now you and I are stuck with it."

I laughed and crossed to the fridge. I might enjoy the chicken and coleslaw occasionally, but I draw the line at butter squeezed out of a plastic tube. I took out Miss Frankie's elegant butter dish, sliced off a generous pat, slathered it on half a biscuit, and took a bite. Not exactly light and fluffy, but childhood memories can't be held to the same standard as adult pleasures. "You want me to help you get rid of it?"

"I would be forever in your debt." She picked up a chicken thigh and studied it with a slight scowl. "I'm sure Bernice is just heartsick that she has to miss this meal. She'd best be feeling better tomorrow because I'm not eating it two nights in a row."

I thought about suggesting that Miss Frankie save the bucket and fixings for Bernice and that we go out to dinner instead, but I was actually looking forward to polishing off a plate. Plus, I thought it would be best to discuss Zydeco's future in private. I dug out a breast for myself and took a bite. The chicken was moist and delicious, even if the coating was heavier than I remembered. The coleslaw had a pleasantly commercial tang, and the beans were both sweet and savory. Mass-produced food to be sure, but the memories it brought back were one of a kind.

"So," Miss Frankie said as she handed me the potatoes. "What did you want to talk about? Is there a problem at Zydeco?"

How to begin? Losing Philippe last year had left her reeling for months. She was getting stronger all the time, but I didn't want to cause a setback by making her worry about money—especially when I knew her own finances were strained. But I couldn't keep her in the dark, so I explained the situation at the bakery and told her about Edie's suggestion to cut staff hours.

Miss Frankie nibbled chicken and swallowed a few bites of potatoes and gravy while she listened. "You need money," she said when I finished.

"No," I said quickly. "I mean, yes, but I'm not asking you to put money into the bakery. What we really need is more business. But we'll find a way out of this hole eventually. I'm really just asking for your reaction to cutting payroll."

She stopped eating and wiped her fingers on her napkin. "Edie does have a habit of seeing the glass half-empty. Is the situation really as bad as she claims?"

"We're not sinking yet," I assured her. "But we can't go on this way for long. We're exploring options to bring in business, and Ox has some ideas he'd like to discuss with the two of us. He wants me to set up a meeting when it's convenient for you."

She slanted a glance at me. "Good ideas?"

I grinned and shook my head. "It really wouldn't be fair for me to tell you what I think before you've had a chance to hear what he has to say."

She drummed her fingernails on the table—slowly. "I surely do hate the idea of changing things at Zydeco," she said after a while. "You know it's not what Philippe would have wanted."

"I don't like it either," I said. "But we can't keep doing the same old thing in the same old way and expecting different results. Aunt Yolanda always told me that's the definition of crazy. And who can say what Philippe would have done? He never had to face a situation like this."

"Maybe you're right," she said, but she sure didn't sound as if she meant it. She put her fork on the table and smoothed her hands over her pant legs. "If we're going to hear Ox's suggestions, I suppose we should do it sooner rather than later. Shall we meet tomorrow morning around nine?"

I hadn't counted on her being so eager, so I didn't answer immediately. I still had to pack for the weekend, which meant doing laundry first. Plus, I'd need at least two new pairs of pajamas. Maybe three. No way was I going on this *honeymoon* with only my old, faded sweats and T-shirts to sleep in. Just thinking about the worn-out elastic at the waistbands made me cringe.

"I'm tied up this weekend," I said when I realized she was waiting for an answer. "How about Monday?"

"If you have an order to fill, I don't mind talking while you and Ox work."

"That's not it," I said. "I've promised to do a favor for a friend. It's going to take me away from the bakery for the next few days."

Miss Frankie's hands stopped moving. "Oh? You're going away somewhere?"

"You don't need to worry about the bakery," I said, hoping to reassure her. "Ox will be taking charge while I'm gone. And I'm not going to disappear completely. I should be there for a few hours every day. Just not full-time. It'll be fine. You'll see."

She smiled, but I could tell she was still worried. "Well, of course it will be, sugar. I just worry that you'll be stretching yourself too thin, that's all. What kind of favor are we talking about? Or can't you talk about it?"

I shook my head and wiped my fingers on a napkin. "I

don't think it's any big secret. You remember Old Dog Leg, the trumpet player down at the Dizzy Duke?"

Concern flashed through Miss Frankie's eyes. "Of course. But what on earth does he need from you? Is he in some kind of trouble?"

"I really don't know. It's hard to say." I explained about the letter he'd received and told her what I knew about Monroe's disappearance forty years ago. "Dog Leg needs someone to find out if this guy is really his brother or if he's an imposter."

"Well, of course he does. The poor man can't do it for himself. But how does he expect *you* to identify his brother?"

"Apparently Monroe has a distinctive birthmark on one shoulder. If we can get a look at that, we'll be able to tell."

Miss Frankie pushed her plate away and stood. "Coffee?"

"Please."

She got the pot started, speaking over her shoulder while she worked. "I'm glad to hear you're not going alone. Is Dog Leg going with you, then?"

"Not exactly. I'm going with Gabriel Broussard. You remember him, don't you? He tends bar at the Dizzy Duke."

She turned abruptly. "Of course I remember him. Are you still seeing him? Socially?"

Something in her tone gave me pause. Had she sounded edgy, or was it my imagination? "We see each other occasionally."

Her lips thinned slightly, making her smile look slightly strained. "Well, why don't the two of you take care of Old Dog Leg's problem tomorrow, then? We can meet with Ox on Saturday."

"We may not be able to get answers that fast," I said. "Dog Leg is worried that we'll spook the guy if he suspects we're checking him out. He's staying at a B and B over on the West Bank. Dog Leg wants us to get a room there and treat this as some kind of covert operation." Hearing myself say it aloud made me laugh at the absurdity of the plan.

Miss Frankie's posture stiffened, and this time I knew I wasn't imagining her reaction. "You'll be sharing a room with Gabriel?"

"Well, yes. We have to. The place is some kind of honeymoon getaway." I carried my plate to the sink, uncomfortably aware of my mother-in-law staring at me through eyes of stone. "It's not a big deal," I assured her. "It's not like we're—you know—*getting a room*. It's just a cover to keep Monroe, or whoever he is, from realizing that we're checking him out."

"But sharing a room . . . I'm not sure that's such a good idea, Rita."

For a while after Philippe died, Miss Frankie had held on to the belief that he and I would have reconciled if he'd lived. Over time she'd begun to accept the idea that I would eventually move on with my life, and she'd seemed accepting of my decisions to date Gabriel and Sullivan. Now I wondered if she was backsliding. It wasn't like Miss Frankie to be judgmental.

I put a hand on her arm and met her gaze. "It's not like that. It's just . . . you know . . . a cover."

"But how is it going to look for you to spend the weekend at some bed-and-breakfast with that bartender?"

"I thought you liked Gabriel."

"Of course I *like* him. It has nothing to do with that. But, really, Rita. Don't you think checking into some hotel together will make you look a bit . . . common?"

Everything inside seized up as if she'd slapped me. And in a way she had. My deepest fear was that she considered me too low class to fit into her world, and she'd just thrown it in my face. I'm pretty sure I stopped breathing for a second, and the greasy food I'd wolfed down turned over in my stomach. "That's your objection? That I'm going to embarrass you?"

She waved a hand between us, seemingly oblivious to the wound she'd just inflicted. "It's not me I'm worried about, sugar. But have you thought about what this will look like for Zydeco? We serve an exclusive clientele. You have to consider how your actions will look to them."

I choked out a laugh. "It's nobody's business what I do in my personal life."

Miss Frankie put one hand over mine. "Sugar, I'm not suggesting that you'd do something inappropriate. I know you better than that. But like it or not, appearances matter, especially to the kinds of people who buy our cakes. You just told me yourself that Zydeco's already struggling to stay afloat. Now is not the time to take chances with our reputation."

I felt my hackles rise and my remaining misgivings about Old Dog Leg's plan evaporate in a wave of irritation and stubbornness. "I'm not asking permission, Miss Frankie. I just wanted to keep you in the loop." My face burned with anger as I turned back to the sink. I would have rinsed my dishes and loaded them into the dishwasher, but Miss Frankie shooed me away and did the job herself.

"I didn't realize you and Gabriel were so serious," she said, not meeting my eyes.

"We're not," I said again. Was she even listening to me? "This isn't about Gabriel or me. It's about helping Old Dog Leg."

"And what about your policeman? What will he think of all this?"

Guilt rolled through me, followed closely by anger and resentment. Did she really expect to have a say in my personal life? "I don't know what he'll think," I snapped. "But that's between Sullivan and me. You don't need to worry about it."

Her face fell, and the hurt in her eyes brought me full circle to guilt again.

"I see," she said. "Well, then, I won't worry any longer."

Two wrongs don't make a right, Aunt Yolanda whispered in my ear, and I barely resisted the urge to beat my head against the wall in frustration. It's bad enough to disappoint one of the mother figures in my life, but both of them at the same time? Brutal.

I took a calming breath and said, "I know you care about me, Miss Frankie. I know you're concerned about Zydeco. But I need you to trust me. I'm not going to do anything to jeopardize the bakery or its reputation."

We stared at each other for a moment while the coffee finished brewing. The gurgle of the coffeemaker scraped at my nerves, and the coffee's earthy scent, usually one I find calming, made a dull ache form between my eyes. After a moment, she turned away and rinsed another plate.

"This isn't like you," I said to the back of her head. "Is there something else bothering you?"

She closed the dishwasher and latched it before she answered. "I guess I'm more tired than I realized. I'm sure to be dreadful company. You'll forgive me if I turn in?"

Confused, I turned toward the door, but I stopped there and asked, "Are we okay?"

She looked over her shoulder and smiled. "Absolutely. I'm sure you'll do the right thing, sugar. Forget I said anything."

Uh-huh. As if that would be easy. "Let me see how things go when I get to the B and B tomorrow. Maybe I'll be able to break away for a while on Saturday so we can meet with Ox."

"That would be lovely. You don't mind letting yourself out, do you?"

And with that, I was dismissed.

I trudged out to the Mercedes and sat there for a long time replaying the conversation in my mind. And the disquiet I'd been feeling earlier grew a whole lot stronger.

Five

I got home a little after ten and spent the next three hours doing laundry and packing for the weekend. It wasn't as easy to put together a wardrobe as I'd expected. I wanted to look good without appearing overly concerned about my appearance, but in the three years since Philippe and I separated, my wardrobe had suffered a slow, steady decline that matched exactly the deterioration of my social life.

Or at least that had been the case until I moved to New Orleans last year. I'd been meaning to update the contents of my closet since, but had been too busy to do anything about it. While I considered and rejected a stream of T-shirts and tops that had been in style a few years ago, I toyed with the idea of calling Sullivan to let him know about my weekend plans. I even got as far as punching in his number a few times, but I always talked myself out of hitting send.

It wasn't that I wanted to hide the truth or that I felt guilty about my decision. Somebody had to help Old Dog Leg, and I'd been elected. And Sullivan was levelheaded and understanding about most things. But I had a few doubts about how he'd react to my plan for the weekend with Gabriel, and after the conversation I'd had earlier with Miss Frankie I wasn't in the mood to defend my decision. I finally decided that it would be easier to let Sullivan know what I'd been up to after it was all over, and climbed into bed a little before 2 a.m. When my alarm went off five hours later, I dragged myself out of bed, wolfed down two cups of coffee and an Asiago cheese bagel with cream cheese while I waited for Gabriel to pick me up.

The Love Nest turned out to be a sprawling old house that stretched out over a couple of lots on the West Bank. The central part of the house, which looked as if it had been built early in the twentieth century, was flanked by a couple of more recent additions. By recent, I meant sometime in the *middle* of the twentieth century.

The freshly painted white clapboards and dark green shutters tried to make the building look cheerful, but its location in the heart of a depressed neighborhood gave it a downtrodden quality. It sat back from the street behind a patchy lawn, in the center of which stood two palm trees so bent by the wind that their trunks formed an off-kilter heart.

Traffic was light for a Friday, so we got across the bridge faster than either of us had anticipated. It was half past noon when Gabriel parked at the curb. Check-in wasn't until one, so we sat there for a few minutes watching the neighborhood stroll by. Or maybe *stroll* is the wrong word. The neighborhood surged past us, bounced past us, danced past us, with everyone moving to the beat of the music that seemed to be playing everywhere.

A handful of musicians sat on one corner blowing the desultory notes of a jazz number on trumpets and a saxophone while only a couple of buildings away a driving hip-hop beat poured from the doors of a tattoo parlor. Two old men sat on the crumbling stoop of a barbershop, smoking cigarettes and watching the neighborhood through narrowed eyes. A few feet away several young women lounged against the side of a building, sharing a can of Coke as they kept an eye on toddlers playing on the sidewalk.

Gabriel slid down on his tailbone and visibly relaxed. I felt my nerves winding tighter by the minute. I hadn't given much thought to the area of town we'd be staying in, but now I wondered if we should have spent more time planning. "Maybe Dog Leg should have asked somebody else," I said, breaking the silence. "You and I aren't exactly going to blend in here."

Gabriel grinned and rolled his head to look at me. "Why? Because we're white?"

I grinned back. "Speak for yourself, gringo. Do you think they'll believe that you and I picked this particular bed-and-breakfast for our honeymoon? I don't want to make them suspicious right off the bat."

"You're letting your nerves show," Gabriel said. "What does anyone have to be suspicious about?"

I waved my hand vaguely. "Oh, I don't know. Everything. Don't you think people will wonder what we're doing here?"

Gabriel cut a glance at me. "Only if you keep looking like we're up to no good." He leaned across the seat and kissed me briefly. *Flip.* He rubbed his thumb gently near the corner of my mouth. "Relax. Act like a bride. You remember how to do that, don't you?"

Oh. Yeah. I felt the tingles, but I swatted his hand away and made a face. "I think my skills are a little sharper than yours. At least I've *been* married."

Gabriel laughed and opened his car door. "There. See? Sniping at me already. Right in character. Relax, Rita. We'll be just fine."

Easy for him to say. He had the gift of making friends wherever he went.

He paused with one foot on the pavement and gave me a look. "You want me to call Dog Leg and tell him we've changed our minds?"

I shook my head quickly. "No, I'm just . . ." But I didn't know how to put my concerns into words. They were so wrapped up in my childhood issues about fitting into a new environment and then the challenges of having married so far over my head, I wasn't even sure they were valid. I shrugged. "No. Of course not. Just do me a favor. Remind me why we're doing this?"

"Because Old Dog Leg needs our help."

"Yeah. That's it. I knew there was a reason." I stepped out into the bright spring sunlight and adjusted my sunglasses against the glare. "So which one of us is going to get Monroe to strip down so we can check for the birthmark on his back?"

Gabriel winked and popped the trunk. "I thought I'd leave that to you, honey."

"Well," I said, "I guess it might be a little less weird for me to try getting him naked than for you to do it."

Grinning from ear to ear, Gabriel pulled our suitcases from the trunk. "Getting the man naked is optional. All we really need is a look at his shoulder. But hey! Whatever floats your boat."

"Leave my boat out of this," I said. While he extended the handles on our suitcases, I closed the trunk. "Can we be serious for a minute? What if Monroe isn't who he claims to be? What are we going to do then?"

"I guess that depends on what else we learn about him along the way," Gabriel said as we started walking. "We don't know what we're going to find here. I think we have to just take it one step at a time."

He was probably right, but I'm not fond of going with the flow. I'm much more comfortable when I have a game plan. He was walking quickly, so I put on my best "wife" face—

whatever that was—and scurried after him to the front door. He held the door for me, and I stepped into a room that smelled so strongly of carnations and roses it was more like a funeral parlor than a lobby.

The hardwood floors gleamed, and sunlight spilled into the foyer through tall narrow windows on two of the walls. Several huge vases filled with massive flower arrangements accounted for the heavy floral scent, and a refreshment station out on a small corner table offered coffee, hot water, and an assortment of tea and cocoa packets. The place seemed a bit faded, but it looked clean and comfortable enough.

An elderly black woman with graying hair cut close to her head looked up as we approached the front desk. She struggled to her feet and shuffled toward us, leaning a set of thick arms on the counter when she reached her destination. She watched us with a scowl so deep it formed several extra chins and hooded—maybe even suspicious—eyes. "Can I help you?"

In spite of her advanced age, her voice was strong and clear, her eyes sharp and bright.

Memories of visits to the principal's office flashed through my head, and I swallowed nervously.

Gabriel seemed oblivious to her pursed lips and no-nonsense expression. He put on his sexy smile and turned up the Cajun accent. "My wife and I would like to book a room for a few days. Do you have anything available?"

His Sexy Cajun act usually renders women weak in the knees, but the woman behind the front desk seemed more annoyed than impressed. She ran a slow look over both of us in turn. "*You* want to stay *here*?"

A big old "I told you so" hovered on my lips, but I swallowed it and nodded. "If you're not completely booked."

She stared us down for another few seconds, then lifted one thick shoulder and reached for a book on the desk behind her. "Should'a made a reservation," she muttered. "But we have a room. Seventy-five a night. Breakfast every morning between six and nine. Don't show up at nine-oh-five and expect to be fed. We don't serve latecomers."

Gabriel didn't blink. I didn't dare. He glanced around the lobby, and I followed his gaze, taking in the furniture, covered in a bold flowered pattern, the polished wood tables, and a bookshelf filled with dog-eared paperbacks. One young couple cooed at each other on the couch, and another huddled near a small alcove, pouring over brochures advertising nearby points of interest and local businesses. They didn't seem to notice us, and that gave me hope that we'd be able to fly under the radar while we were here.

"It sounds perfect," Gabriel said, turning back with a cheesy grin. "Doesn't it, *chérie*?"

"Perfect." I offered my friendliest smile to the she-bear behind the front desk.

She ignored me and growled a question at Gabriel. "You want a street view or a room overlooking the garden? Garden rooms are ten dollars more a night."

"What do you think?" Gabriel asked me.

What I really wanted was the room closest to Monroe Magee, but I couldn't exactly ask for it. I'd seen the street view on the way in. I could only hope the garden would be more visually appealing. "I think the garden sounds lovely."

"Garden it is." Gabriel rested one arm on the counter and lowered his voice a little. "This is our first time away together, so give us the best room you've got."

The woman squared her shoulders and sniffed as if he'd insulted her. "All of our rooms are equally nice."

I started to say that I was sure they were, but another woman—thinner, darker, and a handful of years younger—poked her head through an open door behind the front desk and gave a little squeal. Her hair fell to her shoulders, a riot of thick black curls, and her eyes were wide in her thin face.

"More honeymooners? Oh, Hyacinth, isn't this *exciting*?" She bustled through the door and tossed a stack of folded towels onto one end of the long counter. Her head bobbed, birdlike, on her thin neck, and she chirped her words so fast it was hard to follow what she said. "Sister's right, you know. We have *the* best honeymoon suites in the area, and I'm not lying when I say that."

"I'm sure you're not," I said.

And Gabriel added, "We've heard good things about the Love Nest, haven't we, baby?"

Baby agreed that we had, and the newcomer chirped on like a robin on speed. "Now don't you go worrying about the cost. Our rates are very reasonable." She spread open a brochure in front of us and pointed at a cluster of pictures featuring a room completely decorated in red and white. "The Valentine suite has a king-sized bed, a jetted tub, and a balcony. It's a lovely, lovely room. One of my favorites. Or there's Nights in White Satin," she said, directing our attention to another photo grouping. "Very romantic."

Hyacinth tried to push the brochure away. "Primrose, really. Let these poor children breathe." She sent us a smile that looked almost apologetic. "Ignore my sister. She gets carried away at times. Now, as I said, all of our rooms are nice."

With an annoyed eye roll at her sister, Primrose cut in again. "You might like the Honeymooner better. It runs thirty dollars more a night, but the bed and the jetted tub are both heart-shaped and the room has mood lighting."

"The room," Hyacinth said with a disapproving sniff, "has a dimmer switch."

Primrose shushed her and went on. "We also provide a complimentary bottle of champagne when you check in," she said, flashing a set of dimples. "And we throw in a few other romantic touches, too. I'd just need half an hour to get your room ready before you go upstairs. And, of course, we'll want to give you a proper welcome. If you'll join our little group for cocktail hour at five, we'll toast you and your new marriage in style."

A cocktail party to celebrate our marriage? So much for flying under the radar. I tried begging off. We were here to identify Monroe. Period. "Actually," I said, "we have—"

Gabriel cut me off before I could finish. "We're free all evening," he said. "We'd love to join you. And I think the Honeymooner sounds perfect." He pulled out his wallet and handed a credit card to Hyacinth, turning that cheesy grin on me again. "Don't you, *chérie*?"

Chérie most certainly did not. *Chérie* saw no reason to go overboard with this charade. And she tried to say so. "Gabriel. *Sweetheart.*"

He put a finger on my lips to stop me from speaking and followed up with a chaste kiss. "Really, my love. I insist."

I barely resisted the urge to kick him in the shin—which I could have easily done since he also wrapped one arm around my waist while he cooed like a besotted bridegroom. I might have delivered that kick anyway, but Old Dog Leg's face flashed through my memory at that precise moment, accompanied by a whiff of Gabriel's aftershave. By the time my head cleared, Mr. and Mrs. Gabriel Broussard were registered guests in the honeymoon suite at the Love Nest.

Six

We closed the door to our room behind us nearly an hour later. Aside from the time in the car, it was the first time we'd been alone since we'd committed to three fun-filled days and two romantic nights of wedded bliss. Primrose had insisted on giving us a guided tour of the inn's first floor, including the kitchen, a formal dining room, game room and small library, and the front parlor where we were to meet for cocktails later. We didn't have to be downstairs for the cocktail party until five, which gave us plenty of time to settle on a game plan for finding and unmasking Monroe. Since we'd be the guests of honor at the party, I also thought it would be smart to get our stories straight so we could play the newlywed game convincingly.

Gabriel put the bags on the floor and surveyed the room with hands on hips. He nodded as his gaze traveled over the promised heart-shaped bed, covered with a heaping helping of frilly throw pillows and red rose petals. "These must be why we had to wait to come upstairs," he said, lifting one of the rose petals for a sniff. "They're real."

"I kind of figured that out from the overpowering rose scent." I rubbed my nose and fought a sneeze. "I hope you don't think I'm cleaning those up."

"Let's toss a coin," Gabriel said. "I think that's only fair."

"We wouldn't have to deal with them at all if you hadn't asked for the Honeymooner suite."

"Oh come on," he said with a grin. "Are you trying to tell me you weren't even a *little* curious to see this room in person?"

I shrugged and sat on the edge of the bed to test the mattress. It wasn't great, but it wasn't saggy either. "Not even a little," I said. "I was more interested in Nights in White Satin. It sounded much more practical."

"Practical? For our honeymoon?" He shook his head and tried to look serious. "You worry me, Rita. You saw how excited Primrose was over this room. How could I disappoint that sweet old lady?"

"Primrose does seem sweet," I said. "Hyacinth? Not so much. I'm not sure she even wanted our business."

"Well, she's stuck with us now." Gabriel turned his attention to exploring the room—which wasn't large enough to demand a long look around. White lace curtains hung at two windows. A set of wooden doors led onto a tiny balcony overlooking an overgrown flower garden. Cold air blew inside through a portable window unit, but did little to relieve the stuffiness of a room that I suspected hadn't actually seen any honeymoon action in months.

"And we're stuck with this room that you were so curious about." I kicked off my shoes and flexed, then decided to tackle the subject at the top of my head. "There *is* something I am curious about, though."

He adjusted one of the cooler vents and gave me the eye. "Oh? What's that?"

"You."

He stopped moving for a fraction of a second, then picked up his circuit again. "What do you want to know?"

"This and that. Enough to feel confident as your blushing bride when we walk into the cocktail party later."

Gabriel shrugged. "I think you have that under control already, don't you?"

"No I don't." I shifted on the bed so I could see him better. "In case it's slipped your mind, we're supposed to be in love. I should know more about you than the fact that you tend bar, you clean up nicely, and you have friends in high places." That latter point I'd picked up when he'd taken me to the Captain's Court for the Krewe of Musterion during Mardi Gras. "Just how did you make all those influential friends, anyway?"

He smiled and looked out the window. "I met some of them in school. Grew up with some others. You know . . . I get around."

"So your family has money?"

He rocked up onto his toes and stared at something in the garden. "Define *money*."

His attempt to dodge the question didn't surprise me. In the year since I met him, he'd barely ever talked about his past. Which only intrigued me more. "What kind of house did you grow up in? Large? Small? Outhouse and a well, or running water and indoor plumbing?"

With a chuckle, Gabriel turned away from the window. "Smallish. Plumbing. Doors and windows. All the amenities. No old family, though. Disappointed?"

I thought about my conversation with Miss Frankie the night before and shook my head firmly. "Nope. Where were you born?"

"Slidell," he said, referring to a town about thirty miles northeast of New Orleans.

"And your parents? What should I know about them?"

"They're great. Hardworking. Do everything they can to make the world a better place."

"I guess that means they're still alive?"

He nodded once. "Yeah."

"You could give me a little more, you now. What about the rest of the family? Any brothers or sisters?"

Looking exasperated but resigned, he leaned against the wall and crossed one foot over the other. "Two of each."

For some reason, that surprised me. I wasn't sure whether the fact that he'd never talked about his big family with me said more about their relationships or ours. But I'd think about that later. "Younger or older?"

"I'm the oldest," he said. "Alex comes next, then Francine, Renee, and Raoul."

I committed their names to memory and tried to imagine Gabriel sitting around the dinner table surrounded by family. It wasn't easy. "Are they all like you?"

His lips quirked ever so slightly. "Exactly. Everyone has two arms, two legs, and a face."

"You're so funny." I crossed my legs beneath me on the bed. "Seriously, Gabriel. Why don't you ever talk about them?"

He pushed away from the wall and sat on the pointy foot of the heart. "I don't *not* talk about them. We see each other for most holidays and the usual family occasions like weddings and funerals. But I'm single and working. Alex and Francine are married. Renee's engaged and Raoul is still in school. Our lives are just different."

"Speaking of the *M* word," I said, scooting a little closer, "why haven't you ever been married?"

He turned on the Sexy Cajun grin, probably hoping to

distract me with it. "That information is available on a need-to-know basis."

I batted my eyelashes and cooed, "But, darling, I'm your wife. If anyone needs to know, I do."

Gabriel leaned toward me, so close that his face was barely an inch from mine. I could smell his soap and something faintly minty on his breath. His eyes roamed my face so slowly I could hardly breathe, and for one heart-stopping moment I knew he was going to kiss me—and I mean *really* kiss me. My heart jumped around in my chest, and my mouth went dry.

But Gabriel just tweaked my nose and said, "In that case, I'll tell you everything . . . on our first anniversary."

I swatted his arm as he pulled away. "Jerk."

"I've been called worse. My turn to ask the questions. Let's start with you and the cop. What's the story with the two of you?"

I stared at him, surprised by the unexpected change of direction. "What does that have to do with this?"

"Does he know that you're here? With me?"

The question made me uncomfortable, but I answered it anyway. "Not yet."

"Ah." His dark eyes narrowed. "Are you going to tell him?"

"I don't plan to lie to him, if that's what you're asking. But my friendship with Sullivan has no bearing on this weekend."

"*Au contraire, ma chérie.* If the two of you are serious, if he has a prior claim on your affections—" He broke off with an expressive shrug.

I stood to face him. "First of all, nobody has a prior *claim* on anything about me. Sullivan and I are friends. We see each other occasionally, just like you and I do. No commitment, no promises, no petty jealousy."

Gabriel's eyebrows flew up in surprise. "So you're saying he wouldn't care that you're here with me for the weekend?"

Was I saying that? I honestly didn't know how Sullivan would feel, so I took the easy way out. "I'm saying the topic of my relationship with Sullivan is off-limits for the weekend. Let's stay focused on how we're going to convince these people that we're newlyweds and how we're going to figure out what's going on with this Monroe person."

Gabriel touched my cheek gently. "If you say so."

I pushed past him and checked inside a cheaply constructed armoire for extra blankets and pillows. The way his touch was making my heart race, there was no way I'd survive a night on the same bed with my pride intact. Gabriel would have to sleep somewhere else. Just my luck, there wasn't so much as a piece of lint inside the cabinet.

I turned my attention to the dresser instead. Also empty, but the drawers looked clean enough so I unzipped my bag and asked, "You want the top drawers or the bottom?"

Gabriel had crossed to the balcony doors, which were swollen by age and humidity and apparently stuck shut.

"Does it matter?"

"I guess not. I'll take top. Do you want to shower first in the morning or second?"

Gabriel gave the doors another rattle, but they still didn't budge. "Are you planning to organize every bit of our stay?"

"Only the things that need to be organized. Shall we talk about sleeping arrangements?"

Gabriel finally managed to open the swollen doors, and stepped out onto the postage-stamp-sized balcony. "I'll leave it up to you. Do you want the right side or the left?"

"The middle." I sat on the bed beside my suitcase and frowned. "I thought we might at least have a chair or a couch in the room."

Gabriel leaned on the railing but straightened again quickly when it wobbled under his weight. "Even if we had a couch," he said, "I wouldn't let you sleep on it. I wouldn't want you to mess up your back or something."

"Such a gentleman." I gave the mattress another test bounce, and this time I thought I felt the sharp end of a spring. But at least Gabriel and I were back on familiar ground. "You'll need to sleep on the floor, over by the door. I'll try really hard not to step on your head if I get up in the middle of the night."

"Gee thanks. I can feel the love." He came back inside, leaving the doors open behind him. "Don't worry, Rita. We agreed to keep this thing platonic, and I won't go back on my promise . . . unless you change your mind."

Yeah. That was the problem.

"All we have to do is find the man who wrote that letter to Old Dog Leg and look for the birthmark. Once we do that, we can get out of here if you want," Gabriel said. "In the meantime, let's keep those sweet old ladies happy. They could be serving the guy to us on a silver platter—or in a champagne glass—at this little get-together they've planned."

He had a point, which I acknowledged grudgingly. "Let's hope he's actually there tonight."

"Even if he's not, we're still ahead. We'll have met some of the other guests, and maybe one of them can help us get a foot in Monroe's door."

Just then, a knock sounded on the door. My breath caught, and I wondered if our voices had carried out into the hall. Gabriel crossed the room in three long strides and opened it on Primrose, who held a silver tray loaded with a bottle of cheap champagne and two glasses.

She surged through the door, brushing past Gabriel and heading toward the dresser in the corner. "I brought you that bottle of champagne to start off the celebration!" She shoved a couple of candlesticks to one side and put the tray down.

I watched her closely, trying to determine whether she'd overheard our conversation.

Clasping her hands together over her chest, she turned back to face us. "Look at you two! Aren't you the cutest couple ever?"

I let out the breath I'd been holding and tried to look pleased. "That's very sweet of you," I said, mentally calculating how much champagne I'd need to get through this weekend without losing my nerve.

Her hands fluttered in front of her. "I'm more than happy to do it. Seeing a young couple so happy and in love does my heart good."

Gabriel slid a couple of bills into her hand. "You must see couples of all ages here. Newlyweds. People celebrating anniversaries. My grandparents might like this place, but they'd probably have trouble negotiating the stairs. Do you have any honeymoon suites on the first floor?"

Primrose slipped the money into her pocket and shook her head. "No suites, I'm afraid. Most of our clientele is young. Like the two of you."

Which reinforced my guess that Monroe wasn't here on his honeymoon. "This seems like a big operation for you and your sister," I said. "Do you have help?"

Primrose nodded. "Oh lawd, yes. More than we need, really." She motioned toward the outside doors and continued the tour she'd started downstairs. "I see you've found the balcony. This time of year, the weather is wonderful and cool in the evenings. And there's a lock on the front gate, so you'll be safe to leave the windows and doors open for a while. Let the fresh air inside." She broke off with a little laugh and covered her mouth with one hand. "Listen to me! You're on your honeymoon! You don't want any of those old fools across the way knowing your business."

I glanced at the window, but the only building I could see was one of the additions to the inn I'd noticed earlier. "Isn't that part of the Love Nest?"

"Oh, yes. That's where our regulars stay. If you can call those old coots *regular.*" She laughed at her own joke, then turned serious. "We have a couple of rooms over there, but they're quite small and not at all romantic. Still, if your grandparents are interested in staying here, we might be able to work something out."

"The residents over there . . . will they be joining us for cocktail hour?" Gabriel asked.

"If there's alcohol involved, just you *try* to keep them away. Some of them can be a bit prickly, but don't you worry. They're mostly friends from way back. Nice enough, for the most part. But don't let them bother you none. They give you any trouble at all, you let me or Hyacinth know." She stopped, tilted her head to one side, and corrected herself. "Let *me* know. Hyacinth doesn't like to be bothered with such things." She sobered slightly and asked, "That's not a problem, is it? Should I tell them to stay away?"

"Of course not," I said quickly. "They live here, and I'm sure we'll enjoy meeting them."

I was intrigued by the idea of a group of *old coots* living in the inn. Was Monroe one of the Love Nest's longtime residents, or was he on staff? Maybe Primrose and Hyacinth knew about his connection to Old Dog Leg. Were the three of them working together to scam him?

Primrose let out a little sigh and moved on again. "I think Hyacinth told you about breakfast. If you have any special dietary needs, let one of us know and we'll do our best to accommodate. We have parking for guests behind the house, and you're welcome to spend time in the garden if you'd like. Not that we expect to see much of you while you're here. We all understand. We were all young once."

I stood, uncomfortable on that bed in the wake of Primrose's insinuations. "I do have one question," I said to her. "Where's the TV?"

She looked aghast. "There isn't one, of course. What would be the point?"

Right. No point whatsoever.

"If you really need a television," she said, her voice clouded with disapproval, "you're welcome to use the community set in the parlor. We turn it on at six in the morning, and it goes off at eleven every night. But people around here have their routines, so you may have to watch what they're watching."

Old reruns of *Bonanza* or *Kojak*? No thanks.

Gabriel came up behind me and wrapped his arms around my waist. "I'm sure we can find *some* way to entertain ourselves." He nuzzled my neck, making me seriously reconsider my commitment to the whole platonic thing.

Primrose giggled like a young girl and turned toward the door. "You're a lucky woman, Mrs. Broussard."

Yeah. Wasn't I, though? "Call me Rita. Please."

"Of course. If there's anything else the two of you need, just press zero on the house phone," Primrose said. "One of us will bring it right up."

Yeah. Like I was going to have those old ladies running up and down the stairs on my account.

She finally let herself out into the hallway and closed the door with a soft *click*.

I waited until I heard her footsteps recede before I wriggled out of Gabriel's embrace. "She's gone," I said, keeping my voice low just in case. "We can stop playacting now."

Gabriel pretended to be disappointed. "Wouldn't it be better to stay in character while we're here? I wouldn't want to slip up."

I stuck out my tongue. "Nice try . . . but no." I walked into the bathroom, determined to put some distance between us. I could still hear him laughing, even after I closed and locked the door behind me.

Seven

Gabriel and I were no closer to an agreement on how to proceed when we left our room at five o'clock to go to the cocktail party. He practically skipped down the stairs, eagerly anticipating an adventure. I followed more slowly, unsure about whether we'd be able to plug all the holes in our story and nervous about having to lie. When I was a kid, my aunt Yolanda and uncle Nestor had drilled into me and my cousins the importance of telling the truth. I'd taken the lessons to heart—mostly. Oh, sure, I could omit unnecessary information without hesitation if the occasion demanded. And I was pretty good at justifying those omissions using shades of gray. But outright lying shot straight out of the gray area and into the sin zone, which made me more than a little uncomfortable.

My mind raced with questions I couldn't answer. What would we say when we met the man who called himself Monroe Magee? How likely would he be to talk with us? How would I get him to show me that birthmark if, in fact, he had one? And how would Hyacinth and Primrose react if they caught us lying?

Maybe this wasn't the only way or even the best way to find out what Monroe Magee was up to, but we were here and I was determined not to go back to Old Dog Leg empty-handed. Our success or failure now hinged on whether Gabriel and I could successfully maintain the facade that we were a couple of besotted honeymooners. I had experience on my side. At least I'd actually been on a honeymoon. But Gabriel had enthusiasm on his. He was having much more fun than I was.

"Remember," I whispered as we took the last few stairs, "we're in love. We can hardly stand to be apart. You worship me. You think everything I do is adorable and nothing I do irritates you."

He nodded and spoke out of the corner of his mouth. "The feeling is mutual, I assume?"

"Of course it is . . . darling. Just don't overdo it, please."

Gabriel put an arm around my waist and pulled me close. "Overdo? Me?"

"It's been ten seconds," I pointed out, "and already you've proved my point." I put both hands on his chest and applied gentle pressure. "This is not an open invitation, however."

Gabriel nuzzled my neck again and flashed a wicked grin when I stiffened under the brush of warm lips against my skin. "Will you please stop worrying?" he whispered. "Relax and have fun."

"We're not here to have fun," I reminded him. "We're here to do a favor for a friend."

"We're not saving the world, my love."

I frowned and pulled away. "I don't think you're taking this seriously enough. We might just be saving Dog Leg's world, and I can't concentrate when you do that."

Gabriel let out a long-suffering sigh, but the twinkle in his eye told me he was enjoying my discomfort. "All right," he said. "You win. I'll be serious and subdued. Will that make you happy?"

"Delirious."

"Good." His voice dropped to a whisper. "Then stop frowning."

"I'm not frowning," I whispered back. "I'm worshiping you with my eyes."

"Ah. *That's* what that is. Good to know." His grin came back and he pressed a quick kiss to my forehead, and then we walked into the parlor wrapped around each other like kudzu vines.

We found three old men sitting in the parlor with Hyacinth and Primrose, all chatting softly. One short and wrinkled, one tall and thin wearing a black suit that had clearly seen better days, and the third an enormous man who spread across half the couch. The two young couples I'd spotted earlier were talking to each other in one corner.

I scoured the men's faces, searching for a resemblance to Old Dog Leg. Each looked about the right age, and all three were African American, but none of them bore any real similarities to my friend that I could see. I didn't feel discouraged, though. I hadn't expected to find Old Dog Leg's clone.

The short wiry man, who had more wrinkles than a basset hound, spotted us first as we came through the door. He signaled the others with a jerk of his chin, and they fell silent so abruptly, I figured they must have been talking about us.

Primrose bounded to her feet like a woman half her age and advanced on us with her scrawny arms held wide. "Here they are!" she cried. "Our newest happy couple." She hugged us both briefly, then took each of us by the hand and tugged us toward the small group of senior citizens, all of whom were watching us as if they suspected we were up to no good.

Which, of course, we were.

I flashed my most trustworthy smile. Gabriel grinned like

a used-car salesman who'd just spotted an easy mark. I would have elbowed him in the ribs, but Primrose stood between us, still clutching our hands tightly.

"Y'all get on your feet," she ordered. "We're toasting Gabriel and Rita Broussard, who were married—" She broke off, suddenly confused. "I can't believe I forgot to ask. When *were* you married?"

I gave them the answer Gabriel and I had agreed on. "Yesterday afternoon."

"Just yesterday?" Primrose finally let go of our hands and clasped her own over her heart. "Isn't that sweet?"

The old basset hound scowled from one of us to the other. "And you're just getting here today? You from out of town or something?"

We'd prepared for that question, too. "No, we're from right here in New Orleans," Gabriel said. He leaned around Primrose and winked suggestively in my general direction. "We talked about checking in last night after the wedding, but frankly, it was just too far to drive. I didn't want anything to get between me and my lovely bride."

That was his version of serious and subdued? He'd straight-up lied to me out there on the stairs. I looked him in the eye to let him know I was not amused. "Don't make jokes, honey. These nice people might take you seriously."

Mr. Big regarded me steadily over the frames of his thick-lensed glasses. "You saying you didn't want to enjoy your wedding night?"

Heat rushed into my face, which made Gabriel's eyes dance. "That's not what she's saying at all. We did enjoy it, didn't we, *chérie*? Very much."

"That," I said firmly, "isn't an appropriate topic of conversation." And certainly not the topic I wanted to discuss. I smiled to take the sting out of my reprimand and said, "Let's talk about something else." Like whether they were harboring someone pretending to be our long-lost Monroe. But suddenly swinging the conversation in that direction without raising eyebrows would be next to impossible. Like it or not, I'd have to go with the flow and wait for an opportunity.

Mr. Big looked almost disappointed, but he smiled and said, "The lady's right, son. That's the first thing you gotta learn about being married. The lady's always right."

I shot a grin at Gabriel. "I think you should pay attention to him, sweetheart. It sounds like he knows what he's talking about."

All the men laughed. Hyacinth rolled her eyes, and Primrose fluttered her hands at all of them. "Now, now y'all," she said with a laugh. "Let's not tease our guests. This is their first night with us. We don't want to give them a bad impression."

The laughter died away, and nobody said anything for a moment. After a while, the basset hound cleared his throat. "What made you choose this place? This neighborhood isn't your usual stomping grounds, is it?"

I *knew* they'd be curious. My eyes flashed to Gabriel, but just then the cell phone in my pocket vibrated. I silenced it without looking at the screen. I didn't care who was calling. This was not the time for an interruption. But both the question and the phone call made me nervous. Perspiration beaded on my nose and upper lip.

Gabriel didn't even blink. "You're right. This isn't our neighborhood," he admitted easily. "We're both too busy with work to get away for long, but we did want to disappear for a few days . . . if you know what I mean. Nobody will think to look for us here."

The big guy chuckled. "Smart thinking. You put work first your whole life, you end up nothing but sorry. Ask me how I know."

Hyacinth scowled at Mr. Big, but even so, the look she gave him was several degrees warmer than the frosty one she'd given us when we checked in earlier. "They don't want to ask you, Dontae. Nobody wants to hear your stories tonight."

Primrose turned back to us with a smile that looked a little too bright. "These two squabble like brother and sister," she chirped, "but they're harmless. They've been friends forever." She waved a hand toward the large man and said, "This here's Dontae Thomas. He likes to grumble, so just tune him out if he gets started."

Not Monroe. Strike one.

She motioned toward the basset hound next. "And this is Cleveland Bunch. He's another of our long-term residents."

Strike two. That gave us one last chance for a home run.

"If you should ever want to find Cleveland, he'll be hanging out right here in this room watching his stories on the TV." She put a hand to her mouth and whispered, "He's addicted to soap operas, but don't let on that I told you."

"They're not soap operas," Cleveland protested. "I watch my judge shows. You ever seen one?"

I nodded, but refrained from admitting that I wasn't a big fan.

Gabriel said, "Good stuff," as if he thought the on-camera antics of small claims court had some redeeming social value. I hoped he wasn't serious.

Silence threatened again, so I asked the first thing that came to mind. "You don't have TVs in your rooms either?"

"Oh, I got one," Cleveland said, "but it ain't hooked to the whatchacallit. The cable box."

"It's like a giant paperweight," Dontae said. "No earthly good to anyone."

"So what?" Cleveland shot back. "I don't like being cooped up in there all the time. Sue me."

Frowning at the two men, Hyacinth lumbered to her feet. "All I'm saying is, it wouldn't hurt you to find something productive to do. If you ask me, you ought to take a page out of the professor's book."

Cleveland grinned at her and at least a dozen years fell off his face. "I didn't ask your advice, Hy, and that's why, right there. You won't catch me parading around town the way he does. Instead of busting my chops, you ought to be thanking me for being normal. You don't need more than one crazy fool wandering around this place."

Hyacinth turned away with another expressive roll of the eyes. "Oh, we got more than one. But who's counting?"

I laughed uneasily and turned to the tall man who'd been watching the exchange with a benign smile. "I certainly hope you're not the professor," I said, hoping that my third and last chance would be a hit. I wanted him to introduce himself as Monroe Magee and launch into his life story to boot.

"Gracious, no!" Primrose said with a reedy laugh, and scurried over to perform the introductions. "This is Pastor Rod."

I really hadn't expected fate to throw Monroe into our laps that easily, but I was disappointed anyway.

The pastor smiled at me and leaned up to shake Gabriel's hand, revealing a frayed cuff on the sleeve of his shirt. "Rod Kinkle," he said in a gravelly voice. "Pleased to meet you."

Gabriel let out an appreciative whistle. "You have live-in clergy? That's convenient."

I glanced at the others to see if they'd taken offense, but I must have been the only one who thought Gabriel's comment was a trifle insensitive. I mean, in light of everyone's advanced years and all.

"Pastor Rod doesn't live here," Primrose explained, "but he's around most every day. He's just like one of the family. He likes to offer a prayer for the marriages of our guests. I hope that's all right with you."

Under other circumstances, I'd have agreed without hesitation. Aunt Yolanda had raised me with a healthy respect for the Almighty. But the idea of letting the pastor pray for our make-believe marriage triggered my fight-or-flight response and drove everything else, even Monroe, out of my head for a moment.

I flicked a panicked look at Gabriel, but he was embracing the idea as another leg on his grand adventure. "I think that would be great," he said. "Thank you, Pastor."

Was he kidding?

The two men fell into an easy conversation, but I barely heard a word either of them said. I was too busy trying to think of a way to remove us from the prayer list without giving away the fact that we'd been lying since we walked in the front door.

I'd crossed the line this time. Blessing a fake marriage? I was going to hell for sure and practically sending an engraved invitation for God to strike me down where I stood.

Eight

Just when I thought all was lost, I got a Hail Mary pass in the form of an elderly black man wearing a Confederate army uniform, complete with frock coat and a double row of buttons. He marched slowly, his back ramrod straight, his face devoid of all expression. The uniform was strange enough by itself, but the fact that an African American man was wearing it was stranger still. Was *this* our supposed Monroe Magee?

Behind him, an old woman with caramel-colored skin and gray hair leaned heavily on a walker as she shuffled through the door. Whoever these two were, I owed them big-time.

Primrose looked flustered by their arrival. She ignored the woman and spoke to the Confederate soldier. "Well, Grey, I didn't realize you were coming. I thought you were out."

"Temporary change of duty," he said. "My contributions were not required this afternoon."

"In that getup, it's no wonder," Dontae grumbled. "You ought to be ashamed of yourself."

Grey waved off his comment and headed toward a chair.

"I'm tryin' to give an unbiased account of the conflict," he snarled. "Not that *you'd* understand that."

The woman gave her walker a sharp rap on the floor, demanding everyone's attention. Her body seemed frail, but the sparkle in her eyes made it clear that she had her wits about her. "And what about me, Primrose? I told you I'd be a few minutes late, but you started anyway." She turned to the soldier with a scowl. "Didn't I tell you she'd try to cut me out?"

I opened my mouth to assure her we hadn't actually started anything, but Primrose spoke up first. "*I* told you five o'clock sharp, Lula Belle. It's already ten past." Her demeanor had changed drastically. Gone was her smile and the fluttering of her hands. A look of irritation had settled on her thin face.

"So I'm a few minutes late," Lula Belle groused. "It's not the end of the world. You could have waited."

Primrose lifted her chin defiantly. "*You* could have made more of an effort."

I know it's wrong to find pleasure in someone else's unhappiness, but I was so relieved by the shift of attention away from Gabriel and me, I experienced a moment of gratitude for the bad feelings between the two women. You didn't have to be a rocket scientist to figure out that they weren't the best of friends, but that did make me wonder why they chose to live in the same house. In fact, the dynamic of the entire group confused me.

Strangely enough, Hyacinth, who had seemed irritated by the world in general, now wore an indulgent smile. "Sister, you know Lula Belle does her best."

Primrose *tsk*ed her tongue in irritation. "Her best to make me miserable, you mean. This may come as a surprise to you, Lula Belle, but the world doesn't revolve around you."

Lula Belle's walker thumped on the floor as she inched toward a chair. "Somebody ought to give you the same piece of advice, Primrose dear."

Well now, *this* was fun. I glanced at the others again to see if I was the only one who felt uncomfortable with the bickering, but except for one of the other honeymoon brides, nobody even seemed to notice it except Pastor Rod. He turned a benevolent smile on the two women. "Now, now ladies. The rest of us know that you're longtime friends, but our guests may not understand. We don't want to frighten them away, do we?"

Lula Belle sent Primrose a triumphant smile. Primrose snorted and turned toward the Civil War soldier. "Well, since you're here, Professor, come on in. We want to toast the newlyweds." She picked up a bottle of grocery store champagne and counted the glasses on the tray. "Oh bother," she said with a scowl aimed at Lula Belle. "I'm short. Everybody sit tight. I need to fetch more glasses."

As she scurried out the door, the professor shook Gabriel's hand and bowed low over mine. "Brigadier General Edward Asbury O'Neal at your service."

I was still trying to figure out whether he was serious or joking with the Confederate uniform, but Hyacinth took him to task. "Really, Grey, you couldn't even bother to change before joining us?"

The old man let go of my hand and laughed, not even slightly intimidated by Hyacinth's disapproval. "And be even later? Surely you jest. Even I am not so brave."

The corners of Hyacinth's mouth twitched a little as she filled us in. "He's Brigadier General This tonight. He'll be Private First Class That tomorrow. His real name is Grey Washington, but most everyone calls him Professor. In spite of what you see, he's not really crazy. He just acts like it sometimes."

The bride across the room snickered softly. They were certainly a bunch of characters, but I was only listening to their banter with half an ear. The only person at the Love Nest I really cared about wasn't even in the room.

Or was he?

If Dog Leg's visitor was a con artist, he might be any one of the four men (or even one of the three women) in front of me. But how would we ever figure out if that was the case? I certainly couldn't ask if one of them had recently sent a letter to Old Dog Leg. Even if one of them had, it wasn't like he—or she—would just admit it.

Grey's chest puffed up in mild outrage at Hyacinth's introduction. "Me? Crazy? I beg your pardon!"

Hyacinth flicked one thick wrist to wave away his protest. "He dresses up like that because he volunteers at the library."

Despite his earlier comments about the professor, Cleveland joined in to defend the latecomer. "He volunteers to work with kids whose daddies have run off and whose mamas are working three jobs to make ends meet. Or the ones whose parents are more interested in a crack pipe than math homework."

Grey nodded, and a proud smile tugged at the corners of his mouth. "Someone has to do it. Those children aren't receiving a proper education at school." He pointed a finger at the two young grooms across the room and said, "Make sure you do your duty when the kids come along, you hear me?"

One of the young men nodded solemnly. The other bit back a smile.

Hyacinth shook her head slightly, but I could see the fondness in her expression. "Don't get him started on what's wrong with the schools these days. What he really means is that he's bored out of his skull since he retired and dressing up like that makes him feel important."

"Educating kids is a worthy undertaking," Gabriel said. "You must be very proud of your husband," he said to Lula Belle. "How long has he been doing this?"

Lula Belle laughed. "Oh honey, I'm not married to that old fool. I prefer to keep my options open."

Grey ignored her insult and answered Gabriel's question.

"I've been helping the kids more years than I can count." He glanced pointedly at the others in the group, flipped out the tail of his coat with a flourish, and dropped onto a chair. "It's nice to be appreciated for a change."

With his apparent love of acting, Grey certainly could be planning to slip into the role of Monroe Magee, but would someone who really worked with disadvantaged youth do something so shady? I also ruled out the pastor on principle (not that pastors couldn't be scam artists, but still . . .). That left Cleveland and Dontae as the only real candidates.

Dontae chuckled at Grey's outrage, a deep rumble that seemed to roll like distant thunder in his massive chest. "You always were full of yourself, Professor. But these two lovebirds don't care what you do or why you do it. They've got more important things on their minds."

Grey's eyes clouded, and I sensed another storm on the horizon. "You think *I'm* full of myself?" he said with a laugh of derision. "At least I retired after forty years at Letterman Industries, *with* the gold watch and the certificate for dedicated service. Can you say the same?"

The smile slid from Dontae's round face, a clear sign that Grey's volley had hit its intended target.

Hyacinth clucked like a mother hen. "That was uncalled for, Grey. What's gotten into y'all tonight? Let's just drop it. Our guests aren't interested in your old squabbles."

Oh, but we were. At least I was. The more they all bickered with each other, the more likely Gabriel and I might learn something useful. Neither Grey nor Dontae looked ready to back down, but they retreated to neutral corners just as Primrose bustled back into the room holding more glasses.

Gabriel left my side to take the glasses from her, and Hyacinth sniffed loudly. "There you are," she said, her good humor already gone. "I swear you move a little slower every day. Now, can we get on with this? I have work to do."

The residents of the Love Nest certainly had an odd way of showing their affection, though it really did seem to be affection. I bit back a smile at the look Primrose gave her sister and caught Gabriel ducking his head from the corner of my eye.

Part of me was just as eager as Hyacinth to get this phony toast over with, but I wasn't exactly chomping at the bit to go back upstairs to that tiny room with its heart-shaped bed. And if Monroe was a guest at the Love Nest, I'd never meet him from the privacy of our honeymoon suite. I tried sending a silent signal to Gabriel that we should drag out the cocktail party as long as possible—without letting the pastor bless our counterfeit union. If Gabriel got the message, he didn't signal back.

While Primrose poured champagne and passed around the glasses, I put on my best adoring-bride expression and leaned closer to Gabriel, hoping for a chance to whisper something to him without being overheard. As I did, my cell phone vibrated again. Once again I silenced it without taking it out of my pocket. But two calls coming so close together made me wonder if something had gone wrong at the bakery. Vowing to check who'd called the very second I was upstairs, I accepted my glass and asked as innocently as I could, "So, is this everyone who's staying at the Love Nest?"

Cleveland frowned so hard half a dozen new wrinkles formed. "Everyone who matters."

Lula Belle paused in the act of smoothing one gnarled hand over her pant leg. "That's a mean thing to say."

"It's the truth," he said. "Besides all y'all," using his glass, he gestured at the other two couples and then at us, "*this* is our group."

"The Lord asks us to forgive," Pastor Rod said gently.

Gabriel slipped his free hand around my shoulder and squeezed gently, and I suspected he was as intrigued by this group of senior citizens as I was. Just who did they need to forgive? And for what?

Primrose looked up sharply, but the tone of her voice was even sharper. "Pastor!"

"You know I'm right, Primrose."

"What I know is, this isn't the time or the place to air our dirty laundry." Her smile remained, but keeping it in place seemed to take more effort by the minute. "Now, please. Let's lift a glass to Gabriel and Rita. May your marriage be blessed. May your life together be long and fruitful."

Fruitful?

The real honeymooners and small crowd of old people held up their glasses to a chorus of "hear-hears."

I took one tiny sip of champagne, a little afraid to tempt fate after that toast.

Gabriel slugged down his glass as if Primrose hadn't just tried to curse us into multiplying and replenishing.

Pastor Rod held up his hands and said, "Let us pray."

The champagne toast had been one thing, but if I let a man of the cloth pray for my phony marriage, I'd burn in hell for sure. I was seriously considering shouting *Fire!* and putting an end to my misery when a lanky man with dark chocolate skin and a smattering of even darker brown freckles came around the corner. He paused as if he was surprised to see us there. "Ho! What's all this? You havin' a party without me?"

I'm pretty sure you could have heard the proverbial pin drop in the sudden silence that fell. Nobody moved for what felt like a full minute, and the expressions on the faces of the Love Nest residents ranged from stunned surprise on the womens' faces to anger and resentment on the mens'.

Hyacinth recovered first, carefully putting her glass on the coffee table. She spread a quick warning glance over the group and then turned on a smile that was pure Southern hospitality in action. "Well, of course you're invited, Monroe. Get yourself in here and join us."

Nine

Hyacinth's invitation to Monroe echoed in the uneasy silence. My heart sputtered like a bad engine. I wanted to ignore everyone and everything else and immediately go strike up a conversation with Old Dog Leg's alleged brother, but I didn't want to frighten him off.

Clearly sensing my intentions, Gabriel leaned close and whispered, "Patience, Grasshopper."

I kept my eyes straight ahead, trying not to let my eagerness at Monroe's arrival show.

Monroe didn't seem to notice Hyacinth's lack of enthusiasm, my barely concealed excitement, or the others' grim-faced reactions. He slouched into the room, smiling as if we'd all welcomed him with open arms. "So what's the occasion?"

"A wedding," Grey said in a voice that was almost as tight as his Civil War uniform.

While Monroe went over to Pastor Rod and shook his hand, I cuddled up to Gabriel and muttered under my breath, "I'm betting our Monroe has a history with these people."

Gabriel wrapped his arms around me and spoke into my neck, making me shiver. "Ya think? But that's not our problem. We just need to figure out if he's Dog Leg's brother like he claims to be. They don't look alike, though, do they?"

No, they didn't. Monroe's nose was longer and broader, his skin lighter than Old Dog Leg's. Dog Leg was larger and more sturdily built, and despite the physical challenge of not being able to see, he carried himself with a confidence that seemed to elude Monroe. I watched him closely, looking for some shared trait, but I couldn't spot a single one.

Monroe moved on, putting a hand on Cleveland's shoulder, apparently oblivious to the way Cleveland shrugged it off. He then turned and ran a quick glance over Gabriel and me. "I guess you're the bride and groom?"

Gabriel and I moved toward him as if we were joined at the hip. Gabriel shook the man's hand and introduced us. "And you are—?"

"Monroe Magee." He looked around the room, and his grin grew wider. "I'd ask if you were related to somebody here, but I guess it's pretty obvious you're not part of the family."

Everyone in the room seemed uncomfortable with his observation, but Dontae was the first one to speak. "You always did know the wrong thing to say," he grumbled.

Hyacinth scowled at both men. "Mr. and Mrs. Broussard are guests. They checked in this afternoon for their honeymoon. I'll thank you to treat them the same way you'd treat any of our honeymoon couples."

Monroe looked stricken. "I—I didn't mean anything by it," he stammered. "I was just sayin'." Gabriel and I made "don't worry about it" gestures, but Hyacinth seemed determined to take offense on our behalf.

"Well don't," Hyacinth snapped. "Sister, get Monroe a glass of champagne. Monroe, sit down over there by Dontae."

Monroe shoved his hands into his pockets and slouched toward the couch. "How you doin', Dontae?"

Dontae made a vain attempt to shift to one side and kept his eyes downcast, deliberately avoiding looking at Monroe. "I've been better."

Yep. Something was going on here, and I was dying to find out what it was.

Pastor Rod mumbled something in his hardscrabble voice that I couldn't quite make out. Maybe I was imagining things, but he seemed to be the only man in the room who wasn't all that upset by Monroe's arrival.

Now that they'd recovered from the surprise, the women seemed charmed—other than Hyacinth, whose back and shoulders were rigid, her neck suddenly lined by newly prominent veins. Primrose smiled shyly as Monroe passed her. Lula Belle patted the seat beside her and cooed, "Monroe, why don't you come on over here and sit by me instead?"

Monroe's step faltered slightly. He looked back and forth between the two women, as if he didn't know which of them to go to. His apparent lack of self-assurance made it hard for me to believe that this guy was a con man, but I supposed it could have all been an act.

Lula Belle saw that I'd noticed his confusion and winked broadly at me. "I know I'm bad," she confided in a stage whisper, "but I never have been able to resist a good-looking man."

I bit back a smile. I wouldn't say Monroe was unattractive, but I wouldn't have ranked him as handsome.

Lula Belle crossed her legs and leaned back in a pose that might have been provocative in a younger woman. On her it just looked disturbing.

"Mr. Magee is a lucky man," Gabriel said with a grin.

Pastor Rod laughed at that and shook his head with what

appeared to be fond amusement. "I worry for your eternal soul, Lula Belle. I really do."

She kicked one foot gently. "Don't be such a priss, Rod. Nobody goes to hell over a little harmless flirting." Her jet-black eyes danced with mischief, and she put one hand up to her mouth as if she were about to share a secret with me. "Honestly, the way he takes on these days you'd think the man never did anything in his life but read the Bible."

I smiled uncomfortably, and she turned her attention back to Monroe, who still hadn't made up his mind where to sit.

"Well, Monroe?" Lula Belle prodded. "Are you coming?"

He hunched those shoulders a bit more and turned toward Lula Belle. With a speed that surprised me, Primrose stepped in front of him and handed Monroe his glass, effectively cutting off his route to Lula Belle. I swear she even batted her eyelashes. "Here you go, Monroe. I put those extra blankets you asked for in your room. If there's anything else you need, you just let me know."

"And if you need anything important," Lula Belle cut in, "come to *my* room."

The birdlike woman I'd met that afternoon disappeared in a flash as Primrose gave Lula Belle a look that could have pierced solid steel.

Pastor Rod put a hand on Primrose's arm and frowned at her apparent rival. "Lula Belle . . . please."

She laughed again and patted the back of her hair, completely unfazed by the pastor's disapproval and Primrose's sullen frown. Monroe finally seemed to realize that he was walking through a minefield and changed course to head toward the plate of cheese and crackers Hyacinth had set out on a polished sideboard. He loaded a paper plate and stood with his back to the wall, shoulders hunched, watching the rest of the group with an expression that looked both guarded and wistful, as if he'd finally picked up on the negative vibes that were circulating through the room.

Lula Belle pouted at him, clearly disappointed at his stand-offishness, but Primrose seemed mollified and the mood shifted again. Grey roped Gabriel and one of the bridegrooms into a conversation about the evils of public education. The other couple slipped out with an excuse about dinner reservations, and I tried to figure out a nonchalant way to strike up a conversation with Monroe alone. I was just about to make my move when Lula Belle nudged her walker to one side and sighed softly. "Guess I don't have what I once did. There was a time, Monroe wouldn't have been able to tell me no." She patted the cushion again, this time indicating the coveted spot for me. "*You* won't desert me, though, will you, honey? Sit down here and tell me about you and your man."

I couldn't think of a good reason to refuse, and I didn't want to be rude, so I did as I was told. "What would you like to know?"

"Tell me how you met."

We'd actually met at the Dizzy Duke during a memorial for my ex, Philippe. I hadn't been at my best, but I wasn't going to share one of my top five embarrassing moments with Lula Belle, so I gave her the abbreviated version. "We met one night while he was tending bar."

Lula Belle's eyes narrowed slightly and her mouth pursed. "Oh my. He's a bartender? So he's in that environment every night?"

"Most nights."

Primrose finished offering everyone a top-off on their champagne and came to stand beside me. I started to get up so she could sit, but she waved me back into my seat. I might have insisted, but maybe it wasn't a good idea to put her right next to her arch rival.

Lula Belle nudged me with a sharp elbow. "Oh honey,

you'd better watch out. I never did know me a barman who could keep himself under control. All the women. All the booze." She leaned a little closer and lowered her voice. "All that temptation. Isn't that right, Primrose?"

Primrose didn't answer, but she looked angry enough to kill.

I gave myself a little pat on the back for keeping them apart and told Lula Belle, "It's not like that. Gabriel's not like that." At least, I didn't think he was.

She rubbed my hand softly. "Baby, around alcohol and women it's *always* like that. Have you known him long?"

"Almost a year."

"Mmm-hmmm." She shook her head as if that meant something and flicked a piece of lint from her sleeve. "And he's still attracted?"

"To me?" I tried not to laugh. "As much as he ever was."

The old woman slid a sidelong glance in Gabriel's direction. "Well, that's good, baby, but he's a fine-looking man. Other women are bound to notice. Tell her, Primrose. Tell her how hard it is for a woman to hang on to her man."

I couldn't tell if she was trying to make me feel bad, or if she was aiming at Primrose. Either way, I couldn't wait to end this conversation. I wasn't sure what to think of Lula Belle. She reminded me of Alicia Lopez, a girl from high school who'd spent all four years stealing and then discarding other girls' boyfriends. Aunt Yolanda had always assured me that Alicia would grow out of her toxic behavior, but apparently, that wasn't true of all mean girls.

Lula Belle watched me with those bright little eyes, waiting for some kind of response. I gave her the only one I could come up with. "I trust him."

"Well, of course you do, baby." She rubbed my hand again. "Of course you do. But I'm telling you, I've spent my share of time in joints like that, and I've taken more than my share of men from the naïve women who stay at home thinkin' they've got things under control. All I'm sayin' is, you watch your back." She glanced pointedly at Primrose and lowered her voice conspiratorially. "You don't want to end up old and alone. That's no way to live."

I channeled a little mean girl of my own. "Are you married, then?"

"Me?" She threw back her head and laughed. "I was married five times, and I'm not ruling out going for number six. But I'm talking about ending up like . . . oh, like Primrose, I guess. Poor thing just couldn't keep a man, could you, honey?"

Ouch! I winced involuntarily. Primrose's mouth disappeared in a thin line on her stony face and she drifted away. I didn't blame her.

Hoping to change the subject, I agreed to take Lula Belle's advice, then asked, "How long have you lived here at the Love Nest?"

Lula Belle rolled her eyes toward the ceiling for a moment, calculating. "I guess it's been going on thirty years, ever since the sisters inherited this old house from their grandmother. Seems like forever."

Thirty years under the same roof? It was a wonder she and Primrose hadn't killed each other by now. "And all the rest of these people live here, too?"

"All except Pastor Rod. And Monroe, of course. He just showed up a couple of days ago."

Well now. Here was an opening I could sink my teeth into. I schooled my expression into one of casual interest. "Oh? Is he here on vacation or something?"

Lula Belle shrugged. "I wouldn't know. He hasn't said."

"Oh. I just thought . . ." I broke off and smiled sheepishly. "It's just that you seemed awfully friendly."

"Not especially." She again brushed something from her sleeve. "It amuses me to flirt. No harm, right?" The glitter in her eyes died away, and her smile faded. "Or do you have a problem with that?"

"Not at all," I said. Her sudden mood shift surprised me. I'd already decided that she and I weren't destined to be best friends, but I made a mental note to be cautious around her. "So have all the others lived here as long as you?"

Her eyes narrowed slightly. "Does it matter?"

I shook my head slowly. "Not really. I was just making small talk."

Lula Belle reached for her walker and pulled to her feet. "You know what, baby? I think you should worry less about other people and more about that husband of yours. He's going to break your heart. Mark my words."

It would be a lie to say that she rushed away, but I was too stunned to react until she'd put some distance between us. I ran over our brief conversation in my head, trying to remember exactly what I'd said and wondering what had set Lula Belle off like that.

She'd been friendly as long as she'd been throwing barbs at Primrose and poking her nose into my fake marriage, but the minute I'd asked about Monroe and the folks at the Love Nest, she'd done an abrupt about-face. On the surface my questions seemed innocent enough, though—so why had Lula Belle snapped at me?

She settled near Pastor Rod, her mouth clamped shut tightly, her jet-black eyes hard and angry as she looked back at me. I had no idea what was going on with her, but I had the feeling that Gabriel and I weren't the only people here with something to hide.

Ten

⚜

Cocktail hour at the Love Nest began to break up shortly after my unsuccessful conversation with Lula Belle. Gabriel had escaped Grey and spent the past twenty minutes entertaining the group with fabricated stories about our relationship. Most of them featured me as the comic relief. By the time he finished telling about how I'd asked him out for our first date—a wildly exaggerated version of the actual event—I was seriously contemplating a fake divorce.

As the laughter died away, Dontae got to his feet and lumbered from the room, grumbling about needing dinner. Grey marched out a minute later, and Lula Belle and her walker thumped down the hall right after him.

Using his imagination had apparently made Gabriel hungry, too, because he was asking Pastor Rod about good places in the neighborhood to grab a bite. I saw the thinning crowd as an opportunity to finally talk to Monroe.

"I'll help Hyacinth and Primrose clean up," I said, moving away from the hand Gabriel had on my waist. And I'd start with that cheese-and-cracker platter Monroe was standing next to.

Primrose stopped in the act of picking up a couple of glasses and stared at me in shock. "You'll do no such thing. You're a guest here. *And* you're on your honeymoon!"

Oh, yeah. The bloom had already faded from that rose. "It's okay," I said. "We just got married yesterday, but we've been together for a while now. We're both past the clingy stage. It seems wrong to let you go to so much trouble for us and then not even help carry a few dishes into the kitchen."

Hyacinth swept some crumbs from the coffee table into her hand and then started toward Monroe, who was still shoveling in cheese and crackers as if he hadn't eaten in a week. I wasn't about to let her grab up my one excuse for getting close to the man, so I abandoned Primrose with an apologetic smile and made a beeline for the sideboard.

Hyacinth had at least forty years and as many pounds on me, but she still managed to beat me to the platter. I pulled up just in time to hear Monroe ask, "Any chance you'll let me borrow your van to run an errand tomorrow?"

Hyacinth snatched up the platter and reached for a stack of napkins. "It's not running."

The smile on Monroe's face slipped into confusion. "Oh. I thought you drove it to the market this afternoon."

"It broke down after that," Hyacinth snapped. And then, as she noticed me standing there, she softened her tone a little and added, "I'm sorry, Monroe. I would let you borrow it if I could."

Insincerity rang from every word, but either Monroe was truly unaware or an extremely talented actor. "What's wrong with it?"

"How would I know?" Hyacinth said. "I'm not a mechanic."

"What happens when you try to start it? Does it grind or click?"

"It clicks. I'll have someone look at it tomorrow."

Monroe frowned thoughtfully and glanced toward the door. "Do you want me to take a look at it? I'm pretty good with an engine, you know."

"Absolutely not." She shook her head so hard, her chins wobbled. "You're a guest here. I wouldn't think of it."

Monroe laughed and nudged her with a shoulder. "Aw, come on, Hy. It's been awhile, I know, but you can't really think of me as just a guest."

I'd been right to suspect a history with these people, but it didn't seem like a friendly connection. I felt a protective surge at the thought of any of these people taking advantage of Old Dog Leg.

I couldn't just stand there, obviously eavesdropping, so I looked around for something to do. Hyacinth and Primrose had already cleared up most of the mess, so my options were severely limited. I decided to plump the couch cushions—which I figured could use a little tender loving care after holding Dontae up for the past hour.

I gave the first cushion an enthusiastic whack.

Hyacinth slid a glance at me, which I pretended not to notice. When she spoke again, her voice was so low I had a little trouble hearing her. "You've paid for your room, Monroe, and I've agreed for Sister's sake to let you stay. But don't push me or you'll be sorry."

My heart jumped inside my chest as I whacked the cushion for a second time.

"I'm not trying to push, Hyacinth. You know why I'm here. I'm not going to hurt anybody, I swear. If you're having trouble with the van, let me help. There might be snow on the roof"—he pointed to his head—"but I still know how to do a few things. Give me the key and let me see what I can do."

Pastor Rod excused himself from his conversation with Gabriel and edged into Hyacinth's conversation with Monroe before either of them saw him coming. "I think that sounds like a fine idea, Monroe. You can get the van back on the road and save the ladies a few dollars in the process."

Hyacinth's head whipped toward the preacher so quickly I thought her hair would shift to one side. Her eyes flashed and her nostrils flared, but to my surprise she said only, "That's really not necessary, Pastor."

"Sometimes we're called to serve," Pastor Rod said gently, "and sometimes we're called to be served. You just might be blessing Monroe by letting him offer you a helping hand."

Hyacinth looked unconvinced, but she grudgingly conceded the argument. "If you say so, Pastor. I suppose it wouldn't hurt to let you look at it," she said with an unhappy scowl for Monroe, and then she waved a hand toward a couple of chairs against the far wall. "If you're so het up about serving Sister and me, why don't you start by carrying those extra chairs back to the dining room?"

Monroe trailed her across the room, and since I couldn't race him for the chairs without raising eyebrows, my chance to talk with him walked off with him. I whacked the couch cushion again, this time out of frustration.

As Monroe carried one of the chairs out of the parlor, Cleveland stood to confront Pastor Rod. "What'd you do that for? It's a bad idea to encourage him, if you ask me."

Pastor Rod lifted one shoulder to show his lack of concern. "It'll be fine, Cleveland. You'll see. Monroe just wants to help."

"Yeah? Well, Hyacinth don't need his brand of help. Neither does Primrose. None of us does, in fact. If you ask me, they ought to send that troublemaker on his way tonight."

"I'm not sending him away," Primrose cried, slamming down the glass she was holding. It hit the table and shattered, and a shocked silence fell over the room. Primrose's thin face was tight and angry. Her eyes blazed. "Why do you have to be so mean and hateful?" she shouted at Cleveland. "Just let it go. It's water under the bridge."

The pastor made soothing noises, but nobody was paying attention to him. Gabriel crossed the room to stand by me and mouthed, "These people are crazy." He'd get no argument from me.

Cleveland shook a finger in Primrose's face. "You're too naïve. Always have been."

"Yeah? Well, it's not as if *you've* never done anything wrong," she snarled. "How would you like it if I held all of your mistakes over your head?"

I'd seen Gabriel break up a couple of fights at the Dizzy Duke, but he made no move to come between these two old people, both of whom looked ready to lunge at the other without warning. I took his inaction as a sign that he was as fascinated and curious about their relationships as I was.

The pastor made a more determined effort to soothe the troubled waters. His face set in steely determination, he pushed between Cleveland and Primrose. His voice was gentle but firm. "Now, now. You two have been friends a long time. Don't let this come between you."

Cleveland took a step back and snorted. "It's a bit late for that, don't you think?"

Primrose wrapped her thin arms around herself and sniffed loudly. "Only because you're so completely unreasonable."

They were both still upset, but I thought they looked a little less ready to escalate the hostilities, so I said, "I thought Monroe was a friend of yours. He seems like a nice enough guy."

"How would you know?" Cleveland snarled. "You met him five minutes ago."

Primrose glared at him. "You'd better not let Hyacinth hear you talking to our guests like that." She took a deep breath and brushed a curl from her forehead. "And in answer to your question, Monroe is a perfectly nice man."

I thought she was going to say more, but Hyacinth flew into the parlor at a speed I wouldn't have expected from a woman her size. "What's going on in here?"

"Everything's fine," Gabriel assured her, but he spoke too soon.

Primrose pointed one shaky finger at Cleveland. "Ask him."

Cleveland snorted again. "I didn't say anything the others aren't thinking."

"He's going on about Monroe again," Primrose snapped. She sounded more like a petulant three-year-old than a woman in her seventies. "I'd like to know when *he* became a saint."

Hyacinth's eyes grew wide and round, and she folded her thick arms across her chest. "Did the two of you forget that we have guests?"

"It's okay," Gabriel said. "No harm, no foul."

But Cleveland shoved his finger in Primrose's face. "I'm no saint. Never claimed to be. But at least I ain't a snake."

"That's *enough*!" Hyacinth's warning was so harsh and loud, Primrose flinched and Cleveland backed up a step. Hyacinth took a deep breath and gave a grimace that was probably intended to be a smile but missed its mark by a mile. "We. Have. *Guests.* Whatever the two of you are going on about can wait." She turned to Gabriel and me and sweetened her tone. "I apologize for my sister and my friend. You two run along now and enjoy yourselves. Put our childish squabbling right out of your minds."

I was burning up with curiosity, but I couldn't think of a good excuse for sticking around when Hyacinth was so eager to see us go. Reluctantly, I let her escort me toward the foyer. It wasn't until I was alone with Gabriel and trying to wrap my mind around what had just happened that I realized I owed Primrose and Cleveland a debt of gratitude.

Thanks to their argument, Pastor Rod had forgotten all about praying for our fake marriage.

Eleven

"I *knew* it!" I kept my voice low to prevent being overheard, and tugged Gabriel toward the stairs. "This Monroe guy has some connection to the people here."

"Yeah. But for the record, I'm convinced they're all loony tunes."

I laughed and started up the staircase. "Can we see the garage from our window? I want to watch for Monroe to start working on the van. Maybe we can catch him alone."

"Maybe *I* can catch him alone," Gabriel said. "I don't know what's going on with these people, but I don't want you in the middle of it."

I stopped walking and whipped around to face him. "You're kidding, right? They're not going to hurt anyone. They're . . . *old*! And besides, I wouldn't even be here if you hadn't gotten me involved. You don't get to come riding in on your white horse to save me."

He glanced over his shoulder to make sure we were still

alone. "That was before I met these people. Be a sport. Go on up to the room. I'll go outside and wait for Monroe."

"Not on your life." For the third time in an hour my cell phone buzzed, and this time I welcomed the interruption. I fished it out of my pocket just as the first notes of "Rhapsody in Blue" played, signaling a call from one of Zydeco's staff. I checked the screen, saw that the call was from Estelle Jergens, one of my decorators, and waved the phone in front of me. "Sorry. Business. Very important. You go on up. I'll join you when I'm through." I dashed past him and out the front door before he could stop me.

Getting a call from Estelle didn't really surprise me. She's the oldest staff member at Zydeco and the one I'd vote Most Likely to Panic in a Crisis. I'd have an easier time dealing with whatever was bothering her without Gabriel to distract me. But that was only part of the reason I'd bolted for the door. If Gabriel thought I was going to sit upstairs reading a book while he had all the fun, he was crazier than the residents of the Love Nest.

As soon as I stepped outside, the sounds and smells of the neighborhood hit me and reminded me where I was. A group of young people strolled past the inn, laughing and joking with each other. A couple of young men with loose-hipped walks went by, each with an arm slung around the shoulders of a foul-mouthed girlfriend. Lights and music spilled into the night from the tattoo parlor down the street, and rap music thumped rhythmically from passing cars.

In spite of my tough-girl talk earlier, I felt slightly uneasy in this neighborhood. I slipped into the shadows of the porch so I wouldn't be visible from the street and answered the call. "Estelle? What's up?"

"Rita? Oh thank God. I was starting to worry. I've been calling and calling, but it kept going straight to voice mail."

I was a little out of breath, but I think I managed to sound normal. "That's because I'm taking some time off," I said patiently. "If you have a problem at work while I'm away, you might get a quicker response if you call Ox."

Estelle laughed nervously. "Yeah. I know." She took a couple of raspy breaths and then said, "Look, Rita, I really hate to bother you, but I thought you needed to know about what happened this afternoon."

I didn't say anything for a moment. If there was trouble at Zydeco, she was right that I should know about it. Then again, I wanted the staff to understand that I trusted Ox and they didn't need to run to me with every little thing. "I left Ox in charge while I'm away," I said. "Is this something you can talk about with him?"

Estelle laughed, but she didn't sound amused. "Um . . . no. He's part of the problem."

A warning bell sounded in the back of my mind. "What problem?"

"I don't know the whole story, but Ox and Edie got into it this afternoon over some phone call. They're not talking to each other, or to any of us. And Edie was so upset she went home early."

"You're joking, right? Tell me you're making this up just to freak me out."

"I'm sorry, Rita. I wish I was. Sparkle and I thought you should know."

Sparkle, another one of my decorators (and all Goth despite the frilly name), doesn't make a habit of getting involved in drama. If she was worried, maybe I should be, too. Before I could process what Estelle had said, the front door opened and Monroe stepped out onto the porch. He acknowledged me with a dip of his head and whistled as if he hadn't a care in the world as he gingerly walked down the front steps.

This would have been a great chance to talk with him

alone, but I couldn't hang up on Estelle after what she'd just told me. "What time did Edie leave?"

"A few minutes after three."

Roughly three hours ago, and she was just calling me now? "And who handled the front desk after she left?" It was difficult to follow the conversation. My attention was riveted on Monroe, who followed the walk around the side of the building and disappeared from view.

"Isabeau answered the phones until we closed at five," Estelle said. "We didn't have a lot of work, so it didn't mess things up too badly. But she didn't have Edie's password, so she wasn't able to get into the bakery's e-mail account."

I descended the stairs and moseyed after Monroe, hoping he wouldn't notice that I was following him. "I have the password," I said. "I'll check the e-mail account tonight. Are you still at the bakery now?"

"No. We left right after we closed. Sparkle and I had a drink at the Duke, and that's when we decided I should call you. We didn't want to disturb you, but nobody knows if Edie's coming back tomorrow. She was *really* upset."

Edie had been acting strangely for the past couple of days, and now she'd walked off the job? I couldn't just let that slide. I had to find out what was going on with her, especially if it was spilling over into the workplace. "I'm sure she'll be back," I told Estelle. "I'll talk with both of them tomorrow and make sure we get everything smoothed out."

She let out a sigh of relief. "I sure hope you can get those two to talk to you. I did my best to get some information from Ox, but he blew me off. I'm sure Isabeau knows what happened, but she's not saying a word."

I'd reached the corner of the building. Trying to look like someone out for a casual stroll, I checked to see if Monroe was still in sight. He'd stopped in front of a two-car detached garage where he was now fiddling with a heavy padlock. "I'll take care of it," I promised again. "Try not to worry." I managed to end the conversation a few minutes later, and stood in the shadows, enjoying the cool evening breeze while I tried to shift my mental gears and decide on the best way to strike up a conversation with Monroe.

Turned out, I didn't have to worry. Monroe unlocked the padlock and worked it out of the clasp that held the garage doors shut. Setting the lock aside, he swung open one of the wooden doors and propped it open with a piece of cinder block. As he dragged open the second door, he spotted me and straightened up sharply. "Hey there. What are you doing out here?"

"Phone call," I said, wagging my cell phone in front of me.

He put a second cinder block in place and wiped his hands on the back of his pants. "Don't tell me you're sneaking around on your husband already?"

"It's not like that, cross my heart." I sketched an X across my chest. "You're working on the van?"

"I'm fixin' to take a look. Don't know what I'll find, though." He ran a skeptical look over a maroon van that had seen better days. "Looks pretty sorry, don't it?"

I agreed that it did and slipped my phone in my pocket as I stepped toward the garage. "I'm surprised Hyacinth agreed to let you work on it," I said. "I mean, you *are* a guest here. She was upset by the thought of me gathering a few glasses."

He laughed and reached inside the van to start the engine. It didn't click or grind. In fact, it started smoothly and purred like a contented old cat. Surprise, surprise.

After he listened for a moment, Monroe shut it off again. "I guess technically I am a guest," he said as he unlatched the hood, "but it feels more like family. Me and the Hoyt sisters go way back."

I *knew* it! I just didn't know if that was good or bad news for Old Dog Leg. "So you're in town to visit old friends?"

Monroe glanced around the garage, spotted a toolbox, and carried it toward the van. "In a manner of speaking. I lived in New Orleans when I was younger, but I've been away a long time. Came back to see friends and to find my brother."

He certainly seemed sincere. I hitched myself onto a packing box that looked sturdy enough to hold me and settled in to watch him work. "How long have you been away?"

"Longer than you've been alive, I expect."

"And how long since you saw your brother?"

Monroe spent some time wiggling wires and checking hoses. Had he found something wrong with the van or was he just ignoring my question? Eventually he pulled a rag from his pocket and slowly wiped grease from his fingers. "It's been forty years since I saw anyone from these parts."

I did my best to look surprised. "Why so long?"

He looked at me from the corner of his eye. "Long story."

"I have time," I said. "If you want to talk about it, that is." I tried to sound friendly and compassionate, but his expression grew guarded and withdrawn.

"Not really. But thanks."

Wrong answer. I tried again. "Have you seen your brother yet?"

Monroe ducked back under the hood. "Not yet. Sent him a letter the other day. I'm just waitin' to hear back." He wiggled another wire or two and then looked over at me. "I'll bet that husband of yours is wondering where you got off to. Mebbe it would be best if you was to go back inside."

He wasn't going to get rid of me that easily. I smiled, still trying to give off a friendly vibe. "I'm sure he's not worried."

Monroe put both hands on the van and gave me a steady look. "Mebbe not, but I've been down that road before. I don't want trouble. Not that kind. Or any other, for that matter. I just got my life back. I ain't losing it again."

I wondered what he meant by that, but he made it hard to argue or stretch out the conversation. Was he genuinely worried, or just trying to dodge my questions? I didn't want to leave until I knew for sure, but I didn't want to push and make him completely shut down either.

Reluctantly deciding it might be best to back off for now, I hopped from the box and started toward the open garage doors, then stopped and looked back, intending to apologize for interrupting him. But the words froze in my throat.

Monroe had turned his back on me, and I watched as he unbuttoned his shirt and peeled it off, revealing a white tank undershirt. There, clearly visible on his right shoulder, was a birthmark in the shape of a crescent moon.

Twelve

Monroe really was Old Dog Leg's brother!

I rushed back up to the room, eager to tell Gabriel about my discovery. He wasn't in the Honeymooner suite, so I scoured the inn for him and finally found him in the garden, talking about fishing with Dontae and Cleveland. He was regaling them with a story about catching a small shark while fishing in the Gulf of Mexico—a story that might even have been true. Then again, knowing Gabriel, it could have been a complete fabrication.

"Give you much of a fight?" Cleveland asked, sounding almost breathless with anticipation.

"Just about tore my arm off," Gabriel said. "But it was worth the effort. That thing tasted damn good hot off the grill."

Dontae barked an appreciative laugh and then spotted me. "Uh-oh. Looks like the missus tracked you down." He lumbered to his feet, groaning loudly from the effort. "You tell a mighty good fish story, boy. Mighty good."

Cleveland ran a suspicious gaze over me. "It's bad juju to leave your man alone on your honeymoon." He turned his back on me and spoke to Gabriel in a stage whisper that carried across the space between us. "You want your marriage to work out, set the tone now. You're the man of the house. She ain't." When Gabriel only smiled, Cleveland glanced back at me and added, "I ain't jokin'. You mark my words."

Gabriel put a hand on the old man's shoulder. "Thanks, Cleveland. I appreciate the advice, but I've got this." He winked at me and formed a fist. "Iron fist rules."

"Oh please," I said. "Just try that iron-fist crap with me, Broussard. I guarantee you'll be sorry. Are you ready for dinner? I'm starving."

Gabriel left his new best friends and put his arm around my shoulder. "See, fellas? I've got her right where she wants me."

As we drove a few blocks to a nearby restaurant Pastor Rod had recommended, Gabriel told me about his conversation with Cleveland and Dontae, and a few interesting tidbits he'd picked up about the Hoyt sisters. Primrose had never been married. Hyacinth's husband had died a few years ago.

I forced myself to listen while he talked, but then filled him in on my conversation with Monroe—particularly the exciting news that I'd seen the birthmark.

Gabriel's nonplussed expression pleased me. "I'll be damned," he said.

We pulled up to the restaurant, an Italian place in a run-down strip mall a few blocks from the inn. Without Pastor Rod's recommendation, I would have driven right past the place, but what it lacked in ambiance, it made up for in heavenly aromas.

As soon as we placed our orders, we went back to dissecting everything and speculating about the possibilities for Old Dog Leg and his brother. That is, *I* dissected and speculated. Once the food arrived, Gabriel mostly chewed and emitted an occasional "Mmm-hmm" to maintain the illusion that he was actually listening to me.

I couldn't really blame him. The food was excellent. We shared an order of calamari lightly breaded and cooked tender, not chewy, then dove into bowls of rich, creamy oyster and artichoke soup before moving on to our entrées.

After I'd dissected and speculated through the appetizer and soup, we wound back to the Hoyt sisters.

"I got the impression that Hyacinth and her husband had separated," he said as our server placed our entrées in front of us. "But I don't think they ever divorced."

I'd ordered *cappelini ala Bordelaise*, pasta tossed with toasted garlic and parsley. Gabriel had a slow-roasted *osso buco* with rich *jus* gravy that smelled so good it made my mouth water.

I inhaled the garlicky aroma wafting up from my plate and sighed happily. "They're from a generation that didn't really believe in divorce. I admire that, really."

Gabriel looked up, surprised. "Weren't you and Philippe in the middle of a divorce when he died?"

"We were, but marriage is hard. More work than anyone lets on. Somebody ought to warn people what's in store for them before they say *I do*."

Gabriel grinned slowly. "If they had, would you have listened?"

I shrugged and filled my mouth with pasta and garlic. "Probably not. But that's beside the point. We're not talking about me anyway. So Hyacinth's a widow on a technicality. That actually gives us something in common. Maybe I can use it to get more information out of her."

"Like what?" Gabriel asked. "We found out what we need to know. Our work is done."

I'd been floating in a little bubble of excitement since seeing that scar, but now my bubble popped suddenly. Gabriel was right, but curiosity about those old men and women was eating me alive. I wanted to know what their story was and how Monroe fit into their world. For Dog Leg's sake, of course.

"Is our work done?" I asked. "Don't you think we should find out everything we can for Old Dog Leg while we're here?"

Gabriel shook his head. "No, I don't. He asked us to find out whether Monroe is who he claims to be. And based on what you say you just saw, it appears he is. That's it. The rest is none of our business."

Technically, maybe, but that didn't stop me from wondering about a few things. Like the expressions on peoples' faces when Monroe walked into the parlor earlier. "Hyacinth didn't look all that happy to see Monroe," I reminded him.

"Not our concern."

"And what about Dontae? Did you see the way he acted when he thought Monroe was going to sit on the couch beside him?"

Gabriel arched an eyebrow. "Even if there are bad feelings between Monroe and Dontae, it's not something we need to worry about."

"What about Primrose and Cleveland? I thought they were going to take each other apart. There are bad feelings between those two, and they have something to do with Monroe."

"Maybe. But Dog Leg didn't ask us to pry into Monroe's life. He merely asked us to figure out if the man was really his brother. Now that we've done that, the rest is up to Dog Leg."

I put down my fork, my appetite suddenly gone. "So you're just going to let Old Dog Leg walk into that viper's nest . . . blind?"

Gabriel reached for his wineglass. "Let's review one more time, shall we?"

"Don't you dare patronize me," I warned. "Monroe knows Primrose and Hyacinth from before, and judging from their conversations during the cocktail party, he knew the rest of them, too. If there's an issue smoldering among them, we should find out what it is so Old Dog Leg isn't caught off guard."

"Dog Leg's a grown man, Rita. He doesn't need you to take care of him."

"Some friend you are."

Gabriel laughed and turned his attention back to his meal. "I'm not the kind of friend who pries into things that are none of my business, if that's what you mean. If Dog Leg wanted us looking into his brother's affairs, he'd have asked us to do so. But he didn't."

"Dog Leg doesn't *know* about his brother," I reminded him. "That's the whole point."

But Gabriel wouldn't budge, and eventually he stopped responding altogether to my comments about the interesting old characters at the Love Nest.

I don't mind admitting that his attitude rankled. By the time we returned to the inn, I was thoroughly irritated with him. It was nearly ten when we climbed the stairs to our room in silence, and I escaped into the bathroom to change. I slipped into a pair of comfortable pajama pants and a tank top—not ugly, but also not sexy or suggestive—and emerged from the bathroom to find Gabriel bare chested, a pair of jogging shorts slung low on his hips. Judging from the *zing* I felt when I saw him, maybe it was just as well that I was annoyed with him.

I managed not to look at him—much—and made myself comfortable on one side of that imposing heart-shaped bed, all without saying more than a word or two. But when he lay down on the other side of the bed with his back to me, I broke the silence.

"I thought you were going to sleep on the floor."

He slid a glance over one finely toned shoulder. "If you feel that strongly about not sharing the bed, go ahead. Make yourself comfortable down there. But I paid good money for this room, and I'm sleeping on the bed."

I thought about moving off the bed, but my principles will only stretch so far. I plumped my pillow and tugged the sheet out from under his butt. "Now you're just being selfish."

"Yep." He leaned up and looked me over so slowly I could feel my blood warming. "I could show you how *un*selfish I can be if you're interested."

"Fat chance, Romeo." I rolled onto my side again, and he chuckled as he turned out the light. A whole slew of unspoken words swirled between us, and all of mine were tinged with disappointment and irritation. We'd be checking out in the morning. Gabriel saw no reason to stay longer, and I couldn't stay without him, so that was that.

I must have dozed off quickly, because the next thing I knew, a bloodcurdling scream tore me out of a deep sleep. I bolted upright, startled, frightened, and struggling to get my bearings. I was vaguely aware of Gabriel scrambling off the bed and pulling on a pair of pants as he hurried toward the balcony doors.

Oh, yeah. The Love Nest.

"What was that?" I tried to follow him, but my feet were tangled in a sheet.

"I don't know." Gabriel glanced back at me and barked, "Stay there."

Yeah. Sure. Another scream shattered the night, and I finally managed a coherent thought. "Don't open the door," I warned. "You don't know what's out there."

"It'll be fine," he said as he tried to shoulder open the swollen wooden doors. "Just stay there."

"Are you nuts?" At last I managed to kick my feet free of the bedding and half fell off the bed. I glanced at the glowing numbers on the clock and saw that it was just past midnight. "There could be gang members out there. With guns."

Gabriel tossed a look over his shoulder and hit the doors

again. "Would. You. Just. Stay. Back? I don't want to worry about you getting hurt."

The doors finally swung open, and I could hear a woman shouting for help as I trotted up behind Gabriel. By now, I was awake enough to pinpoint the sound as coming from almost directly below us in the garden.

Apparently, Primrose's locked-gate security wasn't all she'd played it up to be. I could hear voices in the distance, raised in alarm. Lights flicked on in the windows of the old folks' annex across the garden.

Gabriel leaned over the balcony railing, careful not to put his weight on it. "Are you all right ma'am?" he called down.

"No! I need help!" the voice replied. It sounded like Primrose.

We both turned on a dime and bolted across the room. Gabriel was out the door a half step ahead of me, but I was hot on his heels and racing down the hall toward the stairs.

We were halfway there when a door flew open at the other end of the hall. A young woman stumbled out of the room, followed by a rangy young man wearing boxers and a wife-beater T-shirt. I didn't recognize them as one of the other couples I'd seen before, and I wondered if they'd made themselves scarce earlier or if they'd checked in after the cocktail party.

The young man rubbed his eyes and focused slowly on Gabriel and me. "Hey. What's going on?"

Gabriel didn't even break stride. "I think someone's hurt in the garden. I'm going to see if I can help."

The young man started after him, but his companion clutched his arm and stopped him. "No, Antwon. Don't. Please."

Gabriel had almost reached the end of the hall and was about to head downstairs without me. I tried to edge around the young couple, but they were blocking my way and neither was paying the slightest bit of attention to me.

"It's all right, Tamarra," the young man said as he tried to disentangle himself from the woman's grasp. "We'll just go check to see what's going on. If there's trouble, we'll call for help. I promise."

His plan sounded reasonable to me, but Tamarra shook her head wildly. "You could get hurt."

"I've got to go, baby. This place is crazy. You *know* what it's like. God only knows what these people are up to now."

Crazy people up to no good? I shot an "I told you so" look at Gabriel, but he didn't even glance back. "You know the folks who live here?" I asked.

Tamarra stared at me as if she'd forgotten I was standing there. "Of course. My grandmother is the owner. Who *are* you anyway?"

"Rita L—" I caught myself from giving my real last name just in time. "My husband and I are here on our honeymoon. That's him heading downstairs." I pointed toward the top of Gabriel's head, which was the only part of him still visible, and then waved my hands at the blockage they were creating. "Look, I don't know what's going on outside, but I'd feel better if Gabriel didn't go out there alone."

Antwon kissed Tamarra quickly and managed to step clear of her grasp. "She's right, baby. I have to go. Somebody could be hurt. You two stay here. We'll be right back."

He pressed Tamarra toward me and thundered down the stairs behind Gabriel, apparently confident that we'd stay behind like good little girls.

So of course I bolted after them.

Tamarra shouted for me to stop, then changed her mind and ran after me. I could hear her behind me, breathing hard as we ran. By the time we made it downstairs, residents were beginning to wander in from the old timers' wing.

Blinking in the sudden flare of light, Cleveland led the charge—if you could call it that. He was followed closely by Grey, who'd changed from his uniform to flannel pajamas and now looked like an ordinary old man from the current century.

Lula Belle shuffled into the parlor on her walker, wearing a pair of lacy white pajamas that were oddly disconcerting on a woman her age. "What's going on?" She sounded different, and it took me a moment to realize that she'd left her teeth in her bedroom.

"Someone's in trouble," I said as I hurried past. "Gabriel and one of the other guests went to see if they could help."

Lula Belle spotted Tamarra and stopped moving. "Well hello, honey. When did you and your handsome husband get here?"

"A couple of hours ago." Tamarra looked distracted and edgy, but when Lula Belle lifted her cheek for a kiss, Tamarra complied almost without thinking.

"Why didn't somebody tell us you were coming?" Lula Belle fussed. "I would have waited up."

"It was a last-minute decision," Tamarra said with a tight smile. She glanced toward the patio doors and chewed her bottom lip. "You don't think Antwon's in any danger, do you?"

Lula Belle patted her arm reassuringly. "Now, honey, don't you fret. I saw Primrose and Hyacinth outside a little while ago. One of them probably fell, that's all."

That scream hadn't sounded like a twisted ankle to me, but I didn't want Tamarra to get worked up, so I kept my opinion to myself. "That's probably it," I said. "Why don't you stay here with Lula Belle? I'll check on the guys and be back in a minute."

Tamarra seemed relieved by my suggestion, so I pushed out through the doors and set off along the path that led toward our bedroom window. Overgrown shrubbery tore at my clothes as I raced toward the sound of voices. But when I saw Dontae Thomas on the ground, his legs on the sidewalk and his huge upper body in the dirt, my own legs stopped working. The stench of vomit filled the air, and I covered my nose and mouth with a hand to keep myself from adding to it.

Clearly agitated, Antwon was pacing the short length of sidewalk. Primrose and Hyacinth stood to one side clutching each other tightly, their faces frozen in stunned disbelief. Gabriel was hunkered down beside Dontae checking for a pulse.

"What happened?" Antwon demanded. "What in the *hell* happened?"

Tears streamed down Primrose's face. She tried to back away from Antwon's anger, but Hyacinth held her fast and skewered the young man with a look. "I don't know, Antwon, and neither does Primrose. She came outside to throw out the trash and found him like this."

If Primrose had been carting out the trash, I must not have been asleep *that* long. I glanced around to see if anyone was wearing a watch, but it was too dark to tell.

Antwon rubbed his face with both hands and turned to Gabriel. "Is he breathing?"

Gabriel shook his head sadly. "I don't think so, but I can't be sure. I could use some help turning him over."

Antwon looked as if he wanted to refuse, but he just clamped his mouth shut tight and bent to the task. Even with the two men working together, it was a struggle to roll the big guy onto his back. When they finally managed, Primrose let out a strangled cry and even Hyacinth looked rattled.

Grim-faced, Gabriel checked once more for a heartbeat, but I don't think any of us expected him to find one. After a moment, he lowered Dontae's massive arm to the ground and got to his feet to state what was by then obvious to everyone in the garden.

"I think he's dead."

Thirteen

The next few minutes passed in a blur. Antwon called 911 while Gabriel and I helped Primrose and Hyacinth inside and told the others what had happened. When Tamarra heard that Dontae was dead, she dropped like a stone onto the couch beside Lula Belle, who stared straight ahead and clutched her lacy robe together tightly. The other two couples I'd seen when we checked in had made their way into the parlor while I was outside. They hovered in separate corners, looking shell-shocked.

"Are you sure he's . . . dead?" Tamarra asked. "Maybe he's just passed out."

"He's dead, baby," Hyacinth said. "There's no question."

Wrinkles folded over one another on Cleveland's face. "How? How did it happen?"

Grey spoke up from the spot he'd claimed near the window. "I hate to say it, but he was a heart attack just waiting to happen."

"He's right," Antwon said as he came back into the room. "The man ate like there was no tomorrow."

Cleveland blinked several times and blew his nose into his handkerchief. "If I told him once, I told him a thousand times. He was too sedentary. I tried to get him to do something—*anything*. But you know how he was."

Everyone in the group nodded solemnly, and Lula Belle muttered, "Stubborn old fool."

Primrose let out a little sob and mopped her face with a tissue. "Sister is—" She broke off with a shudder. "—*was* always after him to take better care of himself."

Hyacinth sank into a chair and shook her head as if she was having trouble processing the news. "But I just saw him. We all did. He was going to turn in right after dinner."

"Did he say anything to anyone about feeling ill?" Gabriel asked.

Grey turned away from the window with a scowl. "If he had, don't you think one of us would have kept an eye on him?"

"He didn't mean anything by that," I said gently. "How long ago did Dontae go to his room?"

Lula Belle looked at a clock on the mantle. "An hour, maybe."

"Obviously, he changed his mind about going to sleep," Grey said. "What was he doing in the garden? Anybody know?"

Nobody had an answer for that question, and the arrival of the EMTs and a couple of uniformed officers kept us all busy for the next few minutes. Primrose, Gabriel, and Antwon all answered questions about finding Dontae in the garden, while Grey and Cleveland offered insights into Dontae's activities before he died. Hyacinth disappeared into the kitchen to make coffee, and Lula Belle talked quietly with Tamarra.

After a while, the police and the EMTs disappeared into the garden, and I figured that was that. But a few minutes later, one of the uniformed officers came back inside in a hurry, his face a grim mask. He rushed through the parlor and out the front door, dialing a number on his cell phone as he walked. His partner, a short, solid man with blond hair and blue eyes, came in from the garden a moment later.

"My partner is calling homicide," he said to all of us assembled in the room. "They should be here shortly, but I need all of you to stick around and wait for them to arrive."

Cleveland had relaxed into one of the armchairs, but now he shot to attention. "Homicide? Why?"

"Because your friend didn't die from a heart attack, and that's standard procedure when we come across a suspicious death."

Primrose had just come back from the kitchen, carrying a tray loaded with cups and spoons. She gave a choked gasp and dropped the tray with a loud clang and the sound of breaking china. Tamarra immediately went over to help clean up. "Suspicious death? What is he talking about?"

"You heard the man," Cleveland snapped. "He's saying Dontae didn't die of natural causes."

Hyacinth stumbled as she trailed her sister into the room and her eyes widened in horror. "Is that right? You suspect that he was murdered?"

Tamarra popped up as if she was spring-loaded and rushed to the sisters. She put a protective arm around Hyacinth and rubbed Primrose's shoulder with her free hand. "He didn't say that," Tamarra insisted. "Let's not jump to conclusions."

That sounded like good advice to me, but the word *murder* set off a chain reaction. One of the brides, a young woman with full lips, glossy hair, and a voice like fingernails on a chalkboard, let out an earsplitting scream. Her husband, a bullish kid large enough to make up the entire defensive lineup for a football team, gathered her into his arms and shouted something at the emergency technician.

I couldn't hear what it was over the clamor of voices on my end of the room. I spotted Gabriel trying to get between the linebacker and the paramedic, which might not have been the smartest move. I thought about trying to stop him, but I was no match for Mr. Linebacker, and besides, I had my hands full with Lula Belle, who suddenly sagged back against the couch cushions, eyes fluttering weakly.

"Everyone calm down," Tamarra shouted. "The man never said anything about murder—did you?" She pinned the poor paramedic with a stare that clearly said she expected him to agree with her.

"The coroner will have to make the official call," he said, "but it looks like your friend may have been poisoned."

Miss Hysteria's wails grew even louder, and her husband continued his clumsy attempts to console her. The other young woman, a full-figured girl in a short satin nightgown, rose to her feet and proclaimed loudly, "That's it, Michael. We're out of here. Do you hear me?"

"Not just yet," the technician warned. "I'm going to need all y'all to stick around until the detectives arrive."

"Then you *do* think he was murdered?" I asked, in what I hoped was a noninflammatory tone of voice. The EMT didn't reply, but he didn't deny it either.

Lula Belle gripped my hand so tightly, I flinched. Apparently, she was stronger than she'd let on. "Who could have done such a horrible thing? Who would want to?"

Cleveland bleated a harsh laugh. "I think we all know the answer to that, don't we?"

I didn't, but I was interested in his opinion.

Primrose stepped over the tray and broken coffee cups, her expression changing from shock to outrage. "That's ridiculous, Cleveland. Just because you hate Monroe, that's no reason to go around accusing him of murdering Dontae."

Gabriel had maintained his position between Michael the

honeymooning linebacker and the EMT, but as Primrose advanced on Cleveland, he moved to block her path. "You think Monroe did this?" he asked Cleveland.

"Who else would have done it?" the old man snarled.

"Anyone *but* Monroe," Primrose snarled back at the same time that Lula Belle let out a heavy sigh and said, "That man always was trouble."

This from the woman who'd tried to seduce him just a few hours earlier.

Hyacinth managed to pull herself out of her fog and took charge. "Stop!" she ordered. "Right now. I won't have you dredging up the past, Cleveland. Do you hear? And you"—she glared at Lula Belle—"you know better."

Lula Belle clamped her toothless mouth shut tightly, but her beady little eyes flashed with resentment.

Hyacinth didn't care. She turned the full force of her anger on the paramedic next. "You must be wrong, young man. I'm sure Dontae wasn't poisoned. One of those no-good boys from the neighborhood probably mugged him for his medications."

The EMT shook his head. "That's doubtful, ma'am."

"I know you don't want to believe that this could happen under your roof," Gabriel said, "but I think it's unlikely the EMTs would mistake a mugging for murder by poison."

Tamarra urged her grandmother toward a chair. "It's pointless to speculate. We won't know what happened until they do an autopsy."

Everyone fell silent until the EMTs and police officers returned to the scene of the crime in the garden. The instant the door closed behind them, speculation started up again.

"It could have been a mugging," Grey argued. "You don't know this neighborhood. I've told Dontae a thousand times not to go wanderin' around late at night."

"It's not the best neighborhood," Cleveland agreed, using his arms to punctuate the points he was making. "But nothing's actually happened to any of us until now. You think it's a coincidence that Monroe showed up two days ago and now one of us is dead?"

Maybe I should have warned them about talking in front of the police, but my loyalty was to Old Dog Leg, not this crazy bunch of strangers. Besides, this might be my only chance to hear them talk so freely, so I bit my tongue.

Antwon bent to pick up some of the broken china Primrose had left on the floor. "I think we'd all better just calm down. The investigators are on their way, and I called Pastor Rod and asked him to come. Until they get here, let's quit flinging unfounded accusations."

"If they were unfounded," Cleveland grumbled, "I wouldn't make them."

Antwon caught Tamarra's eye and nodded toward the kitchen. "Would you mind grabbing some more cups, babe? I have a feeling it's going to be a long night."

Tamarra gave Hyacinth a reassuring squeeze before trotting off like a dutiful wife. I was so full of questions, I was about to split at the seams, so I offered to help in the hopes of pumping her for information.

Just as I reached the door, Cleveland glared around the room. "Hold on a second," he said. "Where is Monroe anyway?"

I think every head in the place turned, first to look at Cleveland and then to search around the room as if we all expected to find Monroe hiding in a corner or under the couch.

Lula Belle spoke first. "I haven't seen him since cocktail hour. You don't think—"

"You're damn right I do." Cleveland was halfway to the door before the rest of us could react.

Grey hoisted himself up and plodded after him. "I *told* you not to trust him," he said to no one in particular. "A tiger doesn't change his stripes. I don't care how many chances he gets."

Curious about what stripes Monroe might have had to change, I abandoned the idea of making coffee with Tamarra and joined the parade. Gabriel fell into step behind me. "Never a dull moment," he said into my ear.

I whispered over my shoulder, "I told you there was something weird going on here."

"It appears that you're right."

"Why is Cleveland so certain that Monroe killed Dontae?"

"Is that really any of our business?"

I gaped at him. "What do you want to do, tell Old Dog Leg that the good news is Monroe is his brother, but the bad news is he might also be a cold-blooded killer?"

"It's the truth."

"Well, I'm not going to do that to him. Obviously, he cares about Monroe and about the promise he made to his mother. He deserves answers about what happened forty years ago, not more questions."

Gabriel put a hand on my arm and tried to slow me down. "Look, Rita, I think it would be a mistake to get any more involved in whatever's going on here, especially now that there's been a suspicious death."

I shrugged away from his hand and kept walking. "And I think it would be a mistake to pretend that we can just walk away now."

"And what if Monroe is guilty?"

I thought about the conversation I'd had with Monroe in the garage. Admittedly, we'd only spoken for a few minutes, but I just couldn't imagine him ruthlessly poisoning an old friend. Or even an acquaintance. Maybe my feelings for Dog Leg were getting in the way. I didn't really know the first thing about Monroe. I just knew that I didn't want his brother hurt again.

We all trailed Cleveland past the dining room and library and then into a long corridor that led to the annex. He was surprisingly quick for a man his age. Gabriel and I were still at the end of the hall when he started banging on what was presumably Monroe's door.

"Hey! You in there?" *Bang, bang, bang.* "Open this door, you sonofabitch! I know you're in there." *Bang, bang, bang.* "I'm giving you to the count of three and then I'm coming in."

Grey pulled up behind him, wheezing a little. "Can you hear him in there?"

"I can't hear a damned thing," Cleveland complained. *Bang, bang, bang!* "I know you're not sleeping, you little weasel! But you're not getting away this time. I'll kick this door in if I have to. You're gonna pay for what you did."

I was as curious as the next person about why Monroe hadn't made an appearance, but I didn't think vigilante justice was the way to get answers. I wedged myself between Grey and Cleveland, then tried to squirm between Cleveland and the door. "Let's not destroy the property," I said. "I'm sure Hyacinth and Primrose have a key. In light of what the EMT said, it might be best to wait until the homicide squad gets here anyway."

Hyacinth came up behind us, breathing hard from the effort of moving so fast. She didn't even stop to catch her breath, but turned around immediately and headed back down the hall, presumably to get the key. Cleveland glared at me. "If you think we can wait for the police, you don't know Monroe."

"Well, no, I don't. But—"

"He'll run. That's what he does." Cleveland rattled the doorknob again and gave the door another thump with his fists. "That's what he *always* does. I think we're already too late."

Grey wiped sweat from his forehead with a sleeve and elbowed past us. "I'm not waiting for Hyacinth to get back here. Let me at that door. I'll get us inside."

"I don't think that's a good idea," Gabriel said. "Rita's right. Let the police handle it."

But Grey wasn't listening. He threw himself against the door with such force, the doorframe split. Surprised that he was that strong, I skedaddled out of the way just in time for the second lunge, and on the third the door broke open.

I got inside right behind Grey, who stood panting heavily, rubbing his shoulder as he surveyed the empty room. Monroe was nowhere to be seen. In fact, there was no sign that he'd ever been there at all.

Fourteen

After we discovered that Monroe and his things were gone, all hell broke loose. Nothing could have made Monroe look guiltier. Cleveland bellowed like a bull moose, threatening to kill Monroe with his bare hands. Primrose wailed inconsolably. Hyacinth searched the entire ground floor of the inn, as if she thought Monroe might have packed up and moved into one of the closets. Grey bolted into his own room across the hall and began plowing through his nightstand looking for something to dull the pain in his shoulder. Lula Belle disappeared for a few minutes and came back wearing a lavender polyester pantsuit . . . and teeth.

Gabriel and I worked with Antwon and Tamarra to calm everyone down and get them back into the parlor. While Tamarra served coffee that everybody ignored, Antwon ran upstairs to throw on jeans and a T-shirt. I kept an eye on the two miserable honeymoon couples, but I was more concerned about the longtime residents of the Love Nest. They were all advanced in years, and I was worried that Grey had seriously hurt himself when he broke through the door or that one or more of the others might have an adverse physical reaction to all the stress.

Things finally began to settle down, and believing that we had the residents of the Love Nest under control, Antwon, Gabriel, and I took a seat. But only for a minute. In a surprise turn of events, Miss Hysteria quietly huddled up next to her linebacker husband, but Bride Number 2 started ranting about what she called her constitutional right to leave if she wanted to. To make matters worse, our elderly companions kept popping out of their chairs and alternately threatening to leave the room or to find Monroe and commit a second murder.

Confusion reigned until one of the uniformed officers came back inside to see what the commotion was . . . and then things got really weird. As if someone had flipped a switch, the whole bunch of senior citizens stopped wailing and threatening and running around, and sat like a bunch of stone-faced mannequins.

A case of delayed shock? Maybe, but it was hard to believe it would hit five people at once. Which left only one other explanation I could think of: they all knew something and no one wanted to talk to the police about it.

At some point, a uniformed officer who looked about sixteen came to gather our names and other essential information. Gabriel and I gave ours when our turn came—or rather, Gabriel gave his information, while I hesitated for a moment and then introduced myself as Mrs. Broussard, reasoning that I'd tell the truth once I was alone with one of the officers and away from the residents of the Love Nest.

Smart? Maybe not. But in the wake of Dontae's murder and Monroe's sudden disappearance, I had a feeling that the good folks at the Love Nest might not understand our little deception. I also had another reason for keeping up the charade. If the EMT was right and Dontae had been poisoned, one of these old people was probably responsible. I wasn't eager to reveal who I really was and get on that person's bad side.

I don't know how long we sat there before I noticed a flurry of activity in the foyer followed by a tangible change in the energy flow. A moment later Detective Liam Sullivan strode into the parlor and my heart dropped like a rock.

Sullivan might be a good friend—not quite a *friend with benefits*, but close—but he was just about the last person I wanted to see right then. He's six feet of Southern charm when he's not working, but he had his game face on tonight, and that's not so charming. His cool blue eyes roamed the room, taking in the group and sifting details while one of the uniformed cops brought him up to speed. It took him all of three seconds to spot Gabriel and me, and even from a distance I could see his eyes turn from blue to stormy gray.

I stared back, trying to send him a silent message: *Don't ask. I'll explain later.*

Very slowly, Sullivan pulled his gaze away from mine so he could pay attention to the briefing. The officer rattled off the pertinent details. One victim. Suspected poisoning. No other signs of trauma. No sign of forced entry into the garden, leading investigators to believe that the perpetrator had accessed the garden through the house.

"What's he doing here?" Gabriel muttered in my ear.

I'd been so engrossed in my eavesdropping I jumped a little at the unexpected sound of his voice. "It's a suspected homicide," I muttered back when I could breathe again. "I guess he caught the case."

"Is that good news or bad for us?"

"I wish I knew," I whispered. "Just promise me, no wild stories when you talk to the police."

Gabriel tried to look shocked. "Why, my dear Mrs. Broussard, I'll be just as truthful as you are."

I cut a sharp glance at him. "This is no time for jokes, Gabriel. Behave. Please."

"As you wish." He fell silent for about three seconds and then started up again. "Your boyfriend looks angry. Is he going to arrest me?"

"Only if you lie." I nodded toward a female officer who was glaring a warning at us from across the room. "Now stop talking before you get us both in trouble."

Sullivan interrupted the briefing once or twice to ask questions, then jerked his chin toward our small group of witnesses. "Is everyone here a guest of the inn?"

The officer waved toward the sisters at the far end of the room. "Hyacinth Fiske and Primrose Hoyt own the place, and the couple over there is family," he said with a nod toward Antwon and Tamarra. "The older folks are long-term residents. I have a list of names for you." And then he motioned toward us, saying, "These three couples and someone named Monroe Magee are the only registered guests. Magee's missing, and so is the company van. No indication how long he's been gone. Hoffman and I were just about to start interrogating."

That brought Sullivan's attention back to me. "You haven't questioned them yet?" he asked the officer, locking his stormy stare with my increasingly uneasy one.

"No sir."

"Who found the victim?"

"Ms. Hoyt over there."

"Take her statement first," Sullivan ordered. "Have Hoffman interrogate the family and residents. I'll question the guests."

"Yes sir." One by one, the officer pointed to each couple with his pen. "You've got Michael and April Manwaring, Curtis and Deanne Sinclair, and Gabriel and Rita Broussard."

Sullivan's gaze zipped back to mine and the storm clouds turned to ice. "Is that right?"

"Yes sir. All three couples are here on their honeymoons."

Heat rushed to my face, but I refused to look away from Sullivan's gaze.

He didn't blink either.

I was holding my own until Gabriel whispered in my ear again. "I don't think he likes me."

At that, my concentration shattered, and I blinked first. I glared at Gabriel, pouring all of my frustration and apprehension into the look I gave him. "Will you knock it off? This isn't a game."

Gabriel's eyes danced with amusement at my expense. "Yes, dear."

"You're *so* not funny," I said in a harsh whisper. "Now be quiet, please. I'm trying to hear what they're saying."

"Of course, *chérie*." He sat back in his chair, still wearing a cat-who-found-the-cream grin.

Which I ignored.

"Hoffman's using the dining room," the cop was saying to Sullivan. "I was going to set up in the game room. Kitchen okay with you, sir?"

Sullivan parked his hands on his hips and rocked onto the balls of his feet. "Kitchen's fine. Let's start with you, Mr. Broussard. Come this way, please."

He sounded so coplike, I felt a little sick. Gabriel got up to leave the room, but before going, he stopped and planted a kiss on me that might have curled my toes under other circumstances. "Don't you worry, sweetheart," he whispered. "I'll bail you out if I have to."

From across the room, Primrose clapped her hands together as if Gabriel had done something wildly romantic. By the time I extricated myself from his enthusiastic embrace, Sullivan had turned away, which meant that I couldn't see his eyes.

And that did not bode well at all.

Fifteen

❧

Gabriel came back from his interview with Sullivan strangely subdued, but I didn't know whether to feel relieved or worried by the change in him. I thought Sullivan might call me next, but he left me where I was and interviewed one of the honeymooners instead. I waited until they'd disappeared to ask Gabriel how the questioning had gone.

"Well?" I whispered. The Love Nest's permanent residents were still maintaining radio silence.

Gabriel slid down and stretched his legs in front of him. "Fine. No problem."

Well, terrific. But that didn't tell me anything. "What did he ask you?"

Gabriel yawned and rolled his head this way and that, trying to get comfortable. "Oh, you know. How did I know the deceased? What did I see and hear before he died? The usual."

"What did you tell him?"

Gabriel cut a glance at me from the corner of his eye. "The truth. What else?"

I nodded and spent a few seconds processing what he'd said. He'd answered all my questions, but he hadn't told me what I wanted to know. Which, of course, wasn't about the murder at all. "How did he seem?"

Gabriel pretended to be confused. "Seem?"

"You know," I said, growing exasperated. "Was he—" I cut myself off, trying to find the right words. It wasn't easy. I knew Sullivan would have been professional. He wasn't the type to let personal feelings get in the way of his job. But I also knew that he *had* feelings for me, and I didn't want to hurt him. Then again, it wasn't really fair of me to ask Gabriel to dissect Sullivan's reaction to finding us here together. It might seem that I cared more about Sullivan than I did about him. Since I wasn't entirely sure *what* I felt, I slouched down in a posture that matched Gabriel's and settled for a more generic question. "Did he give you any idea what the police are thinking?"

Gabriel smiled and closed his eyes. "Yeah. We had a real heart-to-heart in there."

I studied his expression closely. It gave nothing away. "What does that mean?"

"That was sarcasm, *chérie*. He didn't bring me into the loop. He asked questions. I answered them." He opened his eyes and looked straight at me. "Are you worried?"

His steady gaze disconcerted me, but I tried not to show it. "No. Should I be?"

Gabriel lifted one shoulder in a lazy shrug. "You tell me. Are you worried that he's jealous about us being here together? Or angry?"

Trust him to go straight to the heart of the matter. I shook my head slowly. "No. Not really. Or maybe a little. About the jealousy, not the anger. He's not that kind of guy."

"He's a real prince, I'm sure."

I sat upright in a hurry. "Oh, stop it." My voice came out

louder than I'd intended, and a dozen heads swiveled toward us. I flushed with embarrassment and sank down again. "Maybe you should take lessons from him," I said under my breath.

Gabriel tried to look shocked. "Me? Surely you jest."

"Surely I don't. Sullivan's been a perfect gentleman so far. You're the one who seems to have a problem."

Gabriel closed his eyes as if he thought this was a good time to catch up on his sleep. "What can I say? I don't like sharing." He opened one eye, no more than a slit. "And I'm pretty sure your friend in the kitchen doesn't either."

I didn't say anything because I wasn't sure how to respond to that. Part of me wanted to know exactly what they'd said to each other, and the other part wanted to leave well enough alone—and that's the part that won out. Gabriel dozed off—or at least appeared to—and I let him.

I don't know how long Sullivan kept me cooling my heels, but it felt like hours. One by one the other guests left and came back, settling in quietly after their interviews. By the time he finally escorted me into the kitchen, I was practically jumping out of my skin.

I followed him down the hall without saying a word, which was unusual for me. But once inside the old-fashioned kitchen, I launched into an explanation before the door was completely shut. "It's not what you think."

Sullivan didn't even smile. He just nodded toward a retro fifties-style table flanked by six red vinyl and chrome chairs. "Why don't you have a seat, Mrs. Broussard? Congratulations on your wedding, by the way."

The smell of coffee left too long on the burner stung my nose, but the yeasty aroma of dough rising on the counter gave the kitchen a homey feel. "It's not Mrs. Broussard, and you know it. And there was no wedding. Gabriel and I are just here as a favor for a friend. But I'm sure you know that already." Unless Gabriel had been making up stories again. If so, there was going to be another homicide on the books before the night was over.

Sullivan locked eyes with me. "Is there something you want to tell me? About us?"

"Like what?"

"Oh, I don't know. Like maybe you're serious with Broussard?"

"What? No! I told you, we're only here to do a favor for Old Dog Leg. That's it."

Sullivan ran a look over my pajama pants and tank top. "Interesting," he said, turning a chair around and straddling it. He jerked his chin toward another chair on the other side of the table. "Sit. Please."

I'd been waiting a long time. I was agitated and edgy and I didn't want to sit. But I did want to appear cooperative, so I scooted a chair around so I could look Sullivan in the eye and started talking before he could distract me with questions. "There's something weird going on here, Liam."

"You mean something besides murder? I'm just trying to figure out why I'm even slightly surprised to find you here."

I gave an exasperated eye roll. "Very funny. I had nothing to do with any of this. It's just a horrible coincidence."

Sullivan sat back and folded his arms across his chest. "I'm not a big believer in coincidence, Rita. But why don't you tell me about this favor you're doing?"

I had no idea how much Gabriel had told him, so I filled him in on the plan to figure out whether Monroe was Old Dog Leg's long-lost brother or an imposter. As I talked, I watched Sullivan's face for signs of surprise, irritation, or any other indication that Gabriel might not have been entirely truthful with his answers. But his expression remained infuriatingly blank and professional.

I finished with an account of my conversation with Monroe

in the garage, including seeing the scar on Monroe's shoulder, and Sullivan finally glanced up from his notebook.

"Broussard said that you'd identified Monroe Magee as Dog Leg's brother. He also mentioned that the residents here seem to think Magee's responsible for the body out there in the garden."

"Right. And now he's gone. Again." My stomach knotted just thinking about how disappointed Old Dog Leg would be when we told him.

Sullivan digested that for a moment. "So what's your take? You think Magee's the killer?"

"I've asked myself that question a dozen times in the past couple of hours. My gut reaction is no."

"Never underestimate the value of a gut reaction. So where were you when the victim was being done in?"

"That depends on when it happened," I said. "Do you have any idea how long he's been dead?"

"Nothing official but judging from the amount of rigor mortis, I'm guessing not long."

"Then I was probably upstairs," I said. I didn't actually say that I was in "our" room, but I didn't need to. Sullivan got my drift.

A muscle in his jaw twitched, but he stayed focused on the case. "Did you hear anything? See anything?"

I shook my head. "I was asleep. The scream woke me up. By the time I made it downstairs, both Primrose and Hyacinth were there, and so were Gabriel and Antwon Barnett. Hyacinth told us that Primrose found Dontae when she was taking out the trash."

Sullivan consulted his notes. "That's Hyacinth Fiske and Primrose Hoyt, the owners of the inn?"

"That's right. They're sisters."

"Any chance one of them did this?"

I gave that some thought. "It's possible, but I doubt it. The

119

sisters didn't seem to have any issue with the victim. None of the other permanent residents did either. He wasn't the one they had a problem with."

Sullivan made a note. "I take it someone else was?"

"Just Monroe," I admitted reluctantly. "Most of the Love Nesters seemed a bit unhappy about him reappearing the way he did."

"Most? Does that mean that some were glad to see him?"

I shrugged. "Neither Primrose nor Lula Belle seemed *un*happy. At least not with Monroe. They're not exactly friendly with each other."

He looked surprised. "You think there was some kind of love triangle going on?"

Guilt buzzed up my spine, no doubt caused by what Gabriel had said about sharing. "I wouldn't say that. I don't think Lula Belle is actually interested in Monroe, but she sure was jerking Primrose's chain about him earlier. I don't know how interested Primrose is in him either, to be honest. I only met these people a few hours ago." I waited while he made another note and then asked, "Do you really think Dontae was poisoned?"

"We won't know for sure until we get the results of the autopsy, but all signs point in that direction. There's some facial swelling and signs of diarrhea and vomiting. I'm betting the coroner will find evidence of internal bleeding when he does the autopsy."

"So it was murder?" I asked.

"We don't know that either. He could have ingested the poison accidentally. Then again, someone might have dosed something he ate or drank."

My blood ran cold at the thought that one of the people I'd been drinking champagne with earlier could have killed him. "Do you know when the poison was administered?"

Sullivan shook his head. "If it was poison, we won't be able to say for sure when he ingested it until we know what it was. But judging from the look of the body, I'm betting on something fast acting. Could have been in something he ate or drank at dinner. We'll check the champagne y'all had earlier, but the rest of you are fine, so I doubt it was in the bottle. Someone washed the glasses, so we can't test those. My guys are loading up about half a ton of snacks he had stashed around his room, so it might take awhile to narrow it down."

"You mean the poison could have been injected into his Twinkies weeks ago?"

Sullivan shrugged. "Could have been, I guess. But if somebody hated him enough to want him dead, I'm guessing they wouldn't have waited around long to see results."

I tried to remember the conversations, the looks, the undercurrents I'd picked up on since Gabriel and I checked in. Trying to puzzle through the maze those old people had created left me suddenly exhausted. I sank down in my chair and said, "None of this makes any sense. Judging from what I saw and heard tonight, Monroe should be the one lying dead in the garden, not Dontae."

"And yet here we are." Sullivan offered me a thin smile, the first since he arrived.

I was pathetically grateful for it. "These people have a history," I told him. "I don't know what it is and nobody seems to want to talk about it, but everyone knows each other. Monroe told me that he goes way back with the sisters, and the sisters seem to go way back with everybody else. Lula Belle has been living here for thirty years, and I assume the others have been here about as long, which means that they all moved in here a decade after Monroe disappeared. So how did he know where to find them?"

"Tamarra Barnett says that the sisters inherited this place. She's Hyacinth Fiske's granddaughter. I'm guessing that Monroe knew about the inn before he disappeared."

"Or he's been in contact with someone while he was gone."

I swallowed a yawn and said, "You know who you should talk to? Pastor Rod."

Sullivan glanced at his notes and frowned slightly. "Who's that? His name's not in here."

"He doesn't live here," I explained. "But he was here earlier, and Primrose said he's like one of the family. I'm surprised he's not here. Antwon called him quite a while ago."

"I'll check with the uniforms, but they had instructions not to let anyone in so they may have sent him back home."

"Well, I'd talk to him soon. He seems to know everyone going way back, including Monroe."

Sullivan sat back in his chair and stared at his notebook, filtering the information he'd picked up from the other cops, the witnesses he'd interviewed, and then mixing in what I'd given him.

I forced myself to wait patiently . . . and succeeded for all of about three minutes. "So what's next?" He didn't answer me immediately, so I pushed a little more. "Is this the part where you tell me to go home and mind my own business? Because you know I can't do that. Old Dog Leg is counting on me."

This time, there was no mistaking the smile on Sullivan's face. He stood and looked down at me as he tucked his notebook into his breast pocket. "Actually, Mrs. Broussard, I see no reason for you and your husband to cut your honeymoon short."

My mouth fell open. Literally. "I don't follow."

"My men are running into a brick wall with their investigation so far. Those old people have clammed up completely. Nobody's saying anything significant, except that Monroe is, or is not, without a doubt, guilty. Beyond that, they're closing ranks. Maybe they know who killed their friend. Maybe they only suspect they know. Either way, they're not talking to us. But you're here. You're one of them."

I laughed uneasily. "I wouldn't exactly say *that*."

"You have a foot in the door," he said. "That's more than I've got at the moment. And I know you. You're persistent. That's one of the best and the worst things about you."

My smile faded slowly. "Should I be offended?"

It was Sullivan's turn to laugh. "Not at all. I could tell you to go away and keep out of the investigation, but we both know you're not going to listen to me."

He had a point.

"Look," he said, moving to my side of the table and taking the chair next to mine. "I'm not asking you to do anything dangerous. In fact, I'm not asking you to do anything at all. But if you want to hang out here and keep an ear to the ground, I'm not going to complain. I won't even write you up for using a false name. Maybe you can find out where the residents of the Love Nest were between the hours of ten and midnight."

"You want me to check their alibis?"

"If it comes up in casual conversation."

I didn't even try to stop the grin that spread across my face. I had his permission to stick around and ask questions. It didn't get any better than that. But I wanted to be clear on all points. "And it's okay with you if Gabriel and I keep up the whole honeymoon charade?"

Sullivan shrugged. "Far be it from me to get in the way of true love."

"You're funny."

He leaned a little closer, and for a second I thought he was going to kiss me. But he just looked me in the eye and said, "Be careful, Rita. Somebody may have poisoned that old man."

Once again, I shuddered at the memory of Dontae's body in the garden. "Message received," I assured him.

"And *he* was their friend. If one of them would do that to a so-called friend, there's no telling what they'd do to a relative stranger who gets in their way."

Sixteen

The police eventually cleared out, and the rest of us went back to our rooms. I expected to lie awake for hours, but I fell asleep the minute my head hit the pillow. I didn't wake up until the sun was already high in the sky. Gabriel was cuddled up to me, his solid chest pressed up against my back, one arm slung over my waist.

I spent a few seconds appreciating the moment, then tried inching out from under his arm so I could check the time on my cell phone. I moved slowly and carefully, trying not to wake him. I finally reached my phone and saw that it was already eight thirty and that I had two text messages from Estelle, reminding me of Zydeco's latest crisis, which had flown completely out of my mind during last night's drama. Edie was at work, but the tension between her and Ox was running high. I couldn't ignore the bakery, and I wasn't foolish enough to try resolving a dispute like this one over the phone. Plus, I needed to set up that meeting with Miss Frankie and Ox.

I scrambled out of bed, startling Gabriel awake.

"If there's another dead body," he groaned into his pillow, "wake me when the cops get here."

He looked dangerously sexy lying there half-dressed, with his dark hair tousled and the shadow of a beard making him look like some kind of pirate hero from a romance novel. He reached for me, but I evaded his grasp, which took more self-control than I'd suspected I had.

"We need to get downstairs," I said. "They stop serving breakfast in half an hour, and Hyacinth warned us they don't serve latecomers."

He regarded me blearily. "Breakfast? Seriously? You think they'll be serving food after last night? And would you want to eat anything in a house where someone was fatally poisoned?"

It's true that I was nervous about eating anything in this house after Dontae's untimely demise, but my traitorous stomach had already begun rumbling. "I don't have much of an appetite either, but this might be our only chance all day to ask the others where they were at the time of the murder without being obvious about it. So get up and get dressed."

He rolled over and pulled the sheet up to his shoulders, then groaned again. But a moment later he sat up on the edge of the bed, which I took as a good sign. I carried clean undies, jeans, and a silk blouse of pale peach into the bathroom and locked the door. "What time are you going to work today?"

"Noon. I'm working the early shift."

"Sounds good. I need to catch a ride with you." He didn't argue, so I showered and dressed quickly. While Gabriel showered I pulled my hair up and slapped on a little eye shadow and mascara. About the time I felt satisfied with my appearance, he came back into the room in jeans, pulling a T-shirt over his head. I don't mind admitting, it was a nice bit of scenery and I may have spent a few seconds enjoying the view.

He grinned at me and scooped a lock of dark hair from his forehead. "Like what you see?"

Um. Yeah. I shrugged and headed for the door. "That has never been a problem." I paused with one hand on the door. "Are you coming?"

He stepped into flip-flops. "Let's go. I'm starving."

Gabriel still hadn't told me what he and Sullivan had talked about last night, but he'd been surprisingly receptive to the idea of extending our stay. Maybe Sullivan had enlisted his help, too. I thought about asking, but frankly, I decided it was better to keep my mouth shut.

The aroma of fresh coffee hit me on the second-floor landing, and a bouquet of other mouthwatering scents soon followed. We passed Miss Hysteria and the linebacker as they left the dining room. They both looked exhausted but healthy, which took away some of the worry about eating breakfast on the premises.

Grey and Lula Belle were at the table when Gabriel and I walked into the dining room, and a breakfast fit for royalty waited on the sideboard. A platter of fluffy scrambled eggs, steaming mounds of bacon and sausage, creamy grits, and cinnamon rolls the size of small hams sat beside a silver coffee service and a crystal pitcher of fresh-squeezed orange juice.

I filled a mug with coffee, laced it with French vanilla creamer, and carried it to the table, then loaded a plate, reasoning that even if the killer wanted another victim, he or she was unlikely to want *me* dead and probably wouldn't risk putting poison meant for one person in food meant for everyone.

As I turned back toward the table, Grey gave me a nod and muttered something to Gabriel. Lula Belle bent over her plate and pretended not to see us. Was she feeling guilty about being so nasty to Primrose last night, nervous about being at the inn with a murderer . . . or afraid of being caught?

Antwon and Tamarra wandered in as Gabriel and I sat down, and we all exchanged awkward good mornings. Tamarra greeted Lula Belle with another peck on the cheek and waved away Antwon's offer to bring her a plate.

Like everyone else, Antwon looked tired, but he brought his wife coffee and then helped himself to generous portions of everything. He went back for extra biscuits and butter and spoke to the rest of us as he carried his second plate to the table. "How is everyone this morning?"

Lula Belle dabbed a napkin to the corners of her eyes and let out a shaky sigh. "I'm not doing well at all, baby. I can't believe he's gone. Dontae! Of all people."

Tamarra put an arm around the old woman's frail shoulders and squeezed gently. "Did you manage to sleep?"

"Not a wink." Lula Belle sighed again, and her hand shook a little as she worked the napkin again. "I couldn't close my eyes all night."

Despite how mean she'd been during cocktail hour, I actually felt a little sorry for her.

Grey tore open a biscuit and slathered it with butter. "I didn't sleep either, but Cleveland sure did. He was still sawing logs when I left my room. I heard him all the way out in the hall. Lord, but that man can snore."

Gabriel laughed softly. "I'm not surprised. He sure was wound up last night."

"He gets that way," Antwon said around a mouthful of eggs. "Half the time you have to just let what he says roll off your back." He salted everything on his plate heavily and tried another bite. "I heard the Manwarings say they're checking out this morning. I sure hope the two of you aren't planning to leave."

I shook my head and put my hand on Gabriel's in what I hoped looked like a wifely gesture. "No, we talked it over and decided to stay." I glanced around and tried to turn the attention away from the two of us. "How are Hyacinth and Primrose? Has anyone seen them this morning?"

Lula Belle pretended not to hear me, but Grey glanced toward the kitchen. "Not yet, but they've obviously been busy." He drained his coffee cup and looked around again. "How's the coffee? Any left?"

Gabriel hopped up to get the carafe and refilled the partially empty cups. I hoped his friendly gesture would convince the others to talk to us.

"It must be hard to lose someone you've known for so long," I said. "Almost like losing a member of the family."

Grey nodded and heaped sugar into his cup. "That's exactly what it's like. Hell, I've known Dontae since I was twenty-something. Six? Seven? Maybe even younger. He could be a pain in the neck, but there was nobody I'd trust more. The man always had my back."

Lula Belle blew her nose and nodded. "That's the truth, Grey. The God's honest truth." She hiccupped softly and covered her mouth with her handkerchief, closing her eyes and making a visible effort to pull herself together.

Tamarra made some soothing noises, and then sat back with a weary look on her face. "He was like an uncle to me," she said, turning a sad smile on Grey in the process. "Y'all are just like family. Why would anyone want to hurt him?"

"When did they do it?" Lula Belle asked. "We were together most of the evening."

"We don't know for sure that anyone did anything," I reminded them. And then, hoping I could narrow down their movements during the times Sullivan had mentioned, I asked, "What time did he go to his room? Did anyone notice?"

Grey added a dollop of cream to his cup. "I saw him around ten. He and Cleveland were watching some fool show on the TV set. He was fine then—at least, he seemed to be."

"I wonder if anyone saw him after that," I mused aloud.

Lula Belle waved her napkin around in front of her and leaned her head against Tamarra's shoulder. "I don't think so, but let's not talk about Dontae. It's too awful."

I couldn't tell if she was genuinely distraught or trying to avoid the subject for some other reason, but I didn't want to push too hard and make her stop talking completely. I offered my most sympathetic smile. "I can't even imagine how difficult this must be."

Gabriel wolfed down half a cinnamon roll. "Let's hope the police figure out what happened soon. Do you think Cleveland's right about Monroe?"

Lula Belle lifted her chin and swiped at her eyes. "How would any of us know?"

"You all knew Dontae," I pointed out. "And you also seemed to know Monroe pretty well. And Cleveland seemed so certain . . ."

A look passed between Grey and Lula Belle. It was gone in a flash, but Grey looked sullen when he planted his elbows on the table and said, "Antwon just told you, you can't take Cleveland serious."

They really were circling the wagons, but why? If they hated Monroe so much, why were they protecting him now? "But you have some kind of history," I insisted. "You all kept talking about the past last night."

Antwon looked up sharply. "We don't even know how Dontae was killed. Even if he was poisoned, there's nothing to say it happened here or even that it was done on purpose."

Looking thoughtful, Gabriel ate a slice of bacon and followed it with a sausage link. "Good point. Does anyone know where he went for dinner?"

"He ate where he always ate," Lula Belle said. "Right here."

That surprised me. "I didn't know Hyacinth and Primrose offered dinner service."

"It's for the long-term residents only," Antwon said. "They get breakfast and dinner included in their monthly rent."

"So you all had dinner together?" Gabriel asked.

Grey nodded. "Just like every night. We told the police that, too. At least, I did. And the rest of us are fine, so don't go getting any big ideas."

Lula Belle sniffed loudly. "Why did Monroe disappear? That's what I want to know. Sure looks suspicious."

Grey let out an angry snort and pulled a small packet of jam from a wire basket on the table. "Why does that sonofa-bitch do anything? I guess we know now that all his talk was just that."

Gabriel anticipated Grey's next request and passed him the silver butter dish without being asked. "What talk is that?"

Grey shrugged and helped himself to a thick pat of butter. "Some ridiculous story about wanting to make up for the past. Dontae *said* there was more to the story. I guess he was right."

Antwon shook his head gently. "We don't know that Monroe did anything." Grey sputtered a protest, but Antwon held up both hands to stop him. "I know, I know, it looks bad. But until we know exactly what happened, I think we should be careful about throwing accusations around."

Grey pointed the butter knife at Antwon and snarled, "You climb down off that high horse you're on, boy. You don't know Monroe like the rest of us do and I'm not going to pussyfoot around like the rest of you and pretend like he's an old friend."

Tamarra jumped in to defend her husband. "But Pastor Rod says—"

Grey snorted. "Pastor Rod. Really. Go back and talk to him again—and this time tell him you want the *truth*, not that watered-down version he's been telling himself since he found God."

Tamarra looked wounded. "That's not fair. Just because Pastor Rod has managed to forgive . . ."

"Forgive what?" I asked, but they ignored me.

Lula Belle made a rude noise and cut the younger woman off. "That's enough! Grey, you need to quit running your big mouth. And Rod's not perfect, young lady," she said to Tamarra. "He's got a past like anybody else. You and Antwon would both do well to remember that."

Antwon stiffened. He looked angry, but his voice remained calm. "He's never tried to deny that. But *he* left *his* past behind. That's the difference."

Grey put his knife to work again. "Watch yourself young man. Don't disrespect your elders."

"I didn't mean any disrespect," Antwon assured him. "I'm just saying that I don't think the pastor would lie."

I thought Lula Belle was going to say something more, but just then the door to the kitchen swung open and Hyacinth backed into the room carrying a fresh pot of coffee. As if someone had flipped a switch, everybody in the room fell silent, just as they had last night when the police came.

Hyacinth paused and ran a look over everyone at the table. "What's going on?"

"Nothing," Grey muttered, suddenly fascinated by the jam.

Antwon sawed at a piece of sausage. "Just making small talk, ma'am. How are you this morning?"

Gabriel and I exchanged a glance. Clearly, the others were intimidated by Hyacinth. But was it because she could kick them out of their rooms if they crossed her, or because they suspected her? Could she have poisoned Dontae? Maybe I'd been wrong to tell Sullivan I didn't think she was guilty. She *did* have unfettered access to the food supply, after all.

Grey stuffed the last bit of sausage into his mouth and pushed away from the table. "You ready to head back to your room, Lula Belle? I'll walk with you."

She stood and slipped two muffins into the pocket of her sweater, then pulled her walker around in front of her. "I think that's a good idea. I don't have much of an appetite anyway."

Under Hyacinth's watchful eye even Antwon abandoned his breakfast. Tamarra picked up her cup and followed her husband out the door.

I could only watch helplessly as all four of them left the room. No matter how much I wanted to chase after them and demand answers, I'd have a better chance of finding out what was happening at the Love Nest if I could talk to each of them alone.

But that wasn't going to be easy. I had a feeling that Hyacinth would be watching her little world like a hawk from now on.

Seventeen

Gabriel and I finished breakfast in relative silence. We had plenty to talk about, but I had the uneasy feeling that someone was hovering nearby, waiting to hear what we'd say. Whether it was true or just my imagination, I wasn't about to discuss the case where we could be overheard, and I had too much on my mind to play phony honeymoon. That left work and the weather, both of which we touched on briefly as we ate.

I'd have given anything for a chance to take a good look at the garden, the garage, or Monroe's room, but yellow crime scene tape barred access to everyone but authorized personnel. Even with Sullivan's blessing on our stay here, we couldn't be considered "authorized" by any stretch of the imagination.

It wasn't that I thought I might find evidence the police had missed, but I was curious about what they'd found and where they'd found it. Sullivan might have asked us to keep an ear to the ground and tell him what we learned, but I could hardly expect him to reciprocate by sharing what the police knew. Which seemed a little shortsighted, really. How was I supposed to determine if something I heard or saw was important?

Gabriel and I drove away from the inn around ten. He had switched shifts for the weekend with one of the Dizzy Duke's part-time bartenders, so he was working the Saturday day shift from noon until four. That would give me the same amount of time at Zydeco before I joined him at the Duke so we could talk with Old Dog Leg together. I was all for speaking to him before either of us went to work, but Gabriel had pointed out that Dog Leg was basically nocturnal—he stayed up until the wee hours jamming with the band, then typically slept in until the afternoon. It would be kinder to let him sleep now and talk to him when he showed up at the Duke that evening.

Gabriel let me out in front of Zydeco, and I stood there for a minute, shifting from pretend-bride mode to baker-boss lady. Four hours should give me plenty of time to smooth Ox's and Edie's ruffled feathers, whatever that was about, and it might even leave me time to get Ox together with Miss Frankie so he could pitch his ideas. It sounded good in theory, but in reality I knew it meant that I had three difficult conversations lined up in a row, and I wasn't looking forward to any of them.

"Rita?"

At the sound of my name, I turned to find Dwight Sonntag loping along the sidewalk toward me. Dwight is another old friend from pastry school and one of the most gifted cake artists I know, but anyone meeting him for the first time might wonder about his professionalism. He's tall and thin and . . . well . . . scraggly. Some might even say he's hygiene challenged, but that would be patently untrue. He's very clean. He just doesn't look like he is.

That morning he wore a wrinkled white T-shirt and a pair of jeans so faded they'd long ago stopped looking like denim. Dark stubble left to fend for itself curled randomly across his cheeks and chin, and a pair of flip-flops so old the soles had all but disappeared slapped the pavement as he walked. He held a white bag in one hand, and in the other carried a ginormous paper cup that probably held a gallon of whatever he'd ordered to go with his lunch.

That day's forecast called for a high temperature in the low seventies, which should have been almost pleasant, but New Orleans's fierce sun and heavy humidity made it feel more like the high eighties. Perspiration trickled down my back, and the fabric under my arms had grown damp by the time Dwight reached me.

He slurped noisily and gave me a chin-jerk greeting. "What are you doing here? I thought you were taking some time off."

"I was," I said. "But I have a few hours on my hands, so I decided to stop by."

"Yeah?" He squinted into the sunlight and ran a glance over me. His eyebrows beetled together, forming an unattractive unibrow. "Any special reason, or just because you miss us so much?"

I laughed and started walking toward Zydeco's broad front stairs. "That depends," I told him. "Which one are you more likely to believe?"

Dwight slurped again and matched my stride, but he was still watching me from the corner of his eye. "Somebody told you, didn't they?"

"Told me what?"

"About Ox and Edie. Who was it? Estelle?"

His guess wasn't all that impressive. Neither Ox nor Edie would have called me, and Isabeau would have protected Ox. Sparkle's not the type to squeal, and Abe, our baker, only works during the wee hours when nobody else is around. He usually leaves about the time the rest of the crew shows up, which left Estelle as the most likely candidate.

I grinned and said, "Maybe," as we reached the foot of the

stairs. I stopped there, partly because I wasn't ready to go inside yet, and partly because it was about twenty degrees cooler in the shade. "What happened, anyway? I'd like your take on it before I go in there."

Dwight glanced up at the front door and shook his head slowly. "I wish I knew. One minute they were going over the details for one of next week's orders, and the next Edie was shouting at Ox like a crazy woman. Before I could figure out what was happening, she walked out."

His story matched Estelle's, but it didn't help me. "You have no idea what set her off?"

The unibrow returned. "Not really, although she did call Ox an insensitive ass. Several times."

I laughed. At least *that* sounded like Edie. "Okay," I said. "Well, she's right. He can be insensitive at times. But it's not as if that's a big surprise. And it's never bothered her like that before."

Dwight shrugged. "Maybe not, but it sure bothered her yesterday."

"Yeah, so I gathered. What did Ox say?"

"What could he say? She freaked out on him and left. He was pissed, but it's not as if he could fire her or anything."

Thank the Lord for small favors. Ox might be insensitive, but Edie could also be a pain in the neck. Yet I needed his talent, and her organizational skills had saved my butt more than once in the past few months. "She's inside now, though, right?"

"She was when I left for lunch." He climbed a couple of steps, then stopped and looked back at me. "Sorry I'm not more help."

I waved away his apology and started up the steps behind him. "Don't worry about it. If she's at work and everything's back to normal, I don't want to stir the pot."

"Oh, she's here," Dwight said with a cryptic grin, "but I

never said that things were back to normal." And with that, he bolted up the stairs.

"Dwight! Wait! What did you mean by that?" I raced after him, but he made it inside before I could catch up. By the time I burst through the door into Zydeco's foyer, I was gasping for air and sweating like a long-distance runner. I really needed to visit the gym. Later. When I had some free time.

Edie was sitting at her desk, her usually sleek hair pulled back in an untidy ponytail, her round face drawn and pale. But there was nothing diminished about her attitude. She rolled a glance filled with disapproval over me. "What are you doing here, Rita?"

"It's good to see you, too." I bent at the waist and grabbed my knees, trying to breathe normally. "Where did Dwight go?"

Edie jerked her head toward the employee break room. "He went that way. Want me to call him?"

I shook my head quickly. "No, that's okay. I'll catch him later." I crossed the foyer, with its high white walls and framed pictures of some of Zydeco's most exquisite cakes, and sat across from Edie, hoping I looked casual. "So what's going on this morning? Are you feeling okay?"

Her gaze shot to mine. "I'm fine. Why would you ask that?"

I crossed my legs and reached for a stack of mail tagged for my office. "You look a little pale," I said, tactfully leaving her hair out of the discussion. "Rough night?"

She seemed to relax a little. She even let out a thin laugh. "You could say that."

"If you're not feeling well—" I began.

"I'm fine," she snapped, cutting me off. "If there was something wrong, I'd tell you, *okay*?"

O-kay then. I hesitated over what to say next. I didn't want to poke an angry bear, but the fact that Edie was so clearly on edge meant I couldn't just pretend that nothing had happened. "Why don't you tell me what happened with you and Ox yesterday?"

What little remained of her smile disappeared in a flash. "Who told you about that? Did Ox call you?"

"It wasn't Ox," I assured her. "So tell me, why did you walk out?"

Scowling, Edie swept a stray lock of hair from her cheek. "I can't believe someone called you. You're supposed to be on vacation."

"Yeah. Well. It's not really a vacation. And that's not the point. What got you so angry with Ox?"

Edie chewed her lower lip for a moment and then sighed heavily. "It wasn't a big deal, okay? I was exhausted and worried about the money thing we talked about the other day, and I just blew up. Ox and I have talked it over. We're cool with each other. Let's just drop it." She turned toward her computer as if that put an end to the discussion.

And maybe it did. I just wasn't sure. I freely admit that personnel issues are not my forte. I'm much better at the stuff that doesn't require me to deal with hurt feelings and other emotions. So while I didn't want to overlook something important, neither did I want to turn a minor skirmish into something major.

As I debated my next move, Miss Frankie's ring tone began to play on my cell phone, and I jumped at the excuse to end my conversation with Edie. I worked up an expression that I hoped would pass for regret and held up the phone. "Sorry. I have to take this."

"Fine," Edie said without looking up. "Not a problem."

Sure, I was disappointed in myself for not getting to the bottom of the trouble between Ox and Edie, but not so disappointed that I'd prolong the uncomfortable. I trotted into my office, carrying the stack of mail with me.

"Well, sugar?" my mother-in-law said when I answered.

"I haven't heard from you, and I've been wondering how your weekend is going."

I hadn't been planning to check in with her. Apparently, she'd thought that I would. I tossed the mail into my in-basket and sank into the chair that Philippe and I had shared when we worked together. I didn't want to tell Miss Frankie about Dontae's murder, but if she hadn't heard about it on the news already, she would soon enough. Either way, there'd be hell to pay if I lied to her now.

"Do you want the good news or the bad news?" I quipped.

A heartbeat of silence passed before she said, "I guess you'd better give me both."

Which made me suspect that she hadn't seen the news yet. I opted for the good news first and told her about spotting the scar on Monroe's shoulder.

"So he *is* Old Dog Leg's brother," she said when I wound down.

"Yeah. He is."

"Well, imagine that." I heard the click of her heels and the scrape of a chair on the floor, and I pictured her sitting at her kitchen table to digest the news. "How did Dog Leg react when you told him?"

"We haven't told him yet," I said. "We're planning to fill him in this evening."

"You and Gabriel?"

"Yes."

"But, sugar, why wait? You found out what he wanted to know, didn't you? Why keep the good news from him?"

"Well, there's been a complication. The bed-and-breakfast caters to honeymoon couples, but there are also a group of senior citizens living there on a long-term basis. One of them was killed last night."

She didn't say anything for a moment, but I heard her getting up from the chair and walking across the kitchen. The refrigerator door opened and closed, and I heard the *clink* of ice followed by the *splash* of liquid into a glass. "Killed? How?"

I told her about Dontae's apparent poisoning and Monroe's disappearance. "We haven't told Old Dog Leg yet because we don't know where Monroe is, and right now I think he's the primary suspect."

"Good Lord!" she breathed. "I knew you were making a mistake to get involved in this mess. Didn't I say it would be a mistake?"

She had, but not for those reasons. "Nobody could have foreseen the murder," I pointed out. "But I know that's not why you called." I assumed she was calling about the meeting with Ox, but she surprised me.

"No, it's not. After you left the other night, I realized there was something I forgot to talk with you about," she said. "I know this is late notice, but Bernice has decided to have a barbecue for a few close friends and family on Monday. You can make it, can't you, sugar? I told Bernice you'd bring a cake."

I scrambled to follow the unexpected turn she'd taken. Miss Frankie has a habit of volunteering me for things without asking, but with so much going on I barely even noticed that she was doing it again. "Monday? Is it a special occasion?"

Miss Frankie ticked her tongue. "Is that a serious question? Have you forgotten the holiday?"

I pawed through the piles of paper on my desk, searching for my calendar. "Holiday?"

"Memorial Day! Sugar, are you even listening to me?"

"Of course I'm listening." It was partially true, anyway. "Memorial Day. Picnic at Bernice's. I'm not sure of my schedule, but I'll be there if I can."

"But, sugar, you have to be there. You're bringing the cake."

"The cake?"

140

"The cake for the barbecue. I just told you about it. Honestly, Rita!"

"I'm sorry," I said. "There's a lot going on and I'm a bit distracted. I'll do my best to be there, but even if I can't make it I'll send a cake. Okay?"

"Oh? You have other plans?" It sounded like a simple question, but it was loaded with hidden meaning. Since Philippe died, I'm Miss Frankie's only family. She relies on me more than I ever would have believed possible. I could almost hear her asking why I hadn't told her what I was doing for the holiday and why I hadn't invited her to join me.

Gabriel and I had reservations at the Love Nest for only two more nights. We were scheduled to check out on Monday morning, but what if Sullivan asked us to stick around for another day or two? Helping Old Dog Leg factored higher on my priority list than a picnic, but I wasn't sure Miss Frankie would agree. Tradition is very important to her.

"I'll let you know as soon as I can," I promised, and changed the subject again. "What does your schedule look like this afternoon? I'm at Zydeco now. If you can stop by, we can meet with Ox about his ideas for the bakery."

She refused to follow my lead. "Why don't you check with that policeman of yours? Bernice thinks we should invite him to join us."

Was it really Bernice's idea? Or was it Miss Frankie's way of making sure I wasn't getting too serious with Gabriel? Either way, I wasn't ready for another complication in my love life right now. "It's sweet of Bernice to offer," I said, "but I'm not sure inviting him is a good idea."

"Oh? Why not?" Miss Frankie managed to sound innocently surprised by my response, and maybe even a little disappointed. But again, I wasn't sure why. All I knew was that she'd rather expire in a fiery ball than give anyone the impression that she was less than gracious.

"I'm sure Sullivan will be busy," I said. "He's working the homicide at the Love Nest, and it's a holiday. There'll be crowds. Alcohol. You know how it is."

"Of course." This time, I thought she sounded relieved. Maybe the invitation had been Bernice's idea after all. "You're right. I didn't think of that. Well, that's too bad. I'll let Bernice know that you'll be coming alone."

"If my schedule is clear," I said again.

"Of course. Just let me know."

"And you'll let me know about meeting with Ox?"

"Absolutely. I'll just juggle a few things and head over that way. You check your schedule and let me know about the picnic when I get there."

I might have argued that I needed more time, but she'd already disconnected and I knew that she was probably already calling Bernice to let her know that the cake and I were a lock for Monday's barbecue.

Eighteen

❧

While I waited for Miss Frankie to arrive, I made a few phone calls and dealt with some paperwork. I texted Ox to let him know that Miss Frankie was coming and thought about talking to him about his argument with Edie, but it seemed unfair to confront him about that right before he had to pitch his ideas to Miss Frankie and me. I'd just have to talk with him about that later.

Miss Frankie arrived a little before two. I watched her carefully as we hugged hello and climbed the stairs to the second floor. If she was still angry with me for spending the weekend with Gabriel she hid it well. Her eyes seemed clear and bright, her hair was teased and sprayed, and her greeting was as warm as ever. So maybe there was nothing to worry about.

I'd chosen the conference room for our meeting instead of my office so that all three of us would be on neutral turf. I asked Edie to let Ox know we were ready for him, which she did without incident. While Miss Frankie and I waited,

Edie delivered coffee and slices of the blueberry sour cream coffee cake Abe had made that morning for the staff. I guess she thought we needed something to sweeten the discussion. It was a good choice. The cake is moist and sweet with a slight tang from the sour cream, and it pairs perfectly with a smooth cup of coffee.

After Ox joined us, we spent a few minutes making small talk until I finally got the meeting started. "So, Ox, you wanted to propose an idea for the bakery?"

Ox nodded and addressed Miss Frankie. "I mentioned this to Rita the other day," he said, and proceeded to lay out his idea to introduce a line of moderately priced cakes at Zydeco. "Money's tight. We all know that. Luxury items are the first to go when peoples' budgets are compromised, and those of us who work with luxury items have to compromise if we want to stay in business."

He handed each of us a glossy black folder. "I've mocked up a price list so you can see what I'm proposing. I think you'll see that I'm not suggesting anything too drastic."

Miss Frankie and I opened our respective folders. We spent a few minutes flipping through pages of photographs and sketches, Ox's proposed pricing, and printouts from the websites of rival bakeries to prove that, just like the website and blog we'd set up a few months ago, we were one of the last to jump on this particular bandwagon.

"We'd set a cap on the size, of course. Nothing over two tiers, for example. These cakes would serve between fifty and a hundred. Nothing larger. Nothing difficult to deliver or to set up. A minimum of decoration—no gum paste, no sculpture, no carved shapes, and no base larger than sixteen inches."

Miss Frankie had been studying the contents of the folder, but now she looked up at Ox. "I don't see any price here over a hundred dollars."

For the first time, Ox seemed a little nervous. "That's right. The whole point is to appeal to a different demographic. As you can see, the prices I'm proposing are right in line with the competition."

Miss Frankie looked at me for my reaction. "It's an idea worth considering," I said. "Let's hear Ox out."

Miss Frankie scowled at me, then back at the folder in front of her. "I thought you wanted to add *more moderate* cakes, but this feels like you're trying to move Zydeco into the bargain basement."

That was harsh. I started to respond, but Ox spoke up first. "I'm not talking bargain-basement quality, Miss Frankie. You know how I feel about Zydeco. I don't want our reputation to take a hit any more than you do."

My mother-in-law closed the folder carefully. "What do you think, Rita?"

"I'm still not certain how I feel," I admitted. "On the one hand, I think it sounds like an idea with potential. Sadly, we're going to have to do *something* to keep Zydeco in the black unless a miracle happens and the economy suddenly turns around. If we don't do something like this, our only other alternative is to cut staff, and that's a direction I really don't want to take."

"But wouldn't even that be better than changing Zydeco and damaging its reputation?"

I felt as if a two-ton weight had dropped onto my shoulders. "The staff is like family," I reminded her. "They're depending on us."

"I'm not talking about letting someone go permanently," Miss Frankie said. "But if we make the kind of sweeping changes Ox is suggesting, there might not be anything left. Wouldn't it be better to temporarily sacrifice one or two jobs if by doing that we save the rest?"

A dull ache formed between my eyes. "You're assuming

that adding the new line will be bad for business. What if it actually improves it?"

"By driving away our traditional clientele?" Miss Frankie shook her head and smiled sadly. "Our high-end clients won't bring their business to a bakery that caters to the masses. They pay for exclusivity. I'm surprised at you, Ox. I thought you would understand that."

Meaning, I supposed, that I would not. Unlike me, Ox—or, more formally, Oxford Wyndham III—had been born into privilege, at a level on par with the Reniers. Miss Frankie rarely said or did anything to remind me of my humble upbringing, so her comment knocked the wind out of me for a moment.

Miss Frankie sighed heavily and shook her head. "I'm sorry. I know Zydeco is at a crossroads, but I don't think lowering our standards is the answer. I have to vote no."

Ox ran a hand over his face and let out a breath weighted with frustration. "With all due respect, ma'am, I'm not suggesting that we lower our standards." He pushed the portfolio toward her again and tapped one of the pictures with his finger. "There's nothing mediocre about the product. It's just a less elaborate cake for a more moderate price. The quality would remain the same."

"I know times are tough," Miss Frankie said. "But I feel that what you're suggesting would change Zydeco into something completely different. Philippe didn't want his baby to be just any other regular kind of cake shop. He had dreams. Visions. You've been here from the beginning, Ox. You should know that better than anyone."

Ox dipped his head. "I do know that. But I also know that he wanted Zydeco to be his legacy. If we go out of business after just three years, that's not a legacy, that's a failure."

I could see that both Ox and Miss Frankie were getting irritated, and I wanted to stop the argument before it spiraled out of control. "Zydeco won't go out of business," I assured them both. At least not yet. "Ox, I hear what you're saying, and I agree with some of the points you're making. And Miss Frankie, I know how deeply you feel about Zydeco and how much you want to see it succeed. But I think we should take personal feelings out of the equation and just look at this from a business angle—"

She stopped me before I could go any further. "Maybe you can take your personal feelings out of the equation, sugar, but I'm afraid I can't." She stood and pushed the folder across the table to Ox. "I simply can't change the vision for Zydeco. I'd rather see it fail completely than become something less than Philippe wanted it to be. If you're going to run the business, Rita, you need to understand what Philippe's vision was." With that declaration, Miss Frankie swept from the room and the two-ton weight on my shoulders doubled in size. I blinked back tears of hurt and anger and tried desperately to catch my breath.

Ox waited until the door clicked shut behind her and then sent me a weak smile. "I think that went well, don't you?"

I was in no mood for jokes. I dropped my head onto my desk and groaned. "She's furious."

"She'll get over it."

I rolled my head to one side and looked at him with my one free eye. "You think so?"

"Eventually." Ox glanced over his shoulder at the door and then back at me with a shrug. "In a year. Maybe two."

I groaned again. "She'd rather fire people than change things around here. What am I supposed to do now?"

"Give her some time to cool down," Ox suggested. "Once she gets used to the idea, we can talk about it again."

"She's never going to get used to the idea," I said. "Miss Frankie doesn't adjust. Philippe and I separated almost three years ago, and she still thinks we were just about to reconcile when he died. She conveniently overlooks the fact that the only reason I came to New Orleans at all was to get his signature on the divorce papers. And I'm pretty sure she's completely forgotten that he would have married someone else about two minutes after our divorce was final." I didn't blame her for putting Philippe's former girlfriend out of her mind. I still didn't understand that one, myself.

"Point taken," Ox said with a laugh.

"I'm glad you can be so cavalier about Miss Frankie's reaction," I said. "I'm having a little more trouble shrugging it off."

Ox put a hand on my shoulder and gave it a squeeze. "Hey. Relax. We'll figure something out."

Relax? Had my tightly wound friend really said that? "Who are you and what have you done with Ox?"

He laughed again, and I dropped my head onto the table once more, this time in relief. Ox and I had our differences from time to time, but it was good to know he had my back. "Thanks," I said. "I mean that."

He acknowledged my gratitude with a smile and changed the subject. "So how's the vacation going?"

I wasn't sure the change was an improvement. "Don't ask. It's not really a vacation. Gabriel and I are . . . well, it's a long story."

"I heard. Everybody's talking about it over at the Duke."

"Great," I said sarcastically. "That'll save time having to explain it to everyone here."

"So is this guy Dog Leg's brother or not?"

"Yeah. But it's all really complicated and I don't want to say too much before Gabriel and I talk to Dog Leg."

Ox studied my expression and got serious all of a sudden. "Broussard's not . . . you know . . . being inappropriate with you, is he?"

That finally got a laugh from me. I sat up slowly. "No,

nothing like that," I assured him. "It's worse, actually. Someone died last night. The police think it might have been murder."

Ox did a classic double take. "Say what?"

"One of the permanent residents of the inn. An old man named Dontae Thomas." I poured a second cup of coffee for each of us and grabbed the first real chance I'd had to process what happened last night. "The coroner hasn't done an autopsy yet, but it doesn't look good."

"You're serious?"

"Yeah. Unfortunately."

Stunned, Ox ran a hand over his smooth head and whistled softly. "And you thought this would be a quick, easy favor."

I laughed again. "That's not even the worst part," I said. I argued with myself for a moment about sharing the details, but the temptation to talk it over with a friend got the best of me. "Get this: the others are convinced that Dog Leg's brother is the killer."

Ox sat back in his seat. "Is he?"

I shook my head. "I don't know, but I doubt it. I think Monroe was just in the wrong place at the wrong time. And to complicate things even further, he's gone again. He skipped out before the police got there."

Ox gave a low groan. "You sure know how to pick 'em. I'll give you that. Old Dog Leg's not going to be happy."

"Ya think?" I rubbed my forehead, trying to ease the ache that was growing stronger by the minute. "I know it's not my fault, but I hate knowing that I was *this close* to him and I let him get away."

"You didn't exactly *let* him do anything," Ox said. "So cheer up. Maybe he'll come back again."

"Yeah. Maybe."

Ox shook his head, but he wore an annoying little smile. "So I guess that means the honeymoon is over, huh?"

I had trouble meeting his eyes. "Not exactly."

"What does that mean?"

"It means we're staying at the inn at least another couple of nights, until our reservation is over on Monday."

Ox put the fingers of one hand to his temple, and I wondered if my headache was contagious. "Come on, Rita . . ."

"It's not my idea." I resented him a little for putting me on the defensive. "Detective Sullivan asked me to stay. He wants me to keep an ear to the ground for any potentially useful information."

Ox's gaze flashed to mine. "Is he nuts? You could be hurt . . . or worse."

"It'll be fine," I said with more conviction than I felt. "I promised to help Old Dog Leg, and I want to keep my word."

"Yeah, but you've done that," Ox pointed out with a slight scowl. "Your part is finished. Let the police do the dirty work."

"It's not that simple," I argued. "And it's not as if Sullivan asked me to do anything really dangerous. He just wants me to hang out and see what I can pick up. And it's not as if I'll be there alone. Gabriel will be there with me."

That didn't seem to make a difference. "Not your job," Ox said again.

I didn't know how to explain; I didn't really understand it myself. But I knew I couldn't rest until Monroe Magee's name was clear and he was reunited with his brother. I just hoped nobody else would get hurt in the process.

Nineteen

Ox and I spent the next hour going over the orders we had for the coming week. Several times I thought about bringing up his argument with Edie, but they really did seem to be okay with each other now, so I shelved that conversation. After Ox went back to the design area, I approved a couple of sketches by other employees and tasted Abe's attempt at a sweet tea cake recipe he'd been experimenting with. He'd stirred black tea and vanilla extract into traditional dry ingredients and then topped the cake with lemon sweet tea buttercream. I liked the concept but the cake wasn't up to Zydeco's exacting standards. The tea was overpowering and the lemon frosting needed more punch. I sent it back to the kitchen with my notes, and at four o'clock set off to tackle the most difficult task on my agenda.

I walked the two blocks to the Dizzy Duke, glad to find that the humidity had tempered a bit, thanks to a breeze blowing in off the Gulf. It had been a rough day so far and I hoped that the warm day and cloudless blue sky would lift my spirits.

Within half a block, the stately old antebellum mansions surrounding Zydeco gave way to squat storefronts and sagging old buildings wrapped up in a musty smell that even sunshine and low humidity couldn't dissipate.

Gabriel was behind the bar when I came through the doors, and the house band was running through songs halfheartedly on the stage. A couple of regular customers chatted amiably at the bar, but the rest of the place was empty.

I breathed a sigh of relief when I saw that it was too early for the Saturday night crowd, and hitched myself onto a bar stool. I wasn't in the mood to deal with crowds, and the fewer people around when we talked to Old Dog Leg, the better. Gabriel brought me a Diet Coke without asking and waved away the money I tried to put on the bar.

"Family discount," he said with a grin.

I laughed. "I get a family discount? Why didn't you say so before? I'm going to miss *that* when this is over."

"It's just one of the many perks that come along with the Broussard name."

I removed the straw from my glass and set it aside. "I'd rather discuss those than tell Old Dog Leg we lost his brother. But I guess we'd better get it over with. Is he here?"

Gabriel nodded toward the stage. "He showed up an hour ago. He's pretty eager to talk with us."

"Wish I could say the same." I slid from the bar stool and carried my glass to the back of the house while Gabriel pulled two beers from the cooler and went off to bring Old Dog Leg over to my table.

The expression on the old man's face was both hopeful and cautious, and my heart went out to him. "So?" he asked. "How'd it go?"

"Which do you want first?" I asked. "The good news or the bad news?"

Dog Leg smiled. "If dere's good news, I'll take it."

Okie-dokie. I took a deep breath and plunged in. "We found Monroe, and I saw the scar on his shoulder. It's him."

Dog Leg absorbed that without even a twitch. "Well, well. After all dis time."

"Yeah. I spoke with him alone for a few minutes," I said. "I think he's genuinely interested in reconnecting with you and old friends, but there's more."

"Ah yes. Bad news." Dog Leg sat up a little straighter and lifted his chin. "Might as well give it to me fast."

"One of the other residents at the inn was killed last night," Gabriel said. "It looks like he was poisoned."

Dog Leg's smile faded, but he still managed to look hopeful. "Another guest, you say? But not Monroe?"

"Not Monroe," I assured him.

Dog Leg's sigh of relief was barely audible. "Well. Poor man. Dey know who did it?"

"Not yet," I said.

Dog Leg took a deep pull from the beer in front of him, his hand shaking a little as he brought the bottle to his lips and then set it down. It was the first real sign that he was affected by the news. "And Monroe? He all right?"

"We think so," Gabriel said.

Hope turned to wariness. "But you ain't sure?"

"The thing is," I said, "he disappeared right after we found the body. Everything was gone from his room, and there's been no sign of him since."

The wariness on Dog Leg's face gave way to dejection. "So he's run off again."

"Maybe," I said. "We don't know that he left voluntarily. There's a chance he could be hurt . . ." I broke off, aware that my suggestions weren't exactly optimistic.

Gabriel picked up where I left off. "Or he could be fine and just . . . you know . . . hiding from the police."

Dog Leg looked confused. "Why would he . . . ?" he asked,

but the answer hit him before either of us could speak. "Ahh . . . police t'ink he killed dis man."

"Some of the other residents at the inn seem to think so," I said. "But I'm not so sure. If you're up to it, we'd like to ask you a few questions about your brother. That may help us figure out what really happened."

Dog Leg nodded. "Ask away."

"We think that he knew the people at the Love Nest from before, back when he lived in New Orleans," Gabriel said. "Could we run some names past you and see if any of them sound familiar?"

Dog Leg nodded again. "You can ask, but I didn't know much about his friends back den, and my memory ain't what it used to be."

"That's okay," I assured him. "Just about anything you can tell us is more than we know right now." I took a drink from my Diet Coke and wished I'd asked for a margarita instead. "Monroe told me that he goes way back with the two ladies who own the inn, a couple of sisters named Hyacinth and Primrose. He called them the Hoyt sisters."

Dog Leg rolled the names around in his memory for a few seconds. "Could be. Where'd he know dem from?"

"We don't know," Gabriel said. "Nobody's talking. Their names aren't familiar to you?"

Dog Leg shook his head. "No. Sorry."

"Was Monroe involved in anything strange back then?" Gabriel asked. "Anything he might want to keep hidden?"

"Like what? Somet'ing illegal?"

"Could be," I said. "We're grasping at straws here, but it seems a little odd that nobody over there is willing to talk about the past."

Dog Leg shook his head slowly. "Not dat I know of, but he didn't tell me much about what he did back den. We had our gig at the Cott'n Bott'm, but he came and went. We played.

I was on the trumpet. He was our bass man. Had a few drinks. Monroe kept to himself."

"Sounds like he fits right in with the others at the Love Nest," I mused. "None of them wants to talk either." I rubbed my forehead, still fighting the stress headache. "How about Dontae Thomas? That's the man who died. Does that name ring a bell?"

"'Fraid not. Anybody else?"

"A man named Grey Washington," I said. "They call him the professor. A pastor named Rod Kinkle, and a woman named Lula Belle."

Old Dog Leg had started shaking his head again, but the last name made him stop. "Lula Belle Isaacs?"

Gabriel and I exchanged a glance. "Could be," Gabriel said. "Do you know her?"

Dog Leg nodded slowly. "Back den just about ever' man in New Orleans knew Lula Belle."

Gabriel waggled his eyebrows. "Sounds like we're talking about the same woman."

"She's still around, eh?" Dog Leg said with a chuckle. "I always 'spected she'd go early. Mebbe get done in by a jealous wife."

"Or almost any other woman on the planet," I muttered. "But she's still alive and well. Mostly, anyway. She's pretty elderly now, but she still likes to flirt, and she seemed interested in Monroe last night. Did he know her, too?"

Old Dog Leg shrugged. "I 'spect he prob'ly did. Truth to tell, he wasn't much interested in de ladies back den. And don't take dat de wrong way. I'm not sayin' he was interested in men. He wasn't interested in nobody. Love didn't interest him much."

We were getting nowhere fast. "So he didn't date anyone back then?" I asked. "He wasn't in a relationship with anyone?"

Old Dog Leg shook his head. "None I ever heard him talk about."

I sighed in frustration. "And you have *no* idea why he disappeared the first time?"

Dog Leg's expression drooped. "None at all. I'm sorry Rita. I wish I did."

"When he disappeared, did you try to find him?" I asked. "Did you check with friends? File a report with the police?"

"Of course. I did all dat. Nobody knew a damn t'ing. One day he was goin' to work and comin' to play with de band. Next day he was gone."

It took a second for his words to sink in, but when they did I sat up a little straighter. "Going to work? You mean the band wasn't his job?"

Dog Leg laughed. "Oh no. It paid us some, but not much. Nobody could live on what we made in de clubs."

"Where did he work?" Gabriel asked. "Is it possible that's how he knew the Hoyt sisters or the others?"

Dog Leg nodded slowly. "Possible, I guess. He never did talk much 'bout his work neither. I always figured dat's because it was such a dead-end job. He had dreams, dat boy. Thought he was goin' to be famous. Make it big. Truth was, he could barely pay rent. Had to come to me for extra cash all de time."

"Where did he work?" I asked, feeling cautiously hopeful.

"Had him a job at Letterman Industries workin' in de warehouse. Stock boy, I t'ink he was."

My heart skipped a beat, and I met Gabriel's gaze with wide-eyed excitement. "Isn't that the same place the professor said he used to work?"

Gabriel nodded. "I'm pretty sure it is."

Dog Leg's old face registered excitement. "De professor? What you say his name was?"

"Grey. Washington," I said. "Do you know him?"

Old Dog Leg spent a minute trying to resurrect a memory of the professor but finally shook his head again. "I'm sorry. Wish I could be more help, but I jus' don' know much."

He looked so disappointed I regretted letting him sense my frustration. "It's okay," I said and put my hand on his. "We know more now than we did when we got here. Does Letterman Industries still exist? Maybe the police can get a look at their old employee records."

"'Fraid not," Old Dog Leg said, hosing down my excitement again. "Place burned down 'bout ten years ago."

I sat back in my chair and frowned. "Of course it did. So we're back at square one. Unless you can think of someplace he might have gone? Is there any chance he'd come to your house?"

Faint hope sparked in Old Dog Leg's expression. "He might. But I didn't answer his letter, so I don' know. T'ink you can find him again? Now dat I *know* it's him, I gotta find out why . . ." His voice cracked, and he swiped the corner of his eye with the back of his hand.

Gabriel met my gaze. "What do you think? Can we find him?"

"We can try," I said. I touched Dog Leg's arm gently. "We can *try*," I said again. "But I can't promise anything."

"Understood."

"We don't have a lot to go on," I reminded him.

Apparently, Gabriel was feeling more positive about our chances than I was. "At least now we have a connection between Monroe and the Love Nest gang."

I laughed a little at his use of the word *gang*. "Yeah, they're a rogue band of septuagenarians, running amok and wreaking havoc in the neighborhood—except, of course, they can barely move."

"And one of them might be a heartless killer," Gabriel reminded me.

There was that, of course. And they were still the only people who knew what happened forty years ago to make Monroe Magee their public enemy number one. All we had to do was get them to talk about it.

That ought to be a piece of cake.

Twenty

Traffic was a mess when Gabriel and I drove back to the inn, which gave us plenty of time to rehash the conversation we'd just had with Old Dog Leg. "I think he took it well," Gabriel said as we inched along Saint Charles Avenue. "Don't you?"

"Better than I expected," I agreed. "But I think we may have given him false hope when we told him we'd try to find Monroe."

Gabriel braked for a traffic light—practically unnecessary in the gridlock. "I don't know why you say that. It can't be that difficult to track him down."

"Seriously? The man's an expert at losing himself, or have you forgotten that he disappeared for forty years?"

"There are two things wrong with your argument," he said, giving a little crook of the finger to a car waiting to merge. "When Monroe disappeared the first time, he was a much younger man. And it's a completely different world now than it was then. Somebody somewhere will spot the van he's driving and call the police."

I wasn't so sure. "You're assuming he's still in the van. He could have ditched it and be driving something completely different."

"So the police will track him using credit cards or the GPS on his phone. I'm sure they've got account numbers by now."

"Yeah," I said. "Maybe." I made a mental note, though, to ask Sullivan about the methods he was using to locate Monroe.

It was nearly dark when we finally pulled into the Love Nest neighborhood, which was pulsing with Saturday nightlife. The shopkeepers, old men, and young mothers who'd made up the daytime population had already begun to give way to the nighttime crowd of brash young men and women looking for a good time. I spotted a couple of plainclothes cops going door-to-door and wondered if they were trying to find someone who'd admit to having seen or heard something at the time of the murder. Or maybe they were tracking gang members. Or drug dealers. Whatever it was, I felt safer knowing they were there.

As I turned to look away, I noticed an old man marching along the sidewalk wearing the uniform of a Union infantry soldier: blue wool coat, slouch hat, and polished knee boots. He walked with his head held high and his eyes straight ahead, completely out of place in the foot traffic that swarmed around him.

My heart did a little skippy dance in my chest, and I turned to Gabriel. "It's Grey! Pull over and let me out. Quick, before he sees us and takes off or something."

Gabriel drew his attention from traffic for a split second so he could stare at me, incredulous. "Are you joking? You want me to let you out here? Alone?"

"Just do it. I'll be fine. The police are right over there if I need help."

He made no move to slow down.

"Come on, Gabriel! Pull over and stop. Please. This might be the only chance I get to talk to the professor alone."

I could see Gabriel arguing with himself over the wisdom of letting me get out in that neighborhood without protection. "And how are you going to explain why you're following him?"

"I don't know. I'll pretend to be shopping or something."

Gabriel laughed without humor and glanced at the collection of stores and businesses huddled together along the street. "Shopping. Where? The tattoo parlor?"

"If I have to. I'll tell him I'm picking out a tattoo for you to get. Something romantic, like a snake with my name on it." I reached for the buckle of my seat belt. "Come on!"

He clearly wasn't sold on the idea, but he finally pulled to the side of the road so I could get out. "Just be careful. I'll stay in the area to keep an eye on things and make sure you're safe."

I would have agreed to just about anything if it meant I could get out of the car. "Fine. Just don't let him see you." I slipped between a couple of parked cars and onto the sidewalk, then fell into step behind Grey, who, so far at least, seemed unaware that I was stalking him.

Thankful for small favors, I closed the distance between us and tried to look surprised when I ran into him—literally— as he stopped to inspect something that had attached itself to the bottom of his shoe.

"Excuse me! I didn't see you—" I broke off, tried to look flustered, and then pretended to recognize him. "Oh! Hello. I hope I didn't hurt you."

Grey responded with a sharp salute. "First Sergeant Charles Remond Douglass at your service, ma'am. Are you all right?"

I offered a friendly smile, but he didn't seem to recognize me. I wondered if he was a little unhinged or just still in character from a session at the library. "I'm fine. Thanks. Just a little embarrassed. If I had to run into someone this way, I'm glad it's someone I know."

When he still didn't react as if he knew me, I tried another way to crack his veneer, waving a hand in front of his uniform and going for the flattery angle. "I take it you've been to the library?"

"Yes ma'am. That I have."

"The kids are lucky to have you. Are you going back to the inn now?" He didn't answer, but I thought I saw a flicker of recognition in his eyes, so I jumped on it before it disappeared. "Would you mind if I walk with you, Professor? I lost track of time, and I'm a little nervous walking the streets by myself."

Grey looked uncomfortable with my request, but he was too much of a gentleman to say no. He gave a curt nod and began to walk again.

Score one for me. I fell into step beside him and kept up the conversation. "I'm glad to see that you're going about your regular routine. I was worried about how much Dontae's death had upset everyone."

He slid a glance at me, and I sensed him struggling to maintain his character. "Routine is an important part of a soldier's daily regimen," he said after a moment.

Forget the soldier. I wanted to talk to the old man who'd retired from Letterman Industries. I did my best to look sympathetic, hoping I could draw out the real Grey Washington. "Well, I admire you for staying the course. I'm completely exhausted after being woken up in the middle of the night. I guess you were asleep when they found Dontae in the garden."

Grey picked up the pace, moving so quickly I had to jog to keep up. I could only hope I'd be so agile when I was his age. "I was in my room, yes. I wasn't asleep, though." He dodged a couple of kids sharing a joint and slipped me a look filled with disappointment. I guess he'd been hoping to leave me in his dust.

I pretended not to notice. "Oh? Did you hear anything unusual outside, or did you see anything?"

The disappointment on his face turned into annoyance. "I was reading."

"Is that a no, then?"

He didn't answer. I was still stinging over the way he'd evaded my questions at breakfast, and determined not to let him give a repeat performance now. I tried a more direct approach. "You mentioned last night that you retired from a place called Letterman Industries," I said. "How long did you say you worked there?"

Did I only imagine the slight check in his step? It was hard to tell. "You must have me confused with someone else. My name is Charles Remond Douglass, oldest son of Frederick Douglass. I'm a printer by trade."

Seriously? He was going back to playing this character? Not if I could help it.

He stepped into an intersection without checking for cars. Maybe they'd turned into horse-drawn carriages in his mind. I followed, praying that modern-day traffic would stop in time to avoid hitting us. I was panting from the effort of keeping up with him, and his latest tactic of avoiding talking to me only made me angry.

"Look," I said. "I understand that you like to stay in character, and I know that you're wary of strangers, but I really need answers. I know you worked at Letterman Industries, and I think you worked there at the same time as Monroe Magee. Am I right?"

Grey stepped around another group of teenagers on the sidewalk. They smelled of booze and stale sweat. "You worked at Letterman Industries with Monroe Magee forty years ago," I said again. "Something happened back then to make you angry with Monroe—so angry you're still upset about it. What was it?"

Grey's stride lengthened even farther. "I'm afraid I don't know what you're talking about, ma'am."

Was he actually crazy or just determined not to talk to me? I couldn't keep running, so I tried taunting him. "What's the matter? Are you afraid Hyacinth will find out you talked to me? What do you think she'll do to you?"

His soldier-boy mask cracked a bit more. "Hyacinth? Nothing. She's a wonderful woman."

"She didn't like the fact that you were talking to me this morning," I said. "That was painfully obvious. What is *she* trying to hide, and why are you trying to protect her?"

Grey stopped walking abruptly. "It's not what you think. She's been through enough."

His admission surprised me. I'd gone out on a limb with my question. It wasn't easy to imagine Hyacinth as someone who needed protection. But apparently I'd struck a nerve, so I kept going. "If that's the case, then surely you'll want to protect her and her business from a long, drawn-out murder investigation."

Grey's gaze flickered to mine uncertainly. "*She* didn't do anything."

"You know that for a fact?"

"I know Hyacinth," he said firmly.

"Well, somebody killed Dontae, and whoever it was did it on Love Nest property. Hyacinth and Primrose are going to pay a price for that, even if they're innocent." Which I doubted.

At least, I doubted Hyacinth's innocence. I had a little more trouble casting Primrose in the role of calculated cold-blooded killer. I pegged her as more of a hot-blooded sort, the type to shove someone off the roof in a fit of anger.

Grey shifted his weight from foot to foot and let out a sigh that vanquished the soldier persona and left him deflated. "I fail to understand how talking about the past will prevent an onerous investigation."

"If someone murdered Dontae because of the past, talking about it is the only way to find the killer and bring him—or her—to justice."

"We don't know that Dontae was killed because of the past," Grey argued. "His death could have been an accident."

"You didn't seem to think so this morning. Have you changed your mind, or do you still think Monroe had something to do with Dontae's death?"

Grey glanced up and down the street, as if he wanted to make sure he wouldn't be overheard. But then he clamped his mouth shut and didn't say a word.

"Cleveland seems to think Monroe is the killer," I pushed. "And you said some pretty harsh things about Monroe at breakfast. What happened between the rest of you guys and Monroe in the past?"

Grey started walking again. "I know what you're trying to do, but it's not going to work."

With a little growl of frustration, I jogged after him. "What am I trying to do?"

"You're trying to confuse me. But it's not going to work."

"I'm *trying* to find out why you and Cleveland are so convinced that Monroe killed Dontae. What did he do? Steal your girl? Get a promotion that you thought should have been yours?"

Grey just shook his head.

"He was a brownnoser," I said, ticking off possibilities as we walked. "He lied to the boss about you. He sat around reading magazines while you did all the work. He pilfered office supplies and blamed you."

"He didn't do a damn thing to me," Grey finally snapped. "Okay? I'm fine. I get up every morning, and I go to bed every night. I can come and go as I please and even walk around town dressed up like a goddamn soldier in the goddamn Union Army if I want to. It's not about me, okay?"

I took an involuntary step backward and blinked in surprise. "Then who *is* it about?"

"Not me," Grey said again and turned on his heel. He walked back the way we'd come as if he couldn't get away from me fast enough. Half a block away, I saw Gabriel's car peel off into a parking lot, but I wasn't really paying attention to that. I was trying to read through the lines and figure out what had just set Grey off.

I ran after him before he could shake me. "Are you saying that someone else *can't* do the things you mentioned?"

Grey whipped around once more and pointed his index finger at me. "Stop! Stop right there. I'm through talking to you."

"You can't leave it like that," I argued, but he'd already started walking again.

I considered chasing after him again, but I had the feeling that if I pushed any harder right now I'd lose him for good. In fact, as I watched his rigid back moving away from me, I thought it might already be too late.

Twenty-one

✥

I held back until Grey marched past the parking lot where Gabriel was waiting, then I hurried to the car and slid inside. "Well," I said as I closed the door. "That was interesting."

"He talked?"

"Not as much as I'd have liked, but I think I have an idea about what happened in the past." I buckled my seat belt and told him about Grey's cryptic comments. "I think someone else got hurt or maybe even died back then, and he holds Monroe responsible."

Gabriel actually looked impressed. "That's good, but it still doesn't explain why Monroe would've killed Dontae."

"No, but it might explain why someone might've tried to kill *him*."

"You think Dontae's death was a mistake?"

"Maybe. That would make sense. Nobody seems to have a motive for killing him, but Monroe's a different story, isn't he?"

"So you think it was revenge gone wrong?" Gabriel gave that some thought as he merged into traffic. "If that's the case, why did Monroe come back at all? Surely he knew how the others felt. Why would he take the risk of coming back to see them?"

"Good question. Unfortunately, it's one of about a hundred equally good questions, none of which I have answers to."

"Well, somebody does, and somebody has to be willing to talk. It's just a matter of finding the right person in the right circumstances."

"Yeah, but who?" I watched a well-dressed young woman sail past a handful of scraggly young men in oversized sweatshirts and pants hanging so low they exposed way more Fruit of the Loom than anyone should have to see in public, and I wondered how the seniors at the Love Nest stayed safe in this neighborhood. "Hyacinth certainly isn't going to spill her guts just because I ask her to," I said as Gabriel turned into the inn's parking lot.

"Hyacinth won't," he said. "But Primrose might."

"She might," I agreed. Primrose was way more chatty than her sister. "If she's not too intimidated by Hyacinth. Or maybe I can get Lula Belle to open up. She's not exactly a functioning member of the Grand Sisterhood of Women. I bet she'd throw any of these other women under the bus if they got between her and a man."

Gabriel grinned. "You're probably right. Maybe we can use one of the others as a wedge to get her to open up. The trick will be getting her alone without Hyacinth realizing what you're doing."

That made me nervous. I'll admit it. The woman intimidated me. Of everyone at the inn she was the one I'd vote Most Likely to Casually Poison a Friend. She was also the one with the best opportunity to do it. I wasn't going to make the mistake of underestimating her.

"I guess this means we'll be watching some reality TV in the parlor this evening," I said. "We can't very well look for opportunities to question the others from the privacy of the honeymoon suite."

Gabriel gave a little fist pump. "Yes! I can finally catch up on *Bachelorette Brides from Bogata, the Lost Episodes*!"

I nudged him with an elbow and thanked my lucky stars there was no such show—at least I hoped there wasn't. "You'll tone it down a notch on the whole honeymoon thing, won't you? I need to be able to concentrate on questioning potential murderers. Your stories are a real distraction."

Gabriel pretended to be disappointed. "Way to take all the fun out of it."

"We're not here to have fun," I reminded him. "We're here to figure out how Monroe Magee managed to disappear without a trace while somebody was killing poor Dontae right under our noses." And, hopefully, we could do that before Bernice's barbecue on Monday. I wasn't in the mood to explain to Miss Frankie why I needed to stay at the Love Nest a few days longer.

Gabriel sobered slightly. "You really don't think Monroe did it?"

"I sure don't want to think that he did," I said. "It would break Dog Leg's heart. I suppose that anything's possible, but my gut tells me that Dontae's death was an accident. I think someone meant to rid the world of Monroe and got Dontae instead."

"Don't they say that poison is traditionally a woman's weapon?"

I nodded. "That's the rumor. But we're talking about a bunch of seventy- and eighty-year-olds. If they were thirty or forty years younger, I might be more inclined to rule out the male suspects. But you've seen them. I don't think any of them is strong enough to whack somebody over the head with enough force to do real damage.

"Grey managed to knock down the door to Monroe's room," Gabriel reminded me.

"Point taken. So Grey might have been able to take Dontae out, but I doubt any of the others could and none of them are the gun-toting type. But anyone can use poison."

"Maybe," Gabriel said. "Although if one of them wanted a gun, they wouldn't have any trouble getting one in this neighborhood."

"Yeah, but it's far more likely that one of them grabbed ant poison from the garage and sprinkled it in the sweet tea."

Gabriel conceded the argument with a shrug. "So we keep trying to figure out who hated Monroe the most?"

I nodded and glanced at the inn. "And we pray that we find Monroe before the killer does."

The inn was quiet as a morgue when we went inside. Not a creature was stirring, but the TV was blaring a rerun of *Grey's Anatomy* in the parlor. Gabriel and I settled in to wait. He dozed off a couple of times while I caught up on the antics of Doctors Bailey and McSteamy, the only two characters I've ever been able to work up an interest in. I drifted off during *Private Practice*. At ten, we gave up and climbed the stairs to our room.

Gabriel slept like a baby, but I lay awake for a while, listening for footsteps or voices, or any other sign that we weren't the only two people at the Love Nest. I gave some thought to the cake Miss Frankie had volunteered me to make for the barbecue and jotted a few notes about ingredients and decorations. I'd have to make the cake tomorrow while Gabriel was at work.

When I still couldn't fall asleep, I dug out a paperback I'd slipped into my bag and read until around 2 a.m., at which point I finally drifted off.

I awoke a little before nine on Sunday morning to a gun-metal gray sky and a marshy scent hanging in the heavy air. After staying up so late, I had a hard time jump-starting myself. I resisted Gabriel's repeated urging to get up until the very last minute, then dressed and hurried downstairs to breakfast, but either we'd missed the others or they were still avoiding us.

Just like the previous morning, however, a scrumptious breakfast was laid out on the sideboard: breakfast burritos filled with eggs, cheese, and ham; cheesy grits; flaky biscuits with rich sausage gravy; yam bran muffins; peaches and cream French toast; and a mouthwatering array of fresh fruit. The only difference was that today nobody but us was around to eat it.

Out of curiosity, I poked my head into the kitchen, but other than a few dirty pans waiting for someone's attention, that room was empty, too. I was ravenous and the food looked tempting and smelled even better, but my growing uncertainty over Hyacinth's part in Dontae's death made it easy to pass up.

Gabriel had to work another day shift at the Dizzy Duke, and I wasn't about to stay at the Love Nest alone, so we headed out to the parking lot just before noon. On our way, we glanced into the parlor and saw that it, too, was empty. This morning's selection: an episode of *Rachael Ray* that was playing to nobody. In fact, the entire house seemed silent and deserted. If it hadn't been for the hot breakfast in the dining room, I might have wondered if we'd slept through the apocalypse.

Traffic was light that morning, so we made it across town quickly. Gabriel would be tied up for most of the day thanks to a Hornets playoff game, and I didn't want to be stuck waiting for him, so I had him drop me at home, then drove my Mercedes back to Zydeco while he went on to the Duke alone.

For the first time in months, the parking lot was empty when I pulled in. Seeing that made my stomach knot. Even though Zydeco is technically closed on Sundays, everyone on staff has a key and it's a rare Sunday that no one comes in to catch up on something.

I could have made the cake for Bernice's barbecue at home, but I hardly ever get to work in Zydeco's kitchen and almost never on my own. I planned to take advantage of the quiet to exercise a little creative freedom in the best kitchen I've ever seen.

State-of-the-art ovens line one wall and massive refrigerators take up another. A bank of sinks deep enough to submerge even the largest pot stretch beneath a row of windows, and a massive granite-topped island combined with matching countertops provide more square feet of workspace than I can count. Half a dozen chefs could have worked in there easily.

The design area is brightly colored and cheerful, but the kitchen is all gleaming white and stainless steel. I feel brilliant and creative every time I walk through its doors—and today it was all mine.

It had been awhile since I'd decorated a cake purely for fun and even longer since I'd started from scratch and baked the cake myself. Feeling like a kid in a candy shop, I rummaged through Abe's recipe files until I found Zydeco's recipe for white chocolate raspberry cake: perfect for a Memorial Day barbecue.

I creamed together butter and sugar, added eggs one at a time, taking care to blend each one into the mixture separately. I melted white chocolate in a double boiler and set it aside to cool slightly, and opened the cupboards to look for the remaining ingredients I'd need.

"Rita? What are you doing?"

I squeaked in surprise at the sound of another voice and nearly dropped the vanilla extract I'd just pulled from the shelf. I turned to find Edie in the doorway, watching me with a curious expression.

"Miss Frankie volunteered me to take a cake to Bernice's barbecue tomorrow. I decided to make it here."

"I'm sure there's an extra cake in the cooler," Edie said. "Abe usually keeps a few on hand for emergencies."

I grinned, shrugged, and pulled a set of measuring spoons from a drawer. When I cook, I eyeball measurements, but baking is a more exact science. A careless splash of liquid can change consistency and texture, or alter flavor and ruin a cake.

"I can hardly qualify this as an emergency," I told her. "Besides, I'm having fun. What are you doing here? Don't tell me you have work to do."

Edie moved a couple of steps into the room. "Not really. I just didn't have anything else to do at home."

"Do you want to help?"

She shook her head quickly and a shudder passed through her. "Thanks but . . . sometimes I like to just come and sit. Play around on the computer. Tinker with the calendar. Straighten office supplies. It relaxes me."

I understood in theory. That's what working in the kitchen does for me. But her reaction to helping me bake seemed odd, frankly. Edie hadn't been the most talented pastry chef in our class, but she *had* attended pastry school, after all.

I traded measuring spoons for a dry cup measure, pulled flour, baking powder, and baking soda from the cupboard, then turned to the fridge for the buttermilk. "How did work go after I left yesterday? Did we get any new orders?"

Edie shook her head and dragged a stool up to the island. "I sent out some e-mails to bridal shops like we talked about, and I did some more research on bridal shows in the area. I widened my search area and checked for anything within a four-hour drive. There's not much going on until fall, though."

I measured the dry ingredients into a mixing bowl. "Things will turn around," I predicted. I sounded like a broken record, but maybe if I said it often enough we'd all start to believe it.

"Yeah. I'm sure it will." She made no move to leave, and

just like the other day, I had the feeling something was bothering her.

"Is something on your mind, Edie? You seem worried."

She tucked a lock of straight brown hair behind one ear and smiled a little. "You mean something besides the fact that we're losing money every day?"

I looked away from the measuring cup and connected with her eye to eye. "I don't know. You tell me. What's up?"

She shifted on the stool and then propped her chin in her hand. "I think maybe I should go."

"Go? Go where?" Had I missed her talking about something important to her? Some sort of family occasion? Maybe a wedding or a birthday? I didn't like thinking I'd been too distracted to remember. "If you need some time off, just say so."

She shook her head. "No, I mean *go*. The bakery is in trouble, Rita. Something has to give, and I wonder if maybe it should be me."

I put down the measuring cup and pushed the canister of flour away from the edge of the counter. "You're talking about quitting?"

She nodded, but she looked miserable.

"Are you crazy? Zydeco would fall apart without you."

Her lips curved slightly. "That's nice of you to say, but we both know I'm the fifth wheel here. I'm not good in the kitchen. My decorating skills aren't even mediocre. Philippe was wonderful to offer me a job here, especially after I dropped out of pastry school. But baking really isn't my passion. It never was. My mother thought I could make a go of it, and for her sake I tried, but . . ." She broke off, leaving me to fill in the blanks for myself.

I was a little embarrassed to realize how little I knew of Edie's story. "So pastry school was your mother's idea?"

"She wanted me to be good at something. But I wasn't."

Edie served up a shaky smile. "You and I both know that of everyone here, I'm the most expendable."

My heart was pounding, and my mind was racing. A dozen responses flew through my head, most of them angry and irrational. I took a deep breath and counted to ten, the way Aunt Yolanda had taught me when I was an angry teenager with impulse-control issues. Surprisingly, my voice sounded almost normal when I spoke again. "How long have you been thinking about this?"

"A few days." That lock of hair came loose, and Edie flicked it behind her ear with a little scowl. "I know Miss Frankie shot down Ox's idea during your meeting yesterday. I also know this place can't keep going the way it is or you'll lose it."

"True, but you're Zydeco's organizational backbone. You're the glue that holds the whole operation together."

She waved away my protest. "You can do everything I do. I can't do what you do."

It's no secret that Edie and I have had our difficult moments, but the thought of losing her this way made it hard to breathe. "I think you're overreacting," I said. "Things aren't that bad yet."

"Maybe not, but they'll get that bad if we don't do something soon."

Almost on autopilot I turned back to the bowl I'd left on the counter. I needed to channel my frustration into something productive. I hated that Zydeco was in this position. I hated being forced to make choices I didn't want to make. I wanted the world to right itself and for everything to be okay again. But that wasn't going to happen by sitting back and ignoring it.

"What about your idea of trimming hours from everyone's schedule?" I asked when I could speak again. "I'd rather do that than lose someone."

"That's a temporary solution at best."

"So? We take the temporary solution until we come up with something else."

Edie just stared at me without blinking.

"I'm serious," I said. "If that's what we have to do to keep everyone working, let's do it."

"Nobody's going to be happy with part-time wages," Edie predicted.

"You were all for the idea a few days ago," I reminded her. "Why are you against it today?"

"Because the other day I thought you and Miss Frankie would agree to Ox's solution, and I thought cutting hours could tide us over until the new line took off."

The spoon in my hand stopped moving. "Ox talked his idea over with you before he talked to me?"

"He wanted some figures compiled. I asked why he needed them." She lifted her chin defiantly. "Don't be angry with him. He's trying to help."

"Yeah? Maybe. But this isn't the first time he's gone behind my back to do it." I really had to get things straight with Ox, but that would have to wait. It wasn't even close to being the biggest fire I had to fight.

I added *explain organizational chart to Ox* to my mental to-do list and refocused on keeping Edie happy. But it felt as if I was fighting a forest fire with a garden hose. "I appreciate what you're trying to do. It's incredibly selfless. But please just give me a few days to find another solution, okay? I promise, I'll figure out something."

She shook her head. "We both know that's not going to happen."

"No we don't." I was getting angry now. "At least give me a chance. Don't I deserve that?"

Edie's brows knit over her pert little nose, and she thought for a very long time. "Yeah. Okay." She stood and tugged the hem of her blouse over her hips. "Just don't do anything stupid."

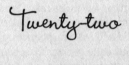

Twenty-two

I pondered options while I finished mixing together the cake, then sat down to make a list of pros and cons while it baked and cooled.

Pros for letting Edie quit: As office manager, she earned one of the largest paychecks on Zydeco's books, factoring in just below Ox's and mine. If she left, we'd save money on salary and benefits every month. Cons: I'd have to take over her duties in addition to my own, and the resulting therapy sessions would negate any perceived financial benefit. Morale would suffer. Plus, everyone at Zydeco loved Edie. They wouldn't respond well if I just let her walk out the door. I didn't need a mutiny on top of an increased workload and unrelenting worries about money. (See note re: therapy above.)

Pros for pushing Ox's agenda: We might pick up new clients willing to pay a moderate price for moderate cakes, and make enough money to keep our real business afloat. Cons: Miss Frankie could very well decide to dissolve our partnership, and I'd end up back in Albuquerque chopping onions for Uncle

Nestor's executive chef at Agave. (Again, refer to previous note about therapy.) Besides, I questioned how many *moderate* cakes we'd have to sell to realize the same profit margin we could pull in from a single exclusive one-of-a-kind cake with its accompanying hefty price tag.

Still contemplating possible solutions, I went back to work on the now-cooled cake, smoothing raspberry filling and a chocolate buttercream between cake layers and covering the three-tier cake with white chocolate buttercream. Tomorrow before the picnic I'd add fresh raspberries, and the result would be a light, delicious cake perfect for a warm spring day.

I left the cake on the counter, clearly marked so nobody would cart it off to the break room as a midday snack, and then did the only thing I could do: I drove over to Miss Frankie's house.

It was shortly after two that afternoon when I pulled into Miss Frankie's driveway. The sky was still overcast, but there didn't seem to be an imminent threat of rain. I waved to Bernice, who was puttering outside in her flower garden next door. She dropped what she was doing and waddled across the lawn toward me. She's a sweet Southern lady with a halo of white hair and an accent as smooth as aged Kentucky bourbon. She's also Miss Frankie's closest friend. That means she takes a lot of pressure off me to be available every time Miss Frankie wants to do something or go somewhere, and puts her pretty high on my list of favorite people.

"You are coming tomorrow, aren't you?" she asked as she puffed up the driveway. "Frances Mae did tell you about the barbecue?"

I hugged Bernice quickly. "She told me."

"And you're coming?"

"If I can. I'll be tied up for most of the morning, but I'll do my best. But don't you worry, Miss Bernice. If I can't be here, I'll at least make sure the cake is. I just finished making it."

Bernice swatted my arm playfully. "Oh you! I'm not worried about the cake. It's you we want. I just hope the weatherman is right and the weather clears." She brushed some dirt from her sleeve and then cut a glance at me. "What kind of cake is it, anyway?"

"White chocolate raspberry with raspberry filling and chocolate buttercream," I said with a grin. "You'll love it."

Her eyes danced with anticipation. "I'm sure I will. And in case you're worried, you won't be the only young person at the party. My nephew and his wife and kids will be here. I just know you'll get along with them like a house afire. Bennie's the sweetest boy."

I'd seen Bennie from a distance a time or two. He was a buttoned-up accountant with thinning hair and pasty skin, and his wife was a plump woman with a hairstyle I don't think she'd changed since high school many years ago. I didn't expect to have much in common with them or their three ill-behaved children, but I smiled politely. Besides, after the company I'd been keeping at the Love Nest, I figured all the people in Miss Frankie's neighborhood would seem like teenagers. "I look forward to it. Do you know if Miss Frankie is home? I need to speak with her about something."

Bernice gave a brisk nod that set her chins wobbling. "I haven't seen her leave, and she didn't say anything about going out this morning, so I expect she's in there." I thanked her and turned to leave, but Bernice laid a hand on my arm and stopped me. "Do try to come tomorrow, honey. Frances Mae is going to need you here."

"I'll do my best," I said again. But I was still weighing the barbecue against my promise to Old Dog Leg, and the scales weren't evenly balanced.

Bernice locked eyes with me. "Good. I'm glad. I know she wants to take flowers to Philippe, and I know it would mean the world if you'd go with her. She's been counting on it for weeks."

Flowers? Agh! My heart fell, and I swear I shrank to about two inches tall. Putting flowers on the graves of loved ones each Memorial Day—even those who hadn't served in the military—was common practice where I come from and it's a tradition that Aunt Yolanda held dear. Every year she'd cut flowers from the garden and spend time selecting the perfect assortment of potted mums from the displays at her favorite grocery store. On the last Monday in May, she'd place flowers on the graves, pulling weeds and clearing away pebbles, twigs, and dead leaves that had blown in over the winter. I, on the other hand, had made it a point to avoid cemeteries and gravesides as much as possible since my parents died, and I hadn't once considered that Miss Frankie would feel different.

"Why didn't she say something to me?"

The clouds parted and the sun hit Bernice in the face. She shook her head and shielded her eyes with one hand. "Oh, you know how she is. She doesn't want you to feel pressured. She doesn't want you to go just out of obligation."

Miss Frankie wanted me to *want* to go. She needed to believe that I cared enough about her son to remember him on a day set aside for remembering. I sighed softly and ignored a twinge of guilt that I'd even consider doing for Miss Frankie what I'd been unable to do for my parents.

Aunt Yolanda had dragged me to the cemetery exactly once after my parents' funeral. I'm ashamed to admit that I'd been surly and uncooperative, and those were the positive qualities I exhibited that day. Realizing the futility in such visits, Aunt Yolanda had pretty much left me alone after that.

I guess the fact that I was even considering going with Miss Frankie was a sign that I'm not twelve anymore.

"I'll do my best," I assured Bernice yet again. And this time I actually meant it.

Bernice patted my arm and toddled back to her garden. I resumed the journey up the driveway.

I spotted Miss Frankie in the kitchen window, so I went around to the back door and knocked softly. I thought she'd seen me walking along the driveway, but she looked up, startled, one hand on her breast as she hurried to let me in. "Goodness, sugar, you just about scared me to death. I didn't know you were coming by. Did I miss your call?"

I kissed her cheek and stepped inside where I found evidence that she'd been in the garden cutting flowers. Mounds of pink magnolia, iris, and camellia lay on the counter, and she'd filled several Mason jars with water.

"I didn't call," I confessed. "I know it's rude to stop by unannounced, but I was out this way, so I took the chance that I'd find you home."

I nodded toward the flowers. "Are those for tomorrow?"

Miss Frankie snipped the stems from a couple of bearded iris and slipped them into one of the jars. "They are."

"Do you want me to go with you to the cemetery?"

Her eyes flashed to mine. "Oh, sugar, would you?"

"Of course." The words came out easily. See? All grown up.

Miss Frankie blinked rapidly and turned away, waving a hand over the garden on the counter. "Are these okay? Is there some other kind of flower you'd like better?"

I didn't have the heart to tell her it didn't matter to me, so I simply said, "Those are lovely."

She lifted her chin and cleared her throat. "If you're sure. I'll have everything ready tomorrow. You won't have to do a thing. We'll go right after the barbecue, if that's all right."

"It's fine," I said.

Miss Frankie finished snipping stems, dusted her hands together, and leaned against the counter. "I don't suppose I need to ask what you're here to talk about, do I?"

"I don't suppose you do," I said. "I just came from Zydeco. Edie tried to quit on me."

That earned a look of surprise. "Did she? Well, I didn't see that coming." Miss Frankie dumped cold coffee from the pot that was sitting on the counter and set about making a fresh one. "You said she *tried* to quit. I guess you didn't let her."

"No I didn't. At least, she agreed to wait for a few days so I could attempt to figure out a better solution."

Miss Frankie didn't say anything until she had the coffee brewing. Somehow I managed not to jump out of my skin while she thought about what I'd said. "You've come to ask me to change my mind about Ox's idea."

"Not exactly." I linked my hands together on the table and tried to marshal my thoughts so I could explain how I felt and sound rational while I did it. "We're at a crossroads, Miss Frankie. You don't want to change Zydeco, and I don't want to lose staff, but clearly we have to do something. I'm hoping we can put our heads together and find a solution we can both live with."

She sat across the table from me. "Well, all right. You probably think I'm being hardheaded."

"I think you're being sentimental, but maybe you're also being smart. What Ox is suggesting would change Zydeco dramatically. I realized as I was driving through your neighborhood this afternoon that you're right about one thing. I'm not sure the change would be a good thing for us. We could lose our client base."

Her lips curved. She seemed pleased that I understood. "And I appreciate how you feel about the staff, Rita. Really I do. That's one of the reasons I chose you to step in when

Philippe died. I wanted someone in charge who would value not only the dream but also the *people* the way Philippe did."

We sat there for a moment with only the sound of brewing coffee breaking the silence. Finally, I said, "Edie thinks she's the most expendable person at Zydeco. I disagree. It's true she's not as accomplished in the kitchen and her decorating skills aren't that great, but she's indispensible at keeping things running smoothly. She understands how things work in the industry, she coordinates the schedule and keeps track of the contracts, and she does a thousand other things I don't have time to do."

Miss Frankie nodded as I spoke and got up to gather sugar, cream, and mugs. "I know she does, sugar. And she's a friend. She's been at Zydeco from the beginning. I understand that."

"So what do we do?"

Miss Frankie pulled a couple of spoons from a drawer and turned back to face me. "I've been thinking about it since I left the bakery yesterday, and I've decided that I'll just have to sell something."

She sounded so matter-of-fact, I rocked back on my chair a little. "You'll what?"

"I'll sell something." She waved a hand to encompass the house, the yard, the car in the driveway. "I might be temporarily cash poor, but I'm not completely without resources."

I didn't know which emotion was stronger, relief or concern. "But what would you sell? Surely not the house."

She laughed and filled our mugs, then carried them to the table. "This house? Never. It would have to be one of my other pieces of property, I'm afraid."

I'd inherited Philippe's personal bank account when he died, but it was just a drop in the bucket compared to the assets Miss Frankie controlled. I'd never asked about the family money, and neither he nor Miss Frankie had ever really talked to me about where their wealth had come from. But there's a time and a place for everything. "What property?"

"Oh, sugar, I have acreage all over this area. Most of the lots have been developed, but a few are still more or less vacant. Unfortunately, most of those aren't worth much. It will have to be one of the others. I'll have to talk to Thaddeus, of course. He has a list of where everything is, and he can get details from the property manager who looks out for it all."

Thaddeus Montgomery was the family attorney. Back when I was pursuing the divorce, he'd been my adversary. But since Philippe died, Thaddeus had become a friend who looked after my affairs as well.

Miss Frankie sounded calm and casual, as if selling off her land was nothing more complicated than returning an unwanted purchase to the local Walmart. I was having trouble wrapping my mind around the concept. "You have so much property, you can't keep track of it?"

Miss Frankie laughed at my confusion. "Honestly, sugar, it's not that big a deal. To me it's just pieces of paper my daddy passed down from his daddy, and his daddy before that."

Bubbling up beneath the confusion I felt another emotion, one I was much more familiar with—guilt. "You want to sell property that's been in your family for generations because the bakery is in trouble? I can't ask you to do that."

"You didn't ask," she said. "I offered. Don't try to talk me out of it. And don't you forget, Zydeco's half mine. It's important to me to keep it the way it was. Philippe had ideas for that place, and when he died I vowed to keep his plans moving forward."

"But you're talking about selling your family property. Land you inherited—"

"I'm talking about the future, not the past. Roots are important, but I'm not going to cling to some old ratty piece of land while you and Zydeco suffer. What kind of family would that make me?"

Tears pooled in my eyes and Miss Frankie's silhouette blurred. I swiped at my eyes and looked around for a tissue. It wasn't just her generosity that had me sniffling; it was the affirmation that she really considered me family. Of course, that was all stirred up with another dash of guilt that I hadn't spared a thought for what she was feeling as we approached Memorial Day, and the certainty that I didn't deserve the bailout she was offering.

And that's exactly what I told her.

She bent down and kissed the top of my head. "Now, now, that's just plain foolish talk. I'll call Thaddeus and get the list, and together you and I can go over the lots he thinks would be best to put on the market. Is that all right with you?"

"You want me to help you decide?" My voice cracked, and I lunged for the paper towels on the counter.

"Well, of course! You're the only family I have. I value your opinion."

I had trouble croaking out the next few words around the massive lump in my throat. "Just tell me where and when."

At that moment I would have promised her anything. You'd think by now I'd know better.

Twenty-three

❧

I hadn't spent more than a few minutes in my own house since Friday morning, so after leaving Miss Frankie's, I stopped home. I planned to do little more than take in the mail and switch which lights I'd left burning to discourage intruders, but when I glanced inside the fridge and realized that I'd left a package of fresh chicken breasts sitting there for two days, I changed my mind.

The chicken wouldn't last another day, and I was in the mood for some alone time, so I bagged the idea of eating out and instead threw together a cilantro almond chicken salad that had recently become one of my favorites.

I coated the chicken (with skin, bone in) in kosher salt and let it sit while I put in a load of laundry. When I finished that, I rinsed the salt from the chicken and poached the breasts with carrot, onion, parsley, and celery.

Leaving the chicken to cool, I switched the laundry to the dryer, then went back and shredded the meat, making sure to carry the skin and bones to the trash outside. There aren't many odors worse than chicken garbage left sitting around.

With the chicken ready, I toasted then slivered the almonds for the dressing, adding garlic, jalapeño, mayo, and sour cream, and folding in cilantro and lime juice to deepen the layers of flavor. I stirred the dressing into the chicken, poured sweet tea over ice, then grabbed a book from the second-floor library and carried the whole thing to the terrace garden on the roof of the house.

Large planters holding a variety of trees and flowering shrubs rim the wrought-iron railing that forms the perimeter of the garden, and stone chairs with colorful cushions ring a round table in the terrace's center. At night, twinkling white lights strung everywhere give the place a fairy-tale look. It's a beautiful space Philippe put together, and I don't spend nearly enough time up there, but after my meeting with Miss Frankie, it seemed like the perfect place to gather my thoughts.

Part of me—the part I'd inherited from my uncle Nestor—was convinced my new life was all too good to be true. But I was slowly learning that my internal worrywart isn't always right. Good things do happen . . . sometimes. I tamped down the hollow, empty feeling of impending doom and settled into my favorite chair with lunch and my book.

I ate slowly, killing time until I could meet Gabriel at the Dizzy Duke. The book was good, an old James Lee Burke I hadn't read. It should have held my attention, but my mind kept wandering from Zydeco to Miss Frankie to the Love Nest and Monroe Magee. I kept thinking about how Grey had alluded to some kind of tragedy in the past, and wondering if he was really crazy or just eccentric.

But just how crazy (or eccentric) was he? Enough to commit murder? What about Cleveland, who had made a lot of noise about how much he hated Monroe? Had he tried to kill Monroe and poisoned Dontae instead? And while I'd ruled out Antwon and Tamarra as possible suspects, because their connection to the others seemed indirect and I'd seen them stumble out of their room the night Dontae died, had I been too quick to cross them off my list?

After a while I gave up pretending to read. I went back inside, folded the laundry, stacked my dishes in the dishwasher, and drove to the Dizzy Duke. I was a few minutes early, but Gabriel's shift was scheduled to end soon and I hoped he might even be able to slip away early. It had been a rough couple of days and I was already exhausted, but if we left now, we might have time to talk with a couple of the Love Nest's residents before they went to bed.

In contrast to my last visit, tonight the bar was full of noisy patrons, most of whom were engrossed in the game on the big-screen TVs at either end of the room. I looked around for Old Dog Leg, but the band hadn't arrived, and I knew he'd probably avoid the crowded bar during the game. It was just as well. I didn't have any news to share with him, and he'd already told me what he knew.

I squeezed between tables, earning jeers from inebriated sports fans who objected to my shadow on the screen, and waited for one of the only empty spots at the bar while a couple of overworked cocktail waitresses shouted orders at the bartenders and complained to each other about rude customers.

It seemed like everyone in the place was shouting, and between the noise and heat generated by so many bodies packed together, my skin began to crawl. I was more than eager to get out of there.

After what felt like forever, Gabriel paused in front of me on his way to deliver a handful of longneck beer bottles to the other end of the bar. "You're early!" he shouted.

"A little!" I shouted back. "How long before you'll be able to leave?"

He glanced at his watch and shook his head. "At the rate it's been going? Never. The game just went into overtime, and the crowd doesn't show any sign of letting up."

My smile faded. "You mean you might not be able to leave at five?"

"I mean I probably won't be able to leave until nine or ten," Gabriel said with a scowl. He hustled away to deliver the drinks and gather money, then came back on his way to the cash register. "I'm sorry about this. Just make yourself comfortable. I'll get away as soon as humanly possible."

Comfortable. Right.

The bar was crowded with basketball fans stacked two deep, and the only empty stools were smack in the middle of the fray. I searched for an available table, but that proved to be a futile effort. I hitched myself onto an empty stool and reluctantly waved away Gabriel's offer to bring me a margarita. He's a true artist at making them, so the offer was more than tempting, but I still had to drive the Mercedes home and besides I had way too much to think about. I needed a clear head, and I'd learned from experience that Gabriel's margaritas and a clear head cannot coexist.

For the first few minutes of the game's overtime, I nursed a Diet Coke and endured jostling from other patrons and cocktail waitresses. During a commercial break, the crowd cleared slightly and I spotted a couple of familiar faces sitting over at Zydeco's usual table near the bandstand. I abandoned my seat at the bar and made my way across the packed room.

Sparkle Starr sat at one end of the table and stared morosely at the drink in front of her. Estelle Jergens sat bolt upright next to Sparkle, chattering nonstop. She looked earnest. Sparkle just looked bored.

Sparkle is in her midtwenties, the daughter of aging hippie

parents who saddled her at birth with a bright shiny name that she's been trying to dim since she became an adult. Her pale face in its goth makeup looked almost translucent in the bar's low light, and locks of fluorescent pink were laced through her otherwise pitch-black tresses. She'd pulled her hair into enormous pigtails high on her head, and her lips were painted stark black. She was wearing a pair of black hip boots covered with spikes and a black trench coat decorated with chains over ebony shorts and a lace tank top. Spiked leather bands covered both wrists so that only the head of her dragon tattoo was visible. I swear she'd used about half a bottle of liquid black liner on her eyes.

Estelle seemed the least likely person on staff at Zydeco for Sparkle to befriend, but Sparkle is actually much nicer than she wants people to think. The two of them had been spending more time together than usual over the past couple of weeks.

Estelle is the oldest member of our little crew; I put her somewhere in her late forties, but I could be off by a few years either way. She's short and round, with a headful of brilliant red curls that spring out in all directions no matter how hard she tries to contain them. She's also seriously fashion challenged. Tonight's outfit featured gray stretch pants, a long blue T-shirt, and brown Birkenstock knockoffs.

Sparkle greeted me with a jerk of her chin but didn't actually make eye contact.

Estelle bounced up out of her seat and lunged toward me. "Rita! I'm so glad you're here." She grabbed me by one arm and pulled me toward the table, bombarding me with questions the whole way. "Did you talk to Ox and Edie? What did they say? What's going on with Edie anyway?"

I slipped out of her grasp and dropped into a chair directly beneath an air-conditioning vent. Thank heaven for small favors. "One thing at a time," I said with a laugh. "I talked to Edie. She's fine. She was just having a bad day."

Estelle dropped into the chair beside me and exchanged a look with Sparkle. "That's what she told you?" Sparkle asked.

Doubt skittered around inside, but I ignored it. "Yes," I said firmly. "And from what I could tell, she was being honest. She and Ox seemed fine with each other today."

They had, hadn't they? Okay, so I hadn't actually asked Ox about their argument, but he would have said something about it if he was worried . . . wouldn't he?

Estelle sat back and folded her arms across her chest. "Well, they aren't fine. At least Edie isn't."

"She's just concerned about the bakery," I assured them both. I didn't want to get into specifics about Zydeco's finances and worry them unnecessarily, but I also didn't want them to start imagining trouble that didn't exist. "You know how slow things have been lately, and you know how Edie is. She likes to be in control, and unfortunately for us, she does not control the economy."

Sparkle's black-lined gaze flickered over my face. I thought she looked skeptical, but she didn't say anything.

Estelle shook her head and set those red curls dancing. "That's not it, Rita. I'm sure it's not. She's been weird the past few weeks. Don't tell me you haven't noticed."

Oh, I'd noticed all right. Especially when she'd tried to give me her resignation earlier that afternoon. But since I had no intention of letting her quit, I thought it best to keep that piece of information to myself. "I'm sure she's fine," I said again.

Estelle scowled so hard wrinkles formed in her forehead. "Well, you're wrong. Tell her, Sparkle."

A shout went up from the game-watching crowd, drowning out Sparkle's response, but I was pretty sure that whatever it was, it had amounted to a big fat "no."

Estelle leaned forward, planting her elbows on the table and getting right in Sparkle's face. "*Tell* her, Sparkle. You have to."

Sparkle gave her a hard-edged stare. "Maybe we should just drop it."

Estelle's eyes grew wide. "Drop it? Are you serious?" She heaved a sigh of frustration and sank back in her chair again, but she kept her gaze locked on Sparkle's face. "If you don't tell her, I will. Something's wrong with Edie and we both know it." She turned on me next, wagging a chubby finger in my face. "And you'd know it, too, if you were paying attention."

"Hey!" I said, offended. "Rude! I am paying attention here."

I really hoped Estelle was making a mountain out of a molehill. What with Dontae's murder, Monroe's disappearance, Bernice's barbecue, Miss Frankie's planned visit to the cemetery, and the guilt I was carrying over the prospect of her selling old family property to help keep our business afloat, I didn't need another serious problem.

Estelle muttered an apology to me—at least I think she did, I had trouble hearing the actual words—but she didn't back down from Sparkle. "Tell. Her."

Sparkle resisted for another minute, but then she looked up at me and said, "I caught her crying in the bathroom a couple of days ago."

"Who?" I asked. "Edie?" No, no, no. That would be bad. Edie's *not* the crying type.

Sparkle nodded, and her expression looked almost apologetic. I wasn't sure which bothered me more: the idea of Edie crying in the ladies' room or the concept of Sparkle apologizing.

I gave my head a little shake, as if that would help me make sense of what I'd just heard. It didn't. "Did she say why?"

Sparkle's lips curved slightly. "Edie? Confide in me? Uh-uh."

Another big play in the game on TV made it impossible to talk for a few minutes. "Are you sure she was crying?" I asked when the noise died away. "Maybe she was just having an allergic reaction to something." Okay, so that was a stretch. I had to pursue every option, didn't I?

"It wasn't allergies," Sparkle said. "She locked herself in the stall when she saw me come in."

Again, not typical Edie-like behavior. "Did you ask her what was wrong?"

Sparkle gave me a *duh* look. "Of course I did. She said it was nothing."

Estelle's eyes bugged out. "As if. You *have* to find out what's going on with her, Rita."

Okay, so maybe there *was* something going on with Edie, but getting answers would be easier said than done. "She has a right to her privacy," I said. "If she doesn't want to talk to me, I can't force her." And besides, dealing with other peoples' emotional issues isn't one of my strengths. Philippe would have been much better suited to having a heart-to-heart with Edie, and not just because he had great people skills. She'd had a thing for him while we were in pastry school, and I was pretty sure it had carried through after he hired her to work at Zydeco. As the woman who'd had him and then let him get away, I was probably the last person she'd confide in.

But even I had to admit that my response sounded like a cop-out. Another wave of exhaustion hit me like a ton of bricks, and suddenly I couldn't wait to get out of the Dizzy Duke's heat and noise. I should have spent more time at home. I needed privacy and space. Time to think and a good night's sleep, not necessarily in that order.

"Keep an eye on things," I said to Estelle. "If Edie is still acting strangely, let me know when I get back to work the day after tomorrow."

"But—"

I stood and cut her off before she could wind herself up any more. "Look, maybe there's something wrong, but there isn't anything I can do about it tonight. Tomorrow's a holiday, and I'll be back to work on Tuesday. Whatever it is, I'm sure it can wait that long."

Estelle shut her mouth and bobbed her head in agreement, but I could tell by the way she set her shoulders and lifted her chin that she wasn't happy. I added her to my growing list of problems to solve and left my empty glass on the table. And then I made my way back to the bar. There might be a big, noisy crowd there, but at least nobody wanted anything from me. For now, maybe that was enough.

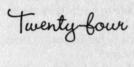

Twenty-four

I was wrong. Going back to the bar was a bad idea. It didn't take long for my already-fraying patience to snap, and I knew I had to leave. I caught Gabriel's eye and motioned him over.

He shoved a few glasses into a sink full of soapy water, dropped a couple of bills into his tip jar, and swiped something from the bar with a cloth before making his way to me. "Change your mind? Ready for a real drink?"

I shook my head. "Listen, you're going to be tied up here for a while, so I think I'm going to head over to the inn on my own. Just come over when you've finished here."

The smile he'd been wearing disappeared. "I don't think that's a good idea. Stick around here. We'll go back together."

"I'll be fine," I assured him.

He wasn't convinced. "I don't like the idea of you there by yourself. Go back to your place. I'll pick you up there."

I shook my head and dropped some money onto the bar. "If I go home, I'll stay there, and we really need to be at the inn tomorrow for breakfast. We lost the whole day today. Tomorrow morning is all we've got before we have to check out."

"So we extend our reservation another day or two." Gabriel leaned in close so I could hear him over the bar noise. "One of those old people killed Dontae. I don't want you going over there alone."

"I'm not planning to talk to anybody tonight," I assured him. "I'm just going to go upstairs to our room and pass out. Feel better?"

"Not much. Just be patient, okay? I can probably slip away in another hour or two."

I swallowed a jaw-cracking yawn. "In another hour or two you'll have to scrape me off the bar to get me out of here. It's already after seven. By the time I get to the Love Nest, all those sweet old people will be in bed anyway. I'll keep my cell phone on all the time and if I run into trouble, I'll call for help. I promise."

One of the other bartenders shouted for Gabriel, and I took advantage of the distraction to slip outside. I knew he wouldn't be happy with me, but the bar was making me claustrophobic and I was way too tired to hang around and make small talk.

It was a cool night, so I rolled down my windows as I drove, and within a few miles the clear air had wiped away some cobwebs. I managed to shelve most of my concerns about the cemetery, the barbecue, and the bakery, which left my head free to tackle the issues surrounding the murder, and Monroe.

I wanted to talk with Lula Belle, so my main focus tomorrow would be getting her alone. Of course, that would only work if Lula Belle actually acknowledged my presence. She was just stubborn enough to try ignoring me again. Good thing I'm stubborn and strong-willed myself. I was determined to outfox that wily old woman.

I also wanted a shot at Primrose without Hyacinth hanging around. She was the one who'd found Dontae's body in the garden. Maybe she'd seen something important. She was also the most likely person to know where Monroe had gone. If she didn't know, I hoped someone had an idea where to look for him.

But all of that could wait until morning. Tonight, all I wanted was sleep.

Or so I thought until I walked into the Love Nest and saw Cleveland in the parlor, remote control in hand. He sat in an overstuffed chair that he'd turned to face the TV, his chin on his chest and his wrinkles bunched up around his neck. And he was completely alone. It was an opportunity I just couldn't resist.

He looked away from the screen when he realized he had company, growling, "I'm not changing the channel. Don't ask."

I returned his unfriendly scowl with my most gracious smile. "I wouldn't dream of it. I'll watch whatever you're watching."

Cleveland snorted softly. "Where's your husband?"

"Working, unfortunately." I turned a flowery chair next to his toward the TV and settled in. "He got called in for a few hours."

"On your honeymoon?"

I shrugged to show it was no big deal. "That's life, isn't it?"

Cleveland mumbled something I couldn't make out and turned back to the TV where a handful of scantily dressed young woman were screaming at each other. Words flashed on the bottom of the screen, translating the dialogue, which was heavily punctuated by the censor's bleeps.

Classy.

"Where is everyone else?" I asked.

Cleveland rolled his eyes toward me. "Who knows? In their rooms, I guess. Now hesh up. You're interrupting my show."

Sorry.

I waited, trying not to look impatient, while the women indulged in more shouting, which resulted in more bleeping.

After a long time, the show broke for a commercial and I took a chance on speaking again. "I was worried about you when you weren't at breakfast the last two mornings. I'm glad to see that you're all right."

With an exaggerated roll of his eyes meant to display tolerance for my ignorance, Cleveland made a point of pressing the mute button. "Why? Can't a man sleep in?"

"Of course. It's just that . . . well, you know . . . after what happened to Dontae . . ."

Cleveland's mouth tightened, and the wrinkles on his forehead sagged. "That's sad news, but there's nothin' I can do about it, is there? What's done is done."

That was an interesting attitude.

"Nothing except help bring his killer to justice," I said, still trying for the gracious effect. "I know the police have been checking alibis. I was upstairs asleep when Primrose found Dontae's body. Where were you?"

"In my room. Alone. Not that it's any of your business."

"Did you hear or see anything out of the ordinary that night?"

"Didn't need to see or hear nothing. I know what happened."

"You think Monroe did it."

"I don't *think* he did it," Cleveland growled. "I know."

"So you actually saw him do it?" I held my breath, wondering if he really did know something or if he was merely jumping to conclusions because he wanted Monroe to be guilty.

Cleveland cut an exasperated glance at me. "No, I didn't see him do it. But I know just the same."

The show came back on, and I had to wait until the next commercial to speak again. "You've known Monroe for a long time, haven't you?"

Cleveland didn't answer immediately but after a moment gave another grudging nod. "Yeah. Awhile."

"Do you have any idea where he might've gone when he left here?"

Cleveland tapped his fingers on the remote. I couldn't tell if he was nervous or irritated. "How would I know that? He was gone for forty years."

"That's true. I just thought you might have an idea that might help the police track him down. Some place he used to go when he lived here before. A friend he might turn to. . . ?"

"Believe you me, if I had any idea where to find him, I'd be singing my head off. Nobody wants that sonofabitch found more'n me."

I believed that, so I pretended to change the subject. "Where did the two of you meet? At Letterman Industries?"

The old man's head whipped around so fast I worried that he'd pulled a muscle. "Who told you that?"

I shrugged, still not sure if my bluff had worked. "I don't remember. I was under the impression that all of you had worked there together. Is that right?"

Cleveland pulled a toothpick from his shirt pocket, put it in his mouth, and spent a minute situating it just so. "What's it to you?"

It wasn't an admission, but it wasn't a denial either. That gave me hope that I was on the right track. "Dontae's murder happened right under our room," I said. "It's freaked me out a little bit. If Monroe really did it, *I* want to see him brought to justice. What did he have against Dontae, anyway?"

Cleveland shrugged and looked away, pretending a sudden deep interest in a commercial for Viagra. Then again, maybe he wasn't pretending.

"He didn't seem angry when I met him the other night," I said. "In fact, if you'd asked me, I'd have put my money on Monroe being the one who ended up in the garden."

Cleveland's wrinkles folded all over themselves. "What do you mean by that?"

I held up both hands to show that I hadn't meant to offend. "I just mean that everyone seemed pretty angry with Monroe that night, not the other way around."

My observation lit a fire in the old man. He aimed the remote at the TV and turned off his show. "You're damn right I was hot under the collar. You woulda been too in my place."

"How so?"

"I thought that dirtbag was gone for good. We all did. And then, out of nowhere, he shows up again without a word of warning? That's bad enough, but he had the nerve to walk around here acting like nothing ever happened. It ain't right."

I did my best to look sympathetic and tossed in what Grey had said on the street last night. "That *was* pretty nervy of him, especially after everything Hyacinth has been through."

Cleveland's eyes narrowed slightly. "You know about that?"

"A little."

"Well, you got that part right. Monroe put her through enough. She didn't need him showing up again after all this time. Nobody did."

He was on the verge of telling me something important. I could feel it. My heart was beating so loud, I was sure he could hear it from where he sat. "How did she react when he came back?"

"How do you think? She lost everything because of that piece of scum."

If Monroe was indeed the intended victim, then I'd just locked down motive, means, and opportunity—the murder trifecta. I could almost hear the theme from *Rocky* playing in my head. All I needed now was evidence that Hyacinth had mistakenly killed the wrong man.

"She was angry. Understandably."

"She never shoulda let him stay. Grey and me, we told her to send him packing. Willie never woulda done what he done if it weren't for Monroe."

My imaginary sound track screeched to a halt. Willie? Who was that? I opened my mouth to ask, but a shrill voice cut me off.

"Cleveland!"

That one sharp word startled both of us, and we turned like guilty schoolchildren to face its source.

Primrose stood in the open doorway, her eyes narrow slits in her stony expression. "That's enough! I'm sure Mrs. Broussard isn't interested in our problems."

Oh, but I was!

Cleveland's eyes flashed as he tossed the remote aside. "Don't tell me what to do, Primrose. You don't own me. It's about damn time you remembered that."

Irritation marred Primrose's normally placid face. She checked to make sure nobody was behind her and took a couple of steps into the room. "That's a damn fool thing to say. I guess you've forgotten the rules of the house. You think you can just plant your scrawny butt on my couch for thirty years and do whatever you want? The past is the past is the past. There's no reason to dig it up and flap it around in front of strangers."

Cleveland blew out an angry breath. "I'm not the one who dug up the past. Your precious Monroe did that the day he walked back through that door."

Her *precious* Monroe?

"I don't know why you insist on blaming poor Monroe," Primrose said with another glance over her shoulder. "You *know* it wasn't his fault."

"I don't know any such thing. *I* was there, Primrose. You weren't. I know who did what."

Were they talking about the night Dontae died, or were they rehashing whatever had happened forty years ago? I wanted to know so badly I could barely sit still, but they were both skittish as newborn colts and I didn't want to spook them.

Primrose put her hands on her hips and got right up in

Cleveland's wrinkled old face. She looked so angry, my breath caught in my throat. "I'll tell you what I know, you old fool. That floozy is the one to blame for what happened. She led the bunch of you around by your noses, and you practically fell over yourselves trying to get her to notice you. Well, look where it got you. First Tyrone and now Dontae. You watch out or you'll be next."

Tyrone?

I heard someone gasp and realized too late that it was me. Primrose and Cleveland whipped around, startled, having clearly forgotten that I was sitting there.

"Well!" Primrose said, shaking her finger at me. "I suppose you think you're smart, listening in to other people's conversations as if it's any of your business."

I shook my head quickly. "No, I—"

"Well, I'll tell you something. If you *are* smart, you'll leave well enough alone. What's done is done. There's nothing you or anybody else can do about it."

That was almost word-for-word what Cleveland had said only moments before, but her version sent a shudder up my spine. Was it a threat or a warning? I wasn't sure, but sweet little Primrose didn't seem so sweet anymore. And I was more determined than ever to figure out what was going on at the Love Nest.

I managed to smile even though my lips felt cold and stiff. "Nothing except help the police bring Dontae's killer to justice. This is all so confusing. Who is Willie and what did he do? What happened to Tyrone, and what does any of this have to do with Monroe?"

Primrose stared at me for one long moment, her eyes again narrowed and her nostrils flaring. My blood ran cold as I looked into her eyes. When she turned on her heel and left the room without answering, the only thing I could do was take a shaky breath and sink back onto the couch to stop my knees from buckling beneath me.

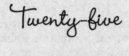

Primrose's anger had rattled me, but it had also chased off my need for sleep. I wasn't about to scurry off to the safety of the honeymoon suite now. I was convinced that I'd just scratched the surface at the Love Nest. There was more to the story, and I was pretty sure that knowing that story was the key to finding Monroe.

I left the parlor and started toward the dining room, but when I noticed the door leading out to the garden inching closed, as if someone had just gone outside, I decided to follow. I had no idea who I was chasing, but I didn't care. Everyone had answers I wanted.

Whoever had come outside before me had already disappeared, so I hesitated for a moment, trying to decide which way to go. The night had grown cooler, and the air was dry. The police had removed the crime scene tape while we'd been gone, but they'd left signs of their presence everywhere. Footprints, trampled flowers, broken edging, snapped twigs, and a couple of soda cans lying in the dirt gave evidence that something had happened out here recently.

I hadn't really looked at the garden the night Dontae died. My mind had been occupied with other things. But as I walked along the overgrown path, I wondered again why he'd been in the garden in the first place. Even excusing its current condition, it was hardly the kind of place someone would actually go to relax. Had he been meeting someone, or had he wandered out here in a stupor after ingesting the poison?

The garden path was poorly lit, and I had to walk slowly in the dim evening light to make sure I didn't trip over an exposed root or the uneven path. As I came around a curve almost obstructed by overgrown bushes, I saw Pastor Rod a few feet ahead, pacing in front of a bench. He cast a furtive look over his shoulder, as if he worried that somebody might be watching him. Which, of course, made me slip into the shadows to avoid being seen.

A moment later, I saw Tamarra hurrying toward him.

Interesting, but I wouldn't have thought it troubling— except for the fact that they'd chosen this particular weed-infested spot to meet.

"Did you hear?" Tamarra said in a voice almost too low for me to make out. "That woman has been asking questions. She cornered the professor on the street last night, and Primrose just told me that she was talking to Cleveland. What do you suppose she wants?"

I had to assume they were talking about me, which nipped in the bud any thoughts I might have had about stepping forward and saying hello.

Pastor Rod sat on the low stone bench and patted the seat beside him. "Maybe it's exactly what she says," he suggested in his distinctive gravel voice. "Maybe she and her husband are just concerned. After all, a man was killed during their honeymoon."

"Maybe," Tamarra said doubtfully. "But she sure has Primrose tied up in knots." She sat beside the pastor. "She asked about my grandpa. How did she know about him?"

Her grandpa? She had to be talking about Willie or Tyrone, but which one? Maybe I *had* been too quick to cross Tamarra off my list of suspects.

Pastor Rod leaned forward with a heavy sigh. He rested his elbows on his knees and buried his face in his hands. His posture conveyed more dismay than I would have expected from a spiritual advisor used to dealing with death, even the unexpected death of a friend. His next words confirmed my suspicions.

"I'm afraid this is what we get for trying to hide the truth," he said as he dropped his hands away from his face.

So he was in on it, too! Whatever *it* was. I felt a flash of disappointment, but I wasn't really surprised. Every time one of these people opened their mouths, it added one more thread in the Gordian knot that was the Love Nest.

Tamarra gave him an impatient look. "With all due respect, Pastor, I don't think that getting philosophical is going to help. The question is, how do we get her to back off?"

He shook his head, and he looked so dejected I almost felt sorry for him. "Don't you think it's time to just let the truth come out? I can't condone lying, Tamarra. I can't turn a blind eye and pretend it's not happening."

Tamarra scooted around on the bench so she could look at him head-on. "You know why. There's nothing anybody can do for Grandpa or Tyrone. It's the rest of you I'm worried about. You've stayed quiet all this time. What good would it do to come clean now?"

That answered the grandfather question: Willie.

"It wasn't an issue before," the pastor said. "The past was dead and buried. Your grandpa paid the price, and Monroe was gone. But now—"

"Nothing's changed," Tamarra insisted. "You know as well as I do that Monroe Magee is responsible for Dontae's death. He's the only one who could have done it. But if you start talking about the past, the police are going to start looking at everybody else—including you."

Pastor Rod rubbed his face again. "Maybe that's for the best. Maybe it's time."

Tamarra stared at him as if he'd suggested that she shave off her eyebrows. "Don't be ridiculous. You've built a new life. Everyone has. The professor is volunteering with kids. Hyacinth and Primrose have this place. You"—she waved a hand toward him—"look at you! How do you think people would react if they knew what your life used to be?"

"God forgives, baby. Don't forget that."

She shook her head firmly. "Maybe *He* does, but regular people don't. Do you really want to see all the good you've done at the church undone because of something that happened forty years ago?"

Pastor Rod closed his eyes. "I made my peace with God before I ever became a pastor. The people who need to know what I did already know about it. Going public now wouldn't change anything."

"If you think that, you're out of touch with reality. The people at that little church look up to you. They think you have answers. They believe what you tell them. But what will they think if suddenly you're dragged into court as an accessory to murder?"

I think my heart stopped then. Murder? Were they talking about Dontae? Without thinking, I leaned a little closer, wanting to make sure I'd heard right. My arm brushed against a shrub, and the whisper of sound made Tamarra sit up and look around.

"Somebody's coming," she said. "And I need to get back inside anyway. Grandma is waiting for me. Just promise you won't say anything. Please. Even if you don't care about your-self, think about the others. Do you want to see all of them suffer?"

Pastor Rod's head drooped, and Tamarra glanced around nervously before putting a gentle hand on his shoulder and then hurrying away.

I stood where I was for a moment, debating whether to let the pastor know I'd heard their conversation or pretend I hadn't. But there were too many secrets and too many ac-cusations to just turn around and walk away. I was dying to know who Tyrone was and what had happened to him. The key to Dontae's death was in those details, I was certain of it.

When I was convinced that we were alone, I stepped out of the shadows and walked quickly across the garden. "Pastor Rod? Are you all right?"

His head jerked up at the sound of my voice, and he made a visible effort to compose himself. "Well hello. Out for a bit of fresh air? Where's your husband? Don't tell me you left him alone."

"Actually, I've been looking for Lula Belle. Have you seen her?"

The pastor nodded slowly. "She's in her room, I believe. She said she was going to lie down for a bit." He scooted over on the bench. "Would you like to join me?"

I had a feeling he was just being polite, but I thanked him and sat before he could change his mind.

"What do you want with Lula Belle?" he asked warily. "If I may ask?"

"I just have a few questions about someone she used to know."

"Maybe I can help. Lu and I have been friends forever."

A chill from the stone bench crept through my jeans. "Maybe you can," I said, suppressing a shiver. "You all knew Monroe Magee when he lived here before, isn't that right?"

Pastor Rod inclined his head a fraction of an inch. "I knew him."

His careful phrasing wasn't lost on me. "And so did the others," I said. "Do you know if Monroe and Lula Belle were lovers?"

The pastor looked a little taken aback. "That's an odd question to ask, don't you think?"

I shrugged. "I guess it is, but I think it's a question you know the answer to."

He actually laughed, which surprised me. "Well, you have me there. But you'll have to forgive me for not indulging in idle gossip."

He was good at dodging my questions, but I didn't let that discourage me. I'd just have to come at him from a different angle. I decided to lay a few cards on the table, in the hopes that it would encourage the same from him. "I heard you and Tamarra talking. Can I ask what happened in the past that she's so determined to keep hidden?"

He dodged again, saying, "You sure do ask a lot of questions."

"What can I say? I have a curious nature."

The pastor's smile faded, and his gaze dropped to his hands. "It's a personal matter. You understand."

I was disappointed but still not ready to give up. I stretched out my legs in front of me and let a little time pass before I tried again. "It sounds like Monroe stirred up some old hurts when he came back. Is that what Tamarra wants to protect all of you from?"

"Tamarra's a sweet girl, Mrs. Broussard. She cares about the people she loves."

I immediately felt guilty for getting on his case about telling the truth while still masquerading as "Mrs. Broussard," but I tried not to let it bother me. It was, you know, for the greater good. "I can tell she does, but keeping secrets isn't always the best way to handle things. Doesn't the Bible say that the truth will set you free?"

The pastor conceded my point with a nod. "It does." He rolled his head on his neck and let out a weary sigh. "Grey said you'd talked to him yesterday, but I was under the impression he didn't give you any information."

"He didn't give me much," I admitted.

"And yet you expect me to spill my guts?"

"Why don't I tell you what I know, and you can fill in the rest."

The pastor didn't exactly agree, but he didn't refuse, so I jumped in and hoped he'd keep his end of my proposed bargain. "I know that Monroe worked at Letterman Industries back in the seventies and that some of the people who live here worked there, too. I know that something happened back then that everybody wants to keep hidden, and I suspect that whatever it was, it had something to do with why everyone is so angry with Monroe, and with Dontae's death. I heard Tamarra say that she's worried that you and the others will be charged as accessories to murder, but I don't know whether she's talking about Dontae's death or whatever happened forty years ago. How am I doing so far?"

The pastor rubbed his neck slowly and let out a sigh that seemed to come up from the depths of his soul. "Sounds like you know quite a bit."

"Not really. Who *is* Willie? Hyacinth's husband?"

"Can I ask where you heard that name?"

"Cleveland mentioned him earlier tonight. Am I right? Was he married to Hyacinth?"

The pastor nodded slowly. "Yes, Willie Fiske was Hyacinth's husband, God rest his soul."

"And Tamarra's grandfather."

"That's right."

"How does Monroe Magee fit into all of this? Why do so many people think that Monroe killed Dontae?"

The pastor linked his hands together over his knees and studied the shadow they made on the ground. "I don't know about Dontae's murder," he said after what felt like forever. "Far as I know, nobody had any reason to want Dontae dead."

"If Monroe didn't kill him, do you think whoever did might have been trying to kill someone else? Like maybe Monroe himself?"

The pastor nodded again. "I think it's possible." He looked up at me and said, "Believe me, Mrs. Broussard, if I *knew* anything at all, I'd come clean immediately."

"But you suspect."

"I suspect."

"And do you know why anyone might've wanted Monroe dead?"

He sent me a ghost of a smile. "That's where it gets tricky."

"So tricky that you'll risk your professional reputation to keep somebody's secret?"

Pastor Rod smiled sadly. "I'm a man of God. I should be above earthly things, right?" He groaned a little as he got to his feet. "It's not somebody else's secret, Mrs. Broussard. It's my secret, too, but it's not about me. Forty years ago, we were all young and stupid. We thought we were invincible, and nobody had any idea that the decisions we made then would have such long-lasting consequences."

I was afraid that he was going to walk away, so again I asked, a little more pointedly this time: "What happened back then?"

He looked down at me, frowning deeply. "Why do you care so much, Mrs. Broussard? You barely knew Dontae, and it's not as if you and Hyacinth are friends."

I thought about telling him about my friendship with Old Dog Leg, but I feared that if the others thought I was on

Monroe's side, they'd never talk to me again. "I don't like unanswered questions," I said. "I lost my parents in an accident the year I turned twelve, and there are still way too many things about *that* that I don't know." I stumbled a bit as I said, "And my first husband was a murder victim, too, so I can't just sit by and let Dontae's death go unsolved. It's easy to see that your friends have been hurt by what happened all those years ago. Maybe talking about it after all this time would help."

Pastor Rod was quiet for a long moment, then seemed to come to a decision. "You're right. We all worked at Letterman Industries together—me, Monroe, Cleveland, Grey, Dontae, and Willie. The pay was horrible. We worked hard, but none of us was ever able to make ends meet."

He sighed again and closed his eyes. "A few of us thought we had a solution to all of our problems. We knew there was a big shipment of stereo equipment at the warehouse—the kind that would bring big money on the streets." He slid a glance at me and almost smiled. "They were some killer eight-track players. Hot stuff back then." His smile slipped away and the sadness returned. "I'm not proud of what we did, but I've made my peace with God."

"And who was Tyrone?"

"The night guard. A friend. But he wasn't in on it. We timed everything perfectly. Knew we'd be in and out before he came by on his rounds. And we would have been."

"What went wrong?"

The pastor opened his eyes and blinked in the darkness. "I wasn't inside, you understand. I was the driver. They called me Hot Rod back then." That ghostly smile made a return appearance. "There was nobody around here better behind the wheel."

"You were a getaway driver?" A sharp laugh escaped my lips.

"I'm a man of many talents," he said. "I wasn't always this old, you know."

"So what happened? What went wrong?"

He shook his head. "Monroe was there. He wasn't really part of our group, but Primrose was sweet on him and she'd already told him too much. We had to pull him in. He tripped an alarm, and Tyrone came back early to check. The others tried to get out before Tyrone realized who they were. They were wearing ski masks, so they should have been able to just disappear. But Monroe panicked, called Willie by name."

My heart dropped like a rock, for Willie, for Monroe, for Pastor Rod, and for Old Dog Leg. "What happened?"

"Tyrone pulled his gun. We were friends, but he was furious. He felt we'd betrayed him, and he wasn't going to let us get away with it." His voice cracked, and an incredible sadness settled over both of us.

"Willie shot him?"

Pastor Rod nodded. "Afterward, he took the fall for all of us. Insisted right up to the end that he was working alone."

"And Hyacinth went along with that?"

"She put up a fuss, but Willie was adamant. She went to the police once, but he told them that she was lying to save him."

I shook my head in disbelief. "And the police believed that?"

"They had their man. They didn't worry about looking any further. That's how things were back then for people like us. I know it was selfish to keep our mouths shut, but Willie was going down for murder anyway. Telling the truth wouldn't have lightened his sentence at all." It was more than selfish, and I wondered if their silence had led to Dontae's murder. Misery and guilt radiated from Pastor Rod's dark eyes. "We promised Willie we'd stick with Hyacinth and make sure she was taken care of. She was too proud to take charity, so one by one, the others moved in here and made sure she had a steady income."

"What about Monroe?" I asked.

"The others wanted to throw him to the wolves, but he ran off. None of us knew where he'd gone. After a while, we went on with our lives as best we could. At least, I did, and I thought the others had."

"And then Monroe came back."

"Only God knows why. He said that he heard about Willie dying in prison. Got some foolish idea that he needed to apologize to Hyacinth."

"He thought an apology would make things better? After all this time?"

Pastor Rod shrugged. "He told me that he'd gone to Oregon and made a new life for himself. He had a wife and a couple of children. Got a good job and tried to put the past behind him. But lately, I guess he's been looking back. It's a side effect of old age, the urge to reach back and fix what you did wrong."

"So he returned to New Orleans and said he was sorry. How did the rest of you react to that?"

"Not well. All of us men were in on that warehouse job together. Monroe was no worse than the rest of us, but he was no better either. Maybe we all kept quiet while Willie took the fall, but the rest of us stuck around to make sure Hyacinth was taken care of. Monroe didn't even bother to do that."

Which explained the hostility I'd sensed the night Gabriel and I checked into the Love Nest. "What else did he plan to do while he was in town? Did he tell you?"

Pastor Rod shook his head. "I don't know. Nothing specific. His wife died last year and the kids are busy with their own lives. He doesn't see much of them and he's lonely. Maybe he just wants to be with friends and family again. A guilty conscience is a stern taskmaster. It'll get you doing things that don't make much sense."

He was about to say more, but the sound of voices nearby reminded us that we weren't alone at the Love Nest. Just like that, the pastor shut down in front of my eyes. "I've said too much. Please, Mrs. Broussard, if you have a heart, let this remain between us."

"I can't promise that," I said. "The police are investigating Dontae's murder. You know it's going to come out eventually."

His eyes looked haunted, his face gaunt. I think he would have sacrificed himself if he thought he could save the others. Just as Willie had tried to do. I thought over what he'd told me. "How does Lula Belle fit into the robbery?"

"She doesn't."

I didn't believe him. "She's here and she's one of you. Primrose clearly blames her for what happened back then."

The pastor's gaze flickered toward mine. "Lula Belle hasn't always behaved with discretion," he said reluctantly. "Her antics caused some dissension between Willie and Hyacinth. And Primrose is very protective of those she loves."

"What kind of dissension, exactly?" As if I couldn't guess.

Pastor Rod shook his head and stood. "I've already said too much."

"Then I'll just ask Lula Belle."

Pastor Rod rubbed his face and groaned. "I wish you'd just drop the whole thing. I think that would be a kindness. But if you insist on talking to Lula Belle, I will ask you to leave her alone tonight. She's not feeling well. She complained of an upset stomach after dinner. Let her sleep. You can talk to her tomorrow."

He put a hand on my shoulder briefly, then left me sitting in the garden while I tried to absorb everything he'd told me. It wasn't until he'd been gone for a few minutes that the importance of what he'd said hit me.

Lula Bella wasn't feeling well. After dinner. In a house where someone else had been poisoned less than forty-eight hours earlier. Not good. Not good at all.

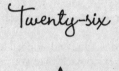

Twenty-six

Panic almost choked me as I raced back along the path and let myself inside. I thought about calling for help, but I didn't know who to trust, so I rushed past the parlor and turned down the corridor into the annex.

I had a feeling of déjà vu as I reached Lula Belle's door and knocked. She was an unpleasant old woman, but that didn't mean I wanted her dead.

"Lula Belle? Are you in there?"

My heart was in my throat and my senses were on such high alert I think I could actually hear the blood pumping through my veins.

"Lula Belle?"

I was so sure she was dying that when the door flew open, I stumbled backward a step in surprise. The last person I actually expected to see was Lula Belle, but there she was, scowling up at me. She wore a pair of silky pajamas and a hairnet, a pair of scuffed purple slippers on her feet.

In the room behind her, I could see a canopy bed heaped

with lacy white throw pillows and an armchair in front of the window. A small closet gaped open, revealing a handful of pastel-colored pantsuits and pairs of shoes. I didn't see any food, any overturned glasses, or any signs that she'd been ill.

"What do you want?" she snarled toothlessly. "You're making enough noise to raise the dead."

I ignored her attitude, relieved that she was feeling well enough to be rude. "Are you all right?"

"I was before you started making such a fuss." She started to shut the door.

I caught it with one hand and stopped her. "Pastor Rod told me you had an upset stomach. Are you *sure* you're okay?"

Lula Belle's lips moved in and out over her gums as she glared at me. "Lordy, child, you're an annoying little thing. You know that, don't you? Can't a woman be indisposed without having a big deal made out of it?"

I let out a relieved laugh, but it sounded more like a nervous titter. "Yes, of course. I'm sorry. I just . . ." I waved a hand, at a loss for words. "I was worried about you."

"Worried? Why?" The light went on in her beady little eyes. "What? You thought somebody tried to poison me?"

"The thought did cross my mind," I said.

Lula Belle threw back her head and laughed, giving me an unfettered view of her toothless mouth. "Oh, that's rich, baby. Really. And just who did you think would be out to kill me?"

I shrugged and then took a chance. "I don't know. Primrose, maybe? It's pretty obvious the two of you aren't exactly friends."

Lula Belle stopped laughing abruptly. "You don't know what you're talking about."

Judging from her reaction, I was almost positive I'd just hit a bull's-eye. "Why does she hate you so much? Is it because she caught you sleeping with her brother-in-law or because you tried to steal Monroe from her?"

Those beady little eyes turned hard. "I never laid a finger on Willie," she said. "Hyacinth was like a sister to me. As for Monroe—" She waved the thought of him away with a flick of her wrist. "I couldn't have stolen him from Primrose because he was never hers to begin with."

"But she was interested in him, wasn't she?"

Lula Belle tilted her head to one side. "Who told you that?"

"Nobody had to tell me," I said. A tiny white lie, but I excused it away with all the others. And besides, what I said next wasn't a lie. "I saw how she looked at him the night we arrived."

A mean little smile curved Lula Belle's mouth. "Primrose imagined a whole lot of things back then. She still does. She makes things up. But it doesn't matter what *she* wanted. Monroe wanted nothing to do with her."

I wondered if that was true or just another mean jab at the woman. "How did she feel about that?"

"What do you mean, how did she feel? She lived in her own little fantasy world. She thought he was madly in love with her."

"What about you and Monroe? Were the two of you an item?"

"Me and Monroe?" Lula Belle laughed again and shook her head. "He wasn't my type, then or now."

"You seemed pretty interested in him the night we met."

"I was yanking Primrose's chain. It's what I do." She put one hand on the back of her head and thrust out a hip in a pose that might have been sexy . . . once. "I never said *he* wasn't interested, did I?"

She'd let go of the door, so I relaxed my hold on it. "He wanted a relationship but you didn't?"

Lula Belle smiled like a cat with a bowl of cream. "Honey, I coulda had any man I wanted back then."

Maybe, but Monroe hadn't seemed especially interested

in her the other night. Maybe he'd just been hiding it well. Maybe *she* was the one living in la-la land. "So why do you dislike Primrose so much?"

Lula Belle lifted one bony shoulder. "She's a troublemaker."

"How so?"

"Why don't you ask her?"

I was getting tired of these people and their secrets. "I'm asking you," I said. "What did she ever do to you?"

Lula Belle's mouth went through its funny set of motions again while she thought about whether to answer me. "She told Hyacinth that I was sleeping with Willie. It was a lie, of course. And thank God Hyacinth believed me. But if Primrose'd had her way, I'd have been out on the curb."

Now I was confused. "She told Hyacinth about you and Willie while you lived here? After Willie went to prison?"

Lula Belle nodded. "That's right."

"I don't understand. Why would she tell her something like that?"

"Because she didn't want me around."

Imagine that.

"Would that really have been so bad?" I asked. "I mean, you've lived here with a woman you hate for thirty years. Wouldn't it have been better to get a place of your own and get away from Primrose?"

"Maybe, but that wasn't part of the deal was it? I couldn't leave."

I assumed it was the same deal Pastor Rod had told me about in the garden, but I asked anyway, just to be sure. "What deal?"

Lula Belle leaned her head against the wall, and for a split second I saw a vulnerable side to her. "We owed Hyacinth. She needed us. I couldn't turn my back on her."

"Because of the robbery and what happened to Tyrone?

Why did you owe her anything for that? You weren't there, were you?"

The old woman's head shot up, and her eyes turned hard and black again. "No, I wasn't, but I knew about it and I didn't try to stop them."

"So you all felt guilty about Willie taking the fall for Tyrone's murder, but not guilty enough to tell the truth? And to ease the guilt you vowed to make sure Hyacinth didn't suffer."

"They aren't going to like you knowing about that," Lula Belle warned.

Something uncomfortable danced across my nerve endings "Who?" I asked. "Who isn't going to like it?"

But I'd crossed the line. Lula Belle was finished talking. She grabbed the door with both hands and gave it a shove that was surprisingly strong for a woman her age.

"Tell me who you're talking about." I tried to stop her, but I was too late. The door banged shut, leaving me alone in the hall surrounded by other closed doors that might have been concealing anything . . . including a killer.

Twenty-seven

❖

Hyacinth was in the dining room clearing away dinner dishes when I returned to the central part of the inn. She moved slowly, her heavy arms jiggling as she worked. Her breathing sounded labored, and she looked angry—or maybe she was just worried. After all, her carefully ordered world did seem to be crumbling around her.

I spent a moment wondering just what kind of life it had been. Her husband had gone to prison for murder, leaving her dependent upon the people who'd helped put him there. When she tried to come forward with the truth, he'd betrayed her by telling the police she was lying. His cohorts had all lived here, paying her way, but the work she did at the inn more than earned whatever they shelled out in monthly rent. And then there was Primrose. I couldn't tell if she helped or hindered Hyacinth's efforts.

Had any of that pushed Hyacinth over the edge? Had living with constant reminders of her husband's mistake been too much for her? It probably would have been for me.

I knocked lightly on the doorframe, and Hyacinth's head jerked up. She scowled when she saw me standing there, but she tried to hide it. "Mrs. Broussard. You're up late. What can I do for you?"

It was barely nine o'clock. Hardly the witching hour. "I'd like to talk with you if you have a minute."

"Oh? What about?"

I nodded toward the annex and tried to keep my voice sounding friendly and unthreatening. "I was just talking with Lula Belle. She told me what happened to your husband."

Hyacinth's attempt at friendliness vanished in a blink. "That's none of your business."

"I realize that," I said, "but if there's a chance that it had any connection to Dontae's death, I think you need to tell the police about what happened back then."

Hyacinth looked away with a huff. "The police don't want to hear what I have to say. They'll believe what they want to."

I could understand why she felt that way, and I decided not to push her. "It must have been difficult for you, being left alone with a child to raise. Is Tamarra's mother still around? Is she any help to you now?"

"What's it to you?"

I moved a little closer. "Nothing, really. But I'm curious by nature and I was brought up to care about other people. Your story intrigues me."

Her eyes flickered to my face briefly. "Maybe you should have been brought up to keep your nose out of other peoples' business."

I laughed softly. "Believe me, my aunt tried hard to teach me that lesson. I just never did get it. I know what it's like to lose someone, Hyacinth. My parents died when I was just a kid and I went to live with my aunt and uncle. I was grateful to have them and I love them with all my heart, but I still struggled with issues of not really belonging. So when I hear about Willie leaving you on your own, with only the people who helped send him to prison as your support system, I can't help but wonder how you and your daughter coped."

She studied me in silence for a moment, and then seemed to thaw a bit. "We just did. We got up every day and put one foot in front of the other. What else you gonna do? I couldn't afford to have a meltdown. Had to keep going for Pearl."

"That's your daughter?"

She nodded. "She died about five years back. Breast cancer. Before she got sick, she helped out here from time to time." She dashed a tear away with the back of her hand. "I miss her, but you can't let yourself get stuck in the bad moments or they'll eat you alive."

I smiled gently. "That sounds like something my aunt Yolanda would say." We both fell silent for a moment and I was optimistic enough to think we'd bonded enough to change the subject. "I'm curious about Lula Belle's relationship with your sister. Can you tell me why they dislike each other so much?"

Apparently, I was wrong. Hyacinth shook her head before I even finished asking. "I can*not*. It's none of your damn business."

No beating around the bush for her. "Look, I know I'm overstepping, but it's possible that someone in this house murdered Dontae. Doesn't it bother you to think there could be a killer living here with you?"

She lifted her chin and stared me down. "So you're just *worried* about me, is that what you want me to believe?"

When she said it in that tone of voice, it did sound a bit far-fetched but I refused to let her intimidate me. "You and the others who are innocent."

"Well, since I don't know who did it, I can't help much, now can I?" She reached across the table for a couple of glasses. "Now if you'll excuse me, I have things to do."

I might not get another chance to talk with her, so I stepped between her and the kitchen door. "You couldn't have been happy to see Monroe Magee walk through your door last week. I know the others blame him for what happened to your husband. Do you?"

Hyacinth froze for a fraction of a second. "Apparently Lula Belle was in the mood to talk."

I didn't want to throw anyone under the bus, so I said, "It wasn't only Lula Belle. I pieced the story together from bits and pieces I've picked up. I'm right, though, aren't I? They all blame Monroe. Do you?"

Hyacinth stacked some plates and sighed heavily. "Monroe was an idiot then, and he's a damn fool now. But do I blame him for Willie going to jail? No, I do not. Willie did what he did on his own. Nobody forced him."

"It didn't make you angry that they let him take the fall for what they all did together?"

"All of my friends going to jail together wouldn't have made life better for me or for Pearl," she said.

Her answer surprised me, mostly because she seemed sincere. "So you don't want Monroe dead?"

"Why would I want that? One death won't make up for another. Now leave me alone. Please."

If she was innocent of murder, I didn't want to hurt her by stirring up the past, but I couldn't just give up and walk away when I was so close to getting answers for Old Dog Leg.

"I've been really curious about Monroe. Do you have any idea where he went after he left here the other night?"

"How would I know?" She brushed crumbs from the table into her hand and dumped them onto the top plate in her stack.

"He took your van. Aren't you anxious to get it back?"

"Of course I am, but the police are looking for him. When they find him, they'll find my van." She dusted her hands together to get rid of the remaining crumbs, then planted her fists on her ample hips. "If I remember right, Monroe had a brother. I don't know if he's still alive, but if he is, maybe that's where Monroe has gone."

It would have been a perfect opportunity to come clean, but I let it slide by. "Did you give the police Monroe's credit card number? Maybe they can track him with that."

She coughed up a laugh. "Credit card? Monroe? Baby, he paid cash. Everybody around here pays cash, 'cept for folks like you."

She lifted the plates and started around me toward the kitchen, so I called out another question before I had time to think it through. "You must have been furious when Primrose told you that Lula Belle was sleeping with your husband."

Hyacinth turned back toward me wearing a look of utter disgust. "Lula Belle and Willie? Are you sick?"

"That's what Lula Belle told me," I said.

To my surprise, Hyacinth threw back her head and laughed. "Sounds to me like somebody's been jerking your chain. Of course Lula Belle ain't never slept with Willie."

"How do you know that?"

"Because, boo, she's Willie's sister."

His *sister*? The image of Lula Belle's toothless mouth open wide with laughter flashed through my head. She'd played me like a fiddle, and I felt like a fool. If she'd lied about that, what else had she lied about?

Hyacinth disappeared into the kitchen, and I climbed the stairs to the honeymoon suite where I pulled on my pajamas and rolled into bed. But I couldn't fall asleep. I kept running over the pastor's story and wondering how the murder of a security guard in the 1970s had led to the murder of one of the men responsible for it forty years later.

Sometime around midnight, Gabriel crept into the room, trying hard not to disturb me. He reeked of stale cigarette smoke and whiskey, with a faint note of his aftershave underneath.

He'd been working for more than twelve hours, and headed straight for the shower. I assumed he was exhausted so instead of waiting up to tell him what I'd learned while he was at the Duke, I curled onto my side and let him sleep.

I woke up with sunshine in my face, still curled on my side but now wrapped in blankets and an arm and a leg that wasn't mine. After the initial shock of finding someone cuddled up beside me, I caught his scent, clean and purely male, and slowly relaxed under the protective barrier he created around me. I didn't often let myself think about everything I'd lost when Philippe and I separated, but this morning I had to admit just how much I'd missed waking up next to someone.

Yesterday had been a rough day, and as soon as I checked the time I realized that we'd slept past breakfast service. We still had a couple of hours until we had to check out, so I tried to move around quietly so Gabriel could sleep. Despite my best efforts, he stirred awake not long after I did. We dressed quickly and I filled him in on what I'd learned the night before while he packed a few things he'd pulled out of his suitcase and I did my hair and makeup. I told him what I knew about Hyacinth and Willie and about the robbery-slash-murder at Letterman Industries. I told him that Pastor Rod wanted to come clean about the past, but that Tamarra was afraid that the police would investigate her grandmother and the others if the truth came out.

I was just about to tell him about Lula Belle and Willie when he came to the bathroom door and met my eyes in the mirror. "I thought you said you weren't going to talk to anyone last night."

"I wasn't planning on it," I said. "But then I saw Cleveland in the parlor and I just couldn't turn around and walk away."

"So you lied to me?"

I turned quickly, completely forgetting that I was holding a mascara wand near my eye. The mascara brushed my cheek, leaving a wet gloppy trail. I turned back to assess the damage and found a long smear of Black Quartz running from the corner of my eye to my ear, but at least I hadn't stabbed myself in the eyeball. "It wasn't a lie," I said as I began cleaning off the smear. "It was a change of plans. You would have done the same thing in my place."

"I doubt it."

"Of course you would. Look at all the great information I got! We know where Monroe went when he left here forty years ago. We know about Tyrone and how he died. We know more about how Lula Belle fits into the picture now . . ."

"And we know that you could have been hurt—or worse." He leaned against the doorjamb, his face drawn into a deep scowl. "Okay, so fate or whatever gave you the opportunity to talk to Cleveland. I'll give you that. But you went looking for the others."

"But—"

"No, Rita. You actively pursued the others. You purposely went looking for possible murderers. Alone. Without backup."

He sounded angry, which shocked me. I tried again to explain. "But I—"

"You said you'd call. What happened to that promise?"

I couldn't look at him, so I focused on scrubbing a particularly stubborn mascara spot off my cheek. "I promised I'd call if I ran into trouble. Which I didn't. So . . . no call." The spot wouldn't budge, so I tossed the cloth aside in frustration. "Why am I under interrogation? I didn't kill anyone."

Gabriel's reflection folded its arms across its chest. "You don't get it, do you?"

"No," I said. "I don't. I'm fine. Nothing happened."

"Well, then, you're lucky. Because even if nobody here poisoned Dontae—which I don't believe for a minute—they're all clearly off their rockers. Something could have happened to you."

"But it didn't," I said again.

"But it *could* have." He grabbed me by the shoulders and looked me in the eye. "The thought of something happening to you makes *me* crazy."

I tried to laugh, but the look on his face and the way his Adam's apple bobbed as he swallowed his emotion, did something I wasn't expecting. "Gabriel, I—"

I wanted to reassure him. I wanted to promise him that I'd never do anything truly reckless. And most of all I wanted to say that I cared about him, too. But the words caught in my throat, and all I could do was look up at him in silence.

He shook his head as if disappointed and let go of me. Turning away, he snatched up his bag from the bed and paused at the door just long enough to say, "You make it damn hard to care about you, you know that, don't you?"

And then he was gone.

Twenty-eight

✠

I can't say that Gabriel gave me the silent treatment after that, but our conversation as we packed up that morning left a lot to be desired. We carried our suitcases to the car and checked out, all with a minimum of small talk. After saying a quick good-bye we drove away from the Love Nest separately, all of which left me feeling edgy and frustrated.

As I crossed town to pick up the cake for Bernice's barbecue, I found myself wishing one minute that Gabriel and I had had more time to settle things between us, and then thanking my lucky stars for the chance to gather my thoughts before I had to see him again. I wondered if I'd overreacted to his concern for me, and then argued with myself for doing so. My uncle Nestor has always been protective of me. Add in four male cousins, all overloaded with machismo, and I'd scarcely had room to breathe when I was a teenager.

Which is why I get so prickly when someone tries to protect me now. It doesn't matter who's doing it, or why. But in trying to set boundaries I could live with, I'd hurt Gabriel. I didn't like feeling responsible for the look in his eyes when he'd walked away from me.

In spite of my mood Bernice's barbecue turned out to be not as bad as I'd feared. The weather cooperated, giving us a day bright with sunshine and only a few harmless clouds overhead. The humidity was in the tolerable range, helped by the fact that Bernice had set a table in the shade of a picturesque live oak.

Her nephew Bennie was a deft hand on the grill, turning out a beer-can chicken that was surprisingly moist and flavorful, along with hot dogs for the kids. Emily, his wife, shucked ears of tender sweet corn and made coleslaw that was both creamy and tangy, with just the right amount of crunch. Despite the dull opinion of them I'd formed from afar, in truth Bennie was actually amusing company, and Emily extremely well-read. The children were every bit as poorly behaved up close as they seemed from a distance, but Bernice had plenty to keep them busy, so even they weren't intolerable.

I stuffed myself on Bernice's potato salad, which was almost as good as Aunt Yolanda's. I'm something of a potato salad snob, and Aunt Yolanda's recipe is the gold standard by which I judge all others.

The potato must be cut into small, bite-sized pieces. The eggs diced, not sliced. Onion, definitely. Celery, a must. Pickles and pickle juice are expressly forbidden. My preferred dressing is half whipped salad dressing, half sour cream, lightly seasoned with salt, pepper, and dry mustard. And, of course, paprika sprinkled across the top, preferably sweet Hungarian.

I could taste vinegar and dill in Bernice's dressing, but she'd used paprika liberally and hadn't broken my personal no-pickle rule, so I could forgive her a few small deviations.

The cake had turned out perfectly; sweet, but not overpoweringly so. The raspberry filling and light chocolate buttercream between the layers held up beautifully, and the white chocolate buttercream on top looked as cool and fresh as it had the day before. I'd finished decorating it with a small cluster of fresh raspberries and matching piping around the edges of the cake, which added color. Several people asked for seconds, which is music to any chef's ear.

It was almost three when Miss Frankie finally looked at her watch and announced that it was time for us to head over to the cemetery. We spent a few minutes saying good-bye, then Miss Frankie and I loaded her car with the jars of flowers she'd so painstakingly prepared the day before and set off. She drove. I watched the world go by and hoped that we'd get through the visit to Philippe's grave with a minimum of emotion. We'd made it through Miss Frankie's birthday, and we'd hobbled through the holidays. But this was the first Memorial Day since his death, and I'd already learned that the firsts were the hardest after someone dies.

It's the same after a divorce, really. The first birthday alone, the first Christmas, the first New Year's Eve—they can blow your recovery out of the water. Old memories tend to creep in uninvited, and the twinges they bring are sharp and painful. Philippe's birthday was coming up in June, and then it would be July, the month he died and we could begin the job of limping through the second year without him. I just prayed it would eventually get easier for Miss Frankie.

We found a parking spot near the Renier family vault and carefully made our way across the uneven ground carrying the flowers. When we reached the vault, Miss Frankie turned her face to the sun and took a couple of deep breaths, then dashed away her tears and put the jar of flowers she was holding on the ground.

While I tried not to think about the fact that Philippe was inside that hot stone structure, Miss Frankie seemed determined to dwell on it. She ran her fingers over the words chiseled into the stone:

PHILIPPE RENIER
BELOVED SON AND HUSBAND

His name was just below his father's, and previous generations were listed above that. Miss Frankie's fingers lingered over the date of Philippe's birth, moved across that tiny dash that encompassed his whole life, and came to rest on the date of his death.

I focused on breathing in and out while she did that, but I hated this place as much as I hated my parents' graves. In my opinion, my parents weren't there. Philippe and his father weren't here. It felt morose to me to focus on their graves and turn them into some kind of shrine. But that's exactly how Aunt Yolanda deals with death, and obviously Miss Frankie felt the same way. I didn't want to ruin the experience for her.

She finally looked away and sent me a tremulous smile. "You must think I'm a silly old bird."

"Not at all," I assured her. "I think you're a grieving mother."

She pulled out a hanky and mopped away a fresh round of tears. "I'd give my own life if I could bring Philippe back. I'm having a little trouble reconciling all of this with God."

Over the years I'd heard lots of meaningless platitudes at funerals, starting with my parents'. I'd listened to people natter on about God's will and how it was their time to go. Wearing kindly expressions, perfectly nice people told me that my parents were in a better place and how God needed them in heaven more than we needed them here . . . yadda, yadda, yadda.

None of it had ever made a bit of sense to me. What kind of selfish God thought he needed my parents more than I did? Who would do that to a twelve-year-old?

I'd spent the next few years angry with God for taking them away and leaving me alone, but I'd finally worked out my own answers to all the questions their accident had left me with. I didn't know if anyone else would agree with me, but at least I'd found a way to live with my personal tragedy.

"Someone chose to end Philippe's life," I said gently. "Just like someone chose to drive drunk and ended up taking my parents' lives. It was horrible and wrong and you have every right to feel angry. I used to think God should have stopped that drunk driver. Now . . . I don't know. But I have to believe that those who hurt innocent people will suffer the consequences of their actions one way or another."

Miss Frankie tried to smile at me, but she failed miserably. "There's no consequence bad enough, if you ask me."

I chuckled softly. "I agree, but maybe that's why you and I aren't in charge of the world. It's taken me a long time to understand that bad things sometimes happen to good people. We can't stop or control it. The only compensation for our loss is that we're given the chance to make something positive out of it."

Miss Frankie's lips trembled a little, and she reached for my hand, clutching it gratefully. "I have you now," she said. "I call that good."

I squeezed her hand in return and blinked to clear my own eyes. "I feel the same way."

"And I think Philippe approves, don't you?"

"I'm sure he does," I assured her. I nodded toward the flowers waiting for us on the sidewalk. "Which of those do you think he wants?"

"He dearly loved magnolias. Let's give him some of those."

We spent a few minutes transferring flowers from the glass jars to the stone pots permanently attached to the front of the vault. Miss Frankie snipped and arranged and moved flowers from pot to pot until she was satisfied, then stepped back to judge the effect from a distance.

"What do you think, sugar?"

"I think it's lovely. Are you finished? Shall I gather the jars?"

She gave a halfhearted nod. "Yes, I suppose there's no sense hanging around, is there?"

I shook my head and kept my mouth shut. I bent to gather the jars, dumped out the excess water, and then extended my arm to Miss Frankie for the walk back to the car.

"Speaking of moving along, I called Thaddeus last night," she said. "He'll have a list of properties for me first thing in the morning. How soon will you be free to look at them with me?"

I almost lost my balance on an uneven piece of flagstone. "So soon?"

"Zydeco's in trouble and you're about to lose staff. We might as well move now, before the need becomes too great. We don't want to end up in a hole we can't climb out of."

I knew she was right, but I still felt guilty at the idea of her selling family land to bail me out. Logically, I knew the fault wasn't all mine, but I couldn't help feeling responsible.

We reached the car, and Miss Frankie leaned against the door, staring out over the cemetery while she waited for me to stow the empty jars in the trunk. After all the drama of the past several nights at the inn—and sharing a bed with Gabriel—I'd been looking forward to spending the evening at home, but the look on Miss Frankie's face convinced me I couldn't leave her alone. "How would you feel about watching a couple of old movies with me tonight?" I asked.

She looked at me from the corner of her eye. "You don't have to stay with me, Rita. I'll be fine."

I pushed away from the car and opened the door for her. "Maybe you will, but I don't want to be by myself. So what do you say? Your place or mine?"

I figured even my aunt Yolanda would understand why I told that lie.

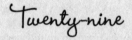

Twenty-nine

Miss Frankie and I spent Monday evening watching those old movies. She dozed off after about an hour, and I tried calling Sullivan to fill him in on everything I'd learned at the Love Nest. He didn't answer, so I left a voice mail asking him to call me.

I got to work early on Tuesday morning, eager for a normal day, one without murder or drama. Solving Dontae's murder wasn't my responsibility, but making Zydeco a success was. I needed to put the Love Nest and Monroe Magee out of my mind and stay focused on my career. It's what any reasonably intelligent woman would do.

Even so, my mind was pulled in a dozen different directions: anxiety about Zydeco, concern over how Ox would react to the news that we'd have to shelve his idea permanently, worry about what Edie would do with her resignation, confusion over my feelings for both Gabriel and Sullivan, not to mention the fear that Miss Frankie might change her mind about selling the property. I needed to clear my head, and working in the kitchen was the one sure way I knew of to do that.

After checking in with Edie—she seemed almost back to normal this morning—I ignored the stack of unopened mail and the blinking light on my phone signaling voice mail and joined the staff in the design room.

Once again, I felt a wave of panic over the thought that I might lose this place, but I shook it off and got to work. Orders might have tapered off, but they hadn't disappeared completely and the staff had their hands full today putting together a bananas Foster cake sculpted in the shape of a dragon in flight for a book launch party in a few days.

The fresh bananas in the filling meant that this particular cake was labor-intensive at the last minute. I wanted to be on the floor and present as we kicked into high gear. With private orders dwindling, getting contracts for corporate events and fund-raisers was more important than ever. I wanted to make sure Zydeco was well represented in front of the city's movers and shakers.

Abe had baked the cake, a delicately flavored rum and cinnamon cake that filled the entire bakery with the most delicious aromas as it cooled. Isabeau seemed a bit subdued as she whisked together the brown sugar buttercream frosting we'd use for the crumb coating and between layers. Estelle had pulled her red curls back under a lime green bandana that almost contained them. She worked slowly and carefully, measuring and double-checking every ingredient as she stirred together the banana slices, brown sugar, nutmeg, and rum for the cake's fresh banana filling.

Ox was out on a wedding consult, so I started rolling out the fondant that would cover the cake. The scents of banana and caramel made my mouth water. I'd had my first bananas Foster experience years earlier at a restaurant in Chicago. I still remembered that first perfect bite, and I'd spent several years trying to recreate it in cake form.

Dwight, with both his shaggy hair and scraggly beard

covered by sanitary guards, carefully cut several fresh cakes into equal layers with a serrated knife and then began the painstaking chore of stacking the layers, separating them with buttercream.

His faded T-shirt was covered by a moderately stained chef's jacket, leaving only his holey jeans and worn-out tennis shoes visible, though even those looked as if he'd found them while Dumpster diving.

Sparkle, working from the one corner of the design room the sunlight never reached, kept her black-lined eyes downcast. She pretended to be riveted on the hundreds of tiny scales she was making for the dragon cake, but I could feel attitude rolling off her in waves.

I ignored Sparkle's vibe for as long as I could, then finally looked up from my fondant and said, "Is everything all right, Sparkle?"

She shrugged and slid a heavy-lidded glance at me, pursing her black-painted lips in an attempt to look bored. It's an expression she uses frequently, and she's good at it. But I've been around long enough now to pick up on her real mood most of the time.

"Sure," she said, her voice flat. "Why wouldn't it be?"

"You seem a little edgy. Is there something I should know?"

She gave another shrug and rolled her eyes away from me. She worked her ruffle stick over one of the dragon wings for a moment, stepped back to gauge her efforts, and then finally spoke again. "I'm just wondering when you were planning to tell us how bad things are around here."

Her question caught me off guard. I didn't like the idea that this was a topic of conversation amongst the staff. "I didn't want to say anything until I had a better idea just what our situation is."

Sparkle's frown deepened. "You talked to Ox and Edie. And Isabeau knows, don't you, Isabeau?"

Isabeau glanced up, clearly uncomfortable. "I might have overheard one or two conversations," she said with a shrug.

"I didn't confide in Isabeau," I said. "I wanted to come to you all with a plan, not just a lot of bad news."

Estelle stopped working and drew closer. "Do you? Have a plan?"

"I'm working on it."

"What about Ox's idea?" Sparkle asked. "What did Miss Frankie say about that?"

I laughed nervously and tried to make a joke. "What part of *confidential* do you people not understand?"

Isabeau's cheeks flushed. Estelle's chins doubled. Sparkle didn't crack a smile. "We're a team," she said. "At least we used to be." She held my gaze, and I could feel the challenge in hers.

I took a deep breath and looked around the room at the others. Isabeau was watching me closely, and Dwight glanced up briefly from his own work. He didn't look happy either.

"Of course we're a team," I said with a nervous smile.

"Then tell us, how did Miss Frankie react to Ox's idea?"

I'd have given just about anything to have this conversation later, when I'd had more time to prepare. "Not well," I admitted. "She's afraid adding a new line of moderately priced cakes will compromise the bakery's integrity."

"In what way?" Estelle asked.

"She thinks we'll lose our high-end customers if we open the doors to . . . others."

Sparkle made a noise with her tongue. "I hate to say it, but she's probably right."

"Oh, I don't know," Estelle said. "If we did it right, we could probably have the best of both worlds."

Dwight laughed and sliced a millimeter of cake from the edge of one tier. "If you think that, you don't know our clientele. Philippe knew what he was doing when he made this place *by appointment only.* It makes the customers feel special, like they have our undivided attention."

"We could specialize Zydeco right out of business if we're not careful," Estelle countered. She swept banana peels into a nearby trash can at her side. "So? What are we going to do?"

I didn't answer right away. I thought I should talk to Ox first—even if he hadn't felt it necessary to extend the same courtesy to me.

"We haven't made a final decision yet," I said, hedging. "Ox's idea is new and different. Miss Frankie wasn't really prepared to consider it. We'll have to discuss it some more before we make a decision."

"And what if she doesn't want to consider it?" Sparkle asked.

I didn't have an answer, but I tried to give the illusion of confidence. "We'll cross that bridge when we come to it."

Estelle's broad face creased, and her eyes narrowed with worry. "What does *that* mean?"

"We're working on it," I assured them all. "Miss Frankie and I are talking about the possibility of selling some property to bring some cash in to bridge the gap until business picks up. Believe me, I'm committed to making sure everyone here keeps their jobs."

"Our jobs?" Estelle squeaked. "Are you talking about letting someone go?"

"No! Of course not. That's not what I meant."

"Who's leaving?" Isabeau asked. "How are you going to decide?"

"It's not going to come to that," I promised. "We'll figure something out."

Dwight locked eyes with me. "Can you promise that?"

I wanted to shout "Yes!" but the word got stuck in my throat. What if Miss Frankie couldn't find a buyer for her land in this depressed economy, or what if it took longer than any of us thought?

"You think that will be enough?" Dwight asked.

"Of course. It has to be."

"That's not exactly a promise," Sparkle said in her trademark monotone. "Things are bad out there. My cousin was vice president at a bank. She lost her job to downsizing and was out of work for almost a year. She finally got a job last month doing tech support for a cell phone company, so she's working nights, never sees her kids, and brings home poverty wages. Plus, she's on Wellbutrin for depression."

Wow! Thanks for the encouraging pep talk. I tried again to get the promise out, but it still wouldn't come.

"I read somewhere that the average time it takes someone to find a job these days is ten months," Estelle said, frowning pointedly at me. "If you're going to fire one of us, you should at least let us get a head start on looking for work. I think you owe us at least that much."

The pressure was starting to get to me. "Will you please stop assuming the worst?" I said, a little too loudly. I lowered my voice and went on. "We'll think of something." And then, because skepticism was shining from every eye in the room, I made a rash promise. "We're not laying anybody off, okay? Miss Frankie and I will find another way around this. I promise."

"You mean that?" Isabeau asked.

"Of course."

Dwight and Estelle exchanged a glance, and Sparkle almost smiled. Whether they believed me or not, they eventually drifted back to work and I did my best to drift with them. I'd crumb-coated the dragon's tail and covered about half of it with fondant when I felt a shadow blocking the light behind me. I looked over my shoulder and found Detective Sullivan leaning against a support beam watching me work.

He looked great. Tall and rugged and solid—which pretty

much sums him up. I hadn't seen him since Friday night, and I was pleased that he'd responded to my phone message with a personal visit. After spending the weekend with Gabriel, though, I felt more awkward in Sullivan's presence than I had in months.

I was ready for a break by then, so I took advantage of the interruption to let the muscles in my hand relax for a few seconds. "How long have you been there?" I asked. "

Sullivan glanced at the clock on the wall. "Not long. I was enjoying watching you do your thing. Is this a bad time?"

I shook my head. "Not really. Do you mind talking while I work, or do we need to go somewhere private?"

"We can talk here. Keep doing what you're doing." He pulled up a stool and sat. "That smells wonderful. What is it?"

"Cinnamon rum cake." I found a paper plate and slid one of the pieces Dwight had carved from the cake onto it. I ladled a dollop of the filling over the top and pushed the plate toward Sullivan, along with a fork. "Try it. You'll like it."

He took a bite and closed his eyes for a moment in appreciation. "That's good."

Which is one of the quickest ways to my heart. I grinned and treated myself to a small piece, too. "Thanks. It's something we've been working on for a while. I'm glad you like it. So what brings you here? Just returning my call, or do you have news about the case?"

Sullivan licked his fork and shook his head. "A little of both, I guess. I spent the day talking to the folks at the Love Nest, and we've been looking for anyone in the neighborhood who saw or heard anything unusual the night of the murder."

"Any luck?"

"Unfortunately, no. The police aren't exactly popular in that neighborhood. It's slow going, and that's being optimistic." His clear blue eyes swept over my face. "How about you? Have you uncovered any useful information?"

"I think so. Tell me, have you run background checks on the residents of the Love Nest?"

"Not yet. Should I?"

I told him everything I knew, leaving nothing out. The robbery. The murder of the security guard. Willie's sacrifice. The way the friends had banded together to support Hyacinth ever since.

"So that's what they're trying to hide," Sullivan said, making a few notes and studying them for a moment.

"Apparently. There could be more, of course. They're full of secrets over there. The only thing I don't know," I said, "is who killed Dontae, and why? And where has Monroe disappeared to now?"

"I'll check out the robbery and murder and see if I can find anything more." He looked away from his notebook and grinned. "You did good, Lucero."

Aw, shucks. I put together a second helping of cake and passed the plate to him. "Any word on how the poison got into Dontae's system?"

"The arsenic was in a bowl of pudding we found in his room. It was in a bowl from the Love Nest, so we're assuming it was made there in the kitchen. Maybe served at dinner. Dontae must have taken his bowl back to his room."

"So the others ate the pudding, as well?"

"We're assuming that at least some of them did, but we don't know for sure. Like I said, we're having a devil of a time getting those old people to talk. Since everyone else is still alive, we're proceeding on the assumption that his portion was the only one with poison in it." Sullivan stopped speaking and attacked the cake as if we weren't discussing a deadly poison.

"What about fingerprints?"

"Unfortunately, there weren't any on the bowl. At least none that help us. We found a couple of clear prints, but they belong to the victim, It looks like he's the one who carried the pudding to his room, but we have no idea who served it." He finished the cake and sat back with a satisfied smile. "You managed to learn a whole lot more than I did. What's your take on Hyacinth Fiske?"

"She's hard to read," I said. "She's had a tough life and she's brusque and bossy, but she doesn't seem to mind that her friends let her husband go to prison alone. She's definitely the head honcho at the Love Nest. Everybody else seems intimidated by her. She probably made the pudding, and she's one of several with the means and opportunity to poison Dontae's bowl, but she had no reason I know of to kill him, and she claims she doesn't hold a grudge against Monroe."

"You believe her?"

"I don't know. Maybe."

One by one, he asked me about the others. I told him about Grey's volunteer service at the library and his penchant for dressing up in costume. Did that make him crazy or dedicated? I still didn't know.

I told him how angry Cleveland was with Monroe, and how he'd threatened to kill Monroe with his bare hands. But had he actually tried? I filled him in on Lula Belle's checkered past, Primrose's avid fantasy life, and the change of heart that had taken Pastor Rod from the getaway car to the pulpit. And I told him about Tamarra, who apparently knew the whole story and wanted desperately to keep it a secret.

"What about alibis? Any luck with those?" Sullivan asked.

I laughed and picked up our empty plates. "I wish. Cleveland says that he was in his room alone. We know that Primrose found the body, and I ran into Antwon and Tamarra coming out of their room at the same time Ga—" I stopped. Flushed. "They were running downstairs at the same time I was. It's not easy to get those people to talk."

"Tell me about it." Sullivan turned serious. "You should

know that we've issued a BOLO for Monroe. He's not being called a suspect yet, but he is considered a person of interest."

I wasn't surprised, but I was disappointed. "Maybe he's running because he knows who did it," I suggested. "And if he knows who did it, maybe he's in danger. Have you even considered that?"

"Of course we have."

"Are you taking precautions to protect him?"

"How, Rita? We have no idea where he is. We're watching the airport, bus stations, and Amtrak, but so far there's no sign of him. Maybe someone is trying to kill him, but we have to find him before we can protect him."

Yeah. I got that. "Maybe you can track down his family. His wife is dead, but he has kids and grandchildren who might be in Oregon somewhere. Pastor Rod said he doesn't see them often, but he may have tried to contact one of them." I felt a little swell of panic start to build in my chest. "It's important to find him, Liam. I don't think Dontae was supposed to die. I think the poison was meant for Monroe. The killer might still be after him. If he's worried for his life, he'll never re-surface."

Sullivan stood and brushed a lock of hair from my cheek with a gentleness that surprised me. "I have some bad news for you, darlin'. I don't think he's going to resurface anyway. At least not in this decade."

That was *so* not the response I wanted. I could only hope that Monroe had lost his edge since the last time he disappeared. But I was afraid that asking all of the NOPD to be on the lookout for him would only push Monroe further underground and almost guarantee that Dog Leg would lose his brother again.

And maybe this time, he'd lose him for good.

I finished work on the dragon's tail and then walked with the rest of the staff to the Dizzy Duke to unwind.

Gabriel was behind the bar looking sexy in a tight black T-shirt and even tighter jeans. The image of him in bed next to me flashed through my head, and I swear I could feel the weight of his leg pinning me against the mattress. Those memories got all wrapped up in confusion over the way we'd parted yesterday and my reaction to seeing Sullivan that afternoon. Gabriel acknowledged my presence with a lift of his chin. I smiled back, but he didn't seem eager to talk to me so I asked for some liquid courage in the form of a margarita, light on the tequila. I figured that gave me an even chance of getting one that would leave me capable of walking when I finished it. Gabriel's a true master at the art of the margarita, and his salt-to-glass ratio is the best I've encountered yet, but I worried that no drink—light on the tequila or otherwise— would be enough to fortify me for what lay ahead tonight.

I carried my margarita to the stage where the band was

setting up for the night. Maybe I should have waited for Gabriel to take a break so we could talk to Old Dog Leg together. Delivering bad news made my breath catch. I'd rather pipe buttercream in a basket-weave pattern over the Saint Louis Cathedral. But I also knew that I had to tell Dog Leg about his brother's part in the robbery and murder of the night security guard forty years ago before the police made a statement.

Old Dog Leg was there with the rest of the band, laughing about something I guess only musicians understand. Eventually the laughter faded and the others drifted away to plug in equipment, tune instruments, and order drinks. I sat on the edge of the stage and watched Old Dog Leg clean his trumpet mouthpiece, waiting for the right moment to let him know I was there.

"You gonna speak up or just watch me?" he asked after a minute or two.

I laughed, a little embarrassed at being caught. "I should know better than to think you're not aware."

"Yeah. You should." He grinned to show that he was teasing and asked, "You got news for me, eh?"

"Yeah. I do. Can we go someplace private?"

Dog Leg tilted his head toward me. "Dat bad, is it?"

"It's . . . sensitive," I said.

Very deliberately he put his trumpet in its case, settled a herringbone newsboy cap on his head, and reached for his white cane. "Okay, den. Let's take a walk."

I led him through the bar and out onto the sidewalk where the air was still and hot and heavy. Dog Leg pulled a handkerchief from his pocket and mopped his face, leaning heavily on his cane as he did. I'd never seen him truly show his age before, and it shook me to see him looking so old now.

"What you find out?" he asked as he put the handkerchief away again.

I glanced around to make sure I could find an empty bench and saw one about half a block away. "Do you want to sit?"

"Not especially. Say what you gotta say, Rita. I can take it."

Maybe he could, but I wasn't so sure I could. Perspiration beaded on my nose and upper lip. From the heat? Or nerves? Maybe both. "I found out that Monroe used to work with several of the people who live at the bed-and-breakfast. Some of the people I mentioned to you last time we talked."

"I remember."

"One of those men told me that forty years ago, they were all involved in a robbery that went bad. A security guard was killed in the process."

Dog Leg's entire body went still. "You sayin' Monroe was part of it?"

"Yeah," I said. "That's why he took off last time."

Dog Leg pushed the hat back on his head, settled it back in place, and then moved it again. "So he was in on a murder."

I couldn't just leave it like that, so I plunged on. "I was told that they'd planned the robbery so they could be in and out before the guard came by on his rounds. But apparently Monroe tripped an alarm accidentally, and the guard came back early. They were disguised and they tried to get out, but Monroe called one of the other men by name. The guard recognized them and pulled his weapon."

"Who shot him?"

"A guy named Willie Fiske. He was the leader of the group, I guess. He took the fall, went to prison, and died there. Willie's widow and his sister-in-law are the ones who own the inn where Monroe was staying. You remember Lula Belle? She's Willie's sister, and she lives there, too, along with some of the men who were in on the robbery."

"Dese people hate my brother."

"I don't know about *hate*, but some of them blame him

for what happened back then, yes. Others claim to be more forgiving. At this point I still don't know who is lying and who is telling the truth."

"And dat's why Monroe ran off."

"I haven't been able to ask him, but that's what I'm guessing."

"Stupid damn fool." Dog Leg mopped his face again and lifted his face to the night sky. "Stupid. I told dat boy a million times you don't trust nobody. I told him everybody's got an angle. I *told* him people would use him. Would he listen to me? No! Monroe never listened to nobody. Always said he knew what he was doing. Didn't need nobody to look after him. Well, look what good it did him. He's in some kind of mess now, too, isn't he?"

"It sure looks like it," I said.

Dog Leg nodded slowly, but I could tell he was having a rough time with the news I'd just delivered. He ran a handkerchief along the back of his neck. "And de man who was killed on Friday night?"

"He was one of the men who took part in the robbery. I still don't know how his death is related exactly, but I'm sure it is." I wasn't so worried about Monroe right then. Dog Leg had my full attention. "Are you all right? Are you sure you don't want to sit down?"

He shook his head. "I'm fine. I'm just wonderin' how my mother ever gave birth to sucha damn fool." He turned his face to the street and tried to compose himself, but anger poured from him as thick and heavy as the humidity in the air. "You still don't have no idea where he is?"

"None," I said. "Apparently, he was married and lived in Oregon for many years. He has children and grandchildren there, so he may be going back home. He hasn't tried to contact you, has he?"

"I'd of told you if he had."

"I really don't know where else to look," I said. "But I hope the police will be able to track him down soon."

"De police? What dey gonna do to him?"

"They'll bring him in for questioning," I said. "Maybe he can help them catch Dontae's killer."

Dog Leg shook his head and gave a sharp laugh. "You t'ink de police gonna just talk to him, you don't know how my world works. Dey t'ink he's guilty of killin' a man, Monroe won't be around to answer questions."

"I'm sure that's not true," I said. "Sullivan's on the case, and you've met him. You know he won't let something like that happen."

But Dog Leg wasn't listening. He let his cane clatter to the ground, and he grabbed my hands in his. "You gotta find him, Rita. Find dat idiot brother of mine 'fore somebody else do."

I didn't have the resources or the time, or any idea where to start. But my mouth and my brain weren't working in sync. My heart took control and I heard myself say, "Okay. I'll try."

I might as well have promised to fly to the moon. I probably had a better chance of succeeding at that.

Thirty-one

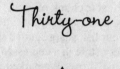

Miss Frankie picked me up promptly at nine on Wednesday morning to go look at the properties she was thinking of selling. I filled a couple of travel mugs with coffee and carried them out to the car, stashing them in cup holders while we buckled ourselves in for the ride.

She was wearing a tan linen pantsuit and a pair of sensible shoes suitable for walking. Her hair had been teased and sprayed so that it would hold up in any weather, and she carried a clipboard loaded with a small stack of papers. I was much more casual in a pair of spice-wash bell-bottom jeans, a striped boatneck T-shirt, and Tory Burch flats I'd picked up at a sale a few weeks earlier.

"I sorted the list by location," Miss Frankie said when she saw me eying the clipboard. "I asked Thaddeus's assistant to print driving directions, so we should be all set. You navigate. I'll drive."

She weaved in and out of traffic while I gave her directions to the first three locations on the list. The first was a small white frame office building located on a busy street corner in the Rivertown District, the second a recently deserted building that had once housed a tire store and a car wash, and the third a small lot on an industrial parkway complete with a tiny two-room building that, according to Miss Frankie's property manager, could be used as a restaurant or a residence. None of the buildings were worth much, but Thaddeus believed the land would bring in a sizeable chunk of cash.

We made notes, discussed options, and headed for the fourth property on our list: a large gutted space that had once been a corner grocery store in a depressed area of town. The clouds gathered as we drove. We parked a couple of blocks from the store and started walking. A block from the car, lightning flashed and the skies opened up, dumping rain on us like someone had overturned a bucket.

Miss Frankie gasped in shock and held her purse over her head. I calculated that the purse would keep her dry for about three seconds and another lightning bolt convinced me we had to find someplace to get out of the storm.

Going all the way back to the car wouldn't be safe, but our other choices were limited. There was a pawnshop of questionable nature across the street, or a bar—equally questionable—on the corner. Neither option appealed to me, but a flash of lightning and the pop and sizzle of a strike nearby convinced me that we needed to get inside fast.

I grabbed Miss Frankie by the hand and tugged her toward our closest option—the bar. "Come on!" I said, wiping rainwater from my face so I could see.

"Where?"

"There." I jerked my head toward the bar, and in doing that I saw a third choice I hadn't previously noticed. Next to the bar sat a small building with a cross on the front. Figuring that a church would be safer than the bar, I changed course and splashed through a puddle that soaked my new shoes and the hems of my pants. Miss Frankie's linen suit was plastered to her, and I discovered that there are limits to even Aqua Net's holding power.

Breathless and laughing a little at our bedraggled appearances, we pushed open the church's door and stepped into a small foyer roughly the size of a postage stamp. A heavy iron candelabrum hung on one wall. Beneath it sat one lopsided chair. I urged Miss Frankie toward the chair and shook rain from my hair while I looked around for someone in charge.

"Hello? Is anyone here?"

I heard a rustling sound and the hush of footsteps on carpet, and then a man came around the corner. He stopped in his tracks when he saw me, and my mouth fell open in dismay when I recognized him.

"Mrs. Broussard! What are you doing here?"

A wave of panic washed over me. I felt like a small child who'd just been caught holding the broken pieces of her aunt's favorite vase. Out of nowhere, I realized I'd been caught in a lie—several of them in fact. I tried to catch Miss Frankie's eye so I could signal her to play along, but she wasn't looking at me. She had collapsed into the chair just a moment before, but now she stood and offered up her charming Southern-hospitality smile. "I'm Frances Renier, Rita's mother-in-law. How do you know Rita?"

Pastor Rod walked past me, hand extended. "Rod Kinkle. I'm the pastor here at the Fifth Street Church. I met Mrs. Broussard this weekend at the Love Nest Bed and Breakfast. She and her husband were on their honeymoon. If you're her mother-in-law, I guess that makes Gabriel your son?"

Of all the churches in all the world, I had to walk into his. *Dear God, please strike me dead. Now!* It was one thing to play honeymoon with Gabriel where it didn't really affect Miss Frankie, but I saw a wounded look slip across her face as Pastor Rod talked, and the game changed in that moment.

She turned toward me slowly. "Gabriel. Yes. The honey-moon." She's always unfailingly polite in public, and I'm sure no one else could have heard the pain in her voice. No one else knew how hard it was for her to pretend that Gabriel was her son, even for a moment. But I knew, and the guilt stole my breath away.

"I can explain," I said again. But before I got a chance, someone else came out of the sanctuary and my explanation was swallowed up by confusion. "Monroe Magee? What are you doing here?"

"What are *you* doing here?" Monroe countered, swearing under his breath when he recognized me. Pastor Rod shot him a warning look.

"We got caught in the storm," I said. "I didn't realize this was Pastor Rod's church." We all stood there for several uncomfortable seconds, waiting for someone to speak. Or maybe I should say, I waited for one of them to speak. Everyone else seemed to be waiting on me.

I mopped rainwater and nervous perspiration from my forehead with a sleeve. I knew I should call Sullivan imme-diately and tell him I'd found Monroe, but I convinced myself that turning in the missing Magee could wait a few minutes. "So this is where you disappeared to," I said, stating the obvi-ous. "Have you been here ever since Dontae died?"

Pastor Rod put a hand on Monroe's shoulder. "It's not what you think. He didn't kill Dontae."

A soft gasp escaped Miss Frankie's lips and too late I remembered I hadn't told her about the murder. She didn't say a word, however, and I made a mental note to thank her for going with the flow. "Maybe not," I agreed, "but running off with the Love Nest's van may not have been the best way to convince people of that."

Miss Frankie looked back and forth between us as we

spoke, and suddenly the light went on in her eyes. "Monroe Magee! Of course, you're the missing brother!"

Monroe flinched as if she'd tried to hit him, but then his eyes narrowed in suspicion. "Wait a minute. What do you know about my brother?"

"I can explain," I said. "But it may take a few minutes, and I think we'd all be more comfortable if we could sit while we talk. Is there somewhere we can go?"

Pastor Rod looked a little less friendly than usual, but he bowed stiffly and led us into the sanctuary. He spent a few minutes turning on lights and air-conditioning to relieve the stuffiness. Miss Frankie and I sat on the front pew. The pastor brought chairs for himself and Monroe so we could face each other.

"Let me start by making a confession of my own," I said when I couldn't avoid it any longer. "My name is not Mrs. Broussard. I'm Rita Lucero. Gabriel Broussard and I are just friends."

Pastor Rod creased his brow in confusion. "You came to the inn for a weekend tryst?"

Lightning flashed again, and a deep peel of thunder shook the windows. "Nothing like that," I said. "We checked in and pretended to be married because Monroe's brother asked us to."

Monroe rocked back in his chair so hard it nearly toppled over. "Donald had you check up on me?"

First of all, *Donald?* And second, his outrage ticked me off. "Can you blame him? You took off without a word, and you stayed away for *forty years.* He didn't even know if you were alive or dead."

"You think I *wanted* to disappear like that? I didn't have a choice! And if he cares that much, why didn't he just come and see me like I axed him to in my letter?"

"Because he wasn't sure it really was you. I mean, what kind of letter was that, anyway? *Hey, I'm back. Stop by if you want.* So he asked us to find out if you were the real deal or a con man up to no good."

Monroe snorted, but a fresh deluge of rain drumming on the roof swallowed the sound. "All he had to do was come and talk to me. He coulda told who I was with one look."

"It's not that simple," I snapped. "He lost his eyesight to glaucoma awhile back. He wasn't sure he could tell just from talking to you, so he told us where to find your birthmark."

Monroe shot a look at his shoulder as if he'd forgotten the birthmark existed, and all of his outrage vanished. "You telling me the truth? Donald's blind?"

"Yes, he is," I said, and Miss Frankie nodded confirmation. "He asked Gabriel and me for help, and we were happy to give it. He's been worried sick about you for forty years, and you haven't even bothered to let him know that you're alive and well."

As I spoke, Monroe began to hang his head, which I thought was exactly what he should have done. He should have felt ashamed of himself. But then I caught the look on Miss Frankie's face and realized that, on the shame front, I wasn't off the hook either.

She cleared her throat and clasped her hands on her lap—the very picture of a genteel Southern lady except for her rain-drenched clothes and her drowned-rat hair. "Now, don't be so hard on the poor man, Rita. I'm sure he has an explanation, just as I'm sure he'll give it to Donald when they finally get together."

A grateful smile tugged at Monroe's lips. "That's right, ma'am. I surely will. Just as soon as I get out of this mess I'm in."

"Monroe is trying to make his life right with God," Pastor Rod said. "He came to me seeking sanctuary. I couldn't turn him away."

I guess I couldn't fault him for that. I'd probably have done the same thing in his place. "I know you haven't notified the police that he's here. Am I right in guessing that you haven't told the others at the Love Nest?"

Pastor Rod shook his head. "I don't think they'd understand."

I had a feeling he was right about that. "Why were you seeking sanctuary?" I asked Monroe. "Because you thought you'd be accused of murder or because you thought someone was trying to kill you, too?"

Monroe looked at me strangely. "Because I know what happened to Dontae."

Miss Frankie leaned forward. "You saw? You know who killed that poor man?"

Monroe shook his head. "No. I wish I did. I was looking at the van that night." His eyes shot to mine, and a little excitement seemed to energize him. "You remember. You were there. Hyacinth said it wasn't working."

"I remember."

"Well, I was late back inside to dinner, so they saved me a plate."

"Hyacinth did? I thought she didn't serve latecomers . . . or guests."

Monroe snorted a laugh. "Yeah. Well, I wasn't really a guest, and I was staying in the annex with the others, so they included me."

"Which is only polite," Miss Frankie put in.

Right. "So Hyacinth saved some dinner for you."

"Truth is, I don't know who made the plate. It was just there in the kitchen, covered with plastic wrap and a piece of paper with my name on it. I was hungry, don't mind telling you that. I put it in the microwave to heat it up and then Dontae came in."

"Into the kitchen?"

He nodded. "Like he was watching for me, you know? He was mad. Said I had no business comin' back to New Orl'ns. He wasn't the only one who felt that way either."

Pastor Rod sighed, and we shared a look of agreement.

"So what else did he say? What did he want you to do?" I asked.

"He told me to get the hell out, so that's what I did."

"But not right then," I said.

"No. Not until later. Only thing I know for sure is, Dontae didn't try to kill me. If he had, he never woulda eaten from that plate."

"The plate that someone left for you in the kitchen?"

Monroe nodded. "He went off on me pretty bad. I didn't have no appetite when he finished, so I just left the plate. He grabbed it and dug in like he hadn't already had a dinner. An hour later, he was dead. But it coulda been me out there in the garden. Maybe it shoulda been me."

"You see why I had to keep quiet about Monroe being here?" the pastor said. "Someone may have tried to kill him, and considering what happened at Letterman Industries, calling the police wasn't an option. I couldn't put him in danger by telling anyone else he was here."

"I understand," I said at the exact moment Miss Frankie said, "You really had no choice, Pastor."

"I'm not so sure about that," I said. "What were you going to do, Monroe? Hide out here for the rest of your life?"

He shook his head and frowned. "No, but I figured I could lie low until the heat was off."

"Maybe," I said. "Sooner or later, someone would have figured out where you were. But here's the thing: the poison wasn't in the dinner. It was in a bowl of pudding Dontae ate while he was in his room. Was that part of the meal?"

Monroe looked shocked. "Pudding? No. I didn't see anything like that."

"Are you sure?" I asked. "Maybe it was in the fridge or something."

Monroe rolled his eyes toward the ceiling as if looking for the answer there. After a minute, he shook his head slowly. "Nope. I woulda noticed that. Got me a bit of a sweet tooth."

If the pudding that Dontae ate wasn't part of Monroe's meal, maybe Monroe hadn't been the intended victim after all. And that was a game changer. "So does that mean someone meant to kill Dontae?" I said.

Pastor Rod looked shaken. "So it would appear, but that doesn't make any sense. Who would have wanted him dead?"

I understood why the idea rattled him. It seemed pretty obvious that someone from the Love Nest had laced that pudding with the poison and then served it up to someone they'd called friend for nearly half a century. How could anyone be that cold? "Did any of the others have issues with Dontae?" I asked gently.

Pastor Rod shook his head. "Not that I know of. We've all been friends for years, but nobody has ever talked to me about having a problem with Dontae."

"What about you?" I asked Monroe. "Do you know if anyone had an issue with Dontae, or did he have any arguments while you were there?"

"Sorry. No. But, you know, I've only been back in town a few days. I barely know any of them anymore. All I know is that about an hour after we talked in the kitchen I saw Dontae go outside. He looked sick. 'Fact, he threw up right there. I figured he got sick on the food that was left for me, and I had a bad feeling about it."

Miss Frankie looked confused. "Why was that?"

"I knew what some of those guys was capable of, didn't I? And you saw the way they acted toward me. I was pretty sure my ass would be grass if I stayed."

"What do you mean by that?" I asked. "What are they capable of?"

Monroe slid a glance toward Pastor Rod and followed up with a shrug. "Couple of 'em used to be pretty hotheaded. You know . . . back in the day."

"Cleveland still gets a little hot under the collar," I said. "Did you see anyone hanging around Dontae's room or hear someone moving around in the hall? Anything?"

Monroe shook his head. "Sorry."

The thought crossed my mind that maybe someone had killed Dontae to frame Monroe, but that seemed like a real stretch. Who would kill a friend to hurt an enemy? Still, there had to be some reason for Dontae's death. *Someone* had put that poison in the pudding and had been careful enough not to leave fingerprints behind. "What else did Dontae say to you that night?" I asked Monroe.

He ran a hand across his face and thought back. "He said I'd ruined everybody's lives." He turned to Pastor Rod as if looking for understanding. "Said it was my fault Willie died in prison. Said if I hadn't tripped the alarm that night, none of it would have happened."

"But they were all in on the robbery," I pointed out. "They were all just as guilty as you were."

"Try telling them that," Monroe said sullenly. "They still think that if I hadn't been there, they'd a been in and out. Nobody woulda been caught. Tyrone wouldn't a been killed."

Pastor Rod nodded slowly. "I've thought about it a lot over the years. Wondering whether things might have turned out differently. It's impossible to say, of course, but some of the guys have convinced themselves that Monroe and Willie were solely responsible for Tyrone's death. They've managed to separate the robbery from the murder in their own minds. I suppose they had to do that to live with the guilt."

Big tears filled Monroe's eyes. "But I didn't know. I didn't *know.* You know that, Rod. You know I didn't do nothin' on purpose." Monroe mopped his face again and his shoulders began to quake. "Tyrone was my friend. I woulda never hurt him. I didn't know Willie and the others was packing."

I froze for a moment while that thought sank in. "Wait a minute. You mean Willie wasn't the only one with a gun that night?"

Monroe blinked a couple of times, confused. "They all had 'em. Dontae and Cleveland both had 'em. So did Grey."

"Did they pull their guns?"

Monroe's shoulders sagged. The more agitated he became, the more he sounded like his brother. "Ever'body did. *Ever'body.* I was da only person in dat whole place didn't have no gun."

My nerve endings tingled, and I leaned forward, wanting to make eye contact so he'd understand how important my next question was. "In that case, are you sure it was Willie who pulled the trigger?"

Monroe looked surprised by my question. He shared a look with Pastor Rod, who now looked pretty rattled himself. "Yeah. I'm sure. He said he done it, didn't he?"

I nodded. "That's what he said, but what if someone else actually took the shot that killed Tyrone?" There had been six men in that warehouse, not counting "Hot Rod," and three of them were now dead. "When you came back to town and stirred up the past, maybe the real killer got nervous. And if Dontae knew the truth, that would give somebody a pretty solid motive for wanting him dead."

Monroe shook his head again. "It wasn't like that. Willie did it. He must have. Why would he go to prison if he didn't?"

"That's a very good question," I said, musing over the

possibilities his story had brought up. "So you don't know for sure who actually killed Tyrone?"

Monroe looked miserable. "Not one-hundred-percent sure, no. But if Willie didn't pull the trigger that night, whoever did would of said something, wouldn't he? He wouldn't of looked Hyacinth in the eye and lied when we were talking about it the other night."

Pastor Rod looked uncomfortable. "No, I'm sure he wouldn't have."

They both had more faith in their friends than I did. "What night did you talk about it?" I asked.

"Wednesday?" Monroe tilted his head and thought. "No, it must of been Thursday. Wasn't it?"

Pastor nodded. "Yes, I believe it was."

"And the very next night, Dontae was killed." Interesting.

Monroe looked back and forth between Pastor Rod and me. "Well . . . yeah. But that's not why. It couldn't be."

The pastor looked away so quickly, I could almost smell guilt on his conscience. "I take it you don't agree, Pastor?"

He met my gaze with obvious reluctance. "I don't know what to think anymore," he admitted sadly. "Our conversation that night may have stirred things up a bit."

"How so?"

"None of us knew that there was any doubt that Willie pulled the trigger and killed Tyrone," he said. "Not until Monroe came back."

Oh, but he was wrong about that. One person had known, and I had a feeling that person was now dead. And I wasn't really any closer to understanding *who* had wanted him that way.

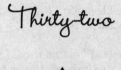

Thirty-two

The storm and meeting up with Pastor Rod and Monroe had put a crimp in our property inspection plans. I placed a call to Sullivan while Miss Frankie and I waited out the rainstorm at the church. His cell phone went straight to voice mail, and his number at the precinct rotated there after several rings, so I figured he was out on a case somewhere. I left messages at both numbers telling him I'd found Monroe and that I had more information about the robbery at Letterman Industries, and I asked him to call me as soon as humanly possible.

When the rain finally abated, I told Monroe to stay where he was and asked Pastor Rod to keep him safe, then escorted Miss Frankie back outside. Neither of us spoke until we were back inside the car, buckled up, and Miss Frankie was merging into traffic. "I'm sorry about that back there," I said. "I know it couldn't have been easy for you hearing the pastor refer to Gabriel as your son."

"No," she said softly. "It wasn't."

"I know you didn't approve of us pretending to be married,

but nothing happened between Gabriel and me. It wasn't like that."

"I believe you." But Miss Frankie clearly wasn't happy. It was written all over her face.

Droplets hit the windshield, signaling that another bout of rain was about to hit. I chewed on my bottom lip for a moment, trying to decide on the best approach to take now. "Miss Frankie, you know I love you," I said, sliding a glance at her to see how she reacted to that.

She blinked, once.

"When Philippe and I got married, I was deeply in love with him. But you also know that when he died, we were in the middle of a divorce. You know he was about to get married again."

I could see Miss Frankie tense, ready to argue, so I rushed on. "I know, I know. It doesn't make any sense to me either, but that's how it was. I get that you want to believe we would have gotten back together if he'd lived, but the fact is, our marriage was over. He'd moved on, and it's time for me to do the same."

"I know that," she said with a heavy sigh. "I do understand how the world works, Rita. And I think I've been quite understanding about your social life."

I smiled a little. "You have been. And for the record, I'm not interested in getting seriously involved with anyone right now. I have too much on my plate trying to get Zydeco back on its feet and establishing my professional reputation here in New Orleans. But I need to believe that you're not going to freak out if I occasionally date someone."

We stopped at a traffic light, and she took her eyes off the road for a moment. Her expression showed no signs of imminent irrational behavior, so I let myself relax.

"My concerns have nothing to do with that," she said. "I told you what worried me. Maybe I'm too stuffy or a bit old-fashioned, but Zydeco's reputation is important to me. I don't want anything to ruin it."

"It's important to me, too," I assured her. "I just . . ." I let my voice trail away while I tried to figure out how to explain what I was feeling.

She took advantage of my silence. "Rita, I don't object to you dating. I know you're going to move on. Just be careful. I don't want to see you get hurt. You're all I have left."

I laughed and put my hand on her arm. "Believe me, I don't want that either. But I have some bad news for you, Miss Frankie. Unless you decide to dissolve our partnership at Zydeco, you're stuck with me. I'm not going anywhere."

Miss Frankie dropped me at home, and I checked my cell phone for messages as I watched her drive away. I wasn't really surprised that I hadn't heard from Sullivan yet. If he was on a case, it could be hours before he called back. But I was worried about Monroe and Pastor Rod. If I'd found them at the Fifth Street Church, someone else could, too. I ran over what they'd told me as I let myself inside. Those old people had kept their secret for forty years without killing one another, so it seemed reasonable to assume that Monroe's return was the catalyst that had prompted one of them to strike out.

According to Pastor Rod, nobody had doubted Willie's guilt until Monroe came back to town. That fact brought me back to Hyacinth over and over again. Her husband had gone to prison and died there for a crime he might not have committed. How had she reacted to that news forty years after the fact? Had she found out that Dontae let Willie take the fall for something he had done? Had that pushed her so far over the edge she'd laced Dontae's pudding with poison to retaliate?

I puttered around the house for a while and then called

Sullivan's cell phone again, still hoping to run my ideas past him. Once again my call went straight to voice mail so I left another message asking him to call and disconnected before I remembered our conversation the day before when he'd mentioned going back to the Love Nest this afternoon. Determined to help the police unmask the killer before he—or she—could find Monroe at Pastor Rod's church, I left the house and drove to the Love Nest.

Hyacinth was dusting in the parlor when I walked in the front door.

She looked up with what for her passed as a smile, but it faded as soon as she saw me. "You're back."

I glanced into the other rooms I could see from where I stood, hoping to see Sullivan interrogating one of the residents, but I couldn't see anyone at all. Now that I was face-to-face with Hyacinth, I was a little nervous about admitting I was there to tell the police I thought she was a cold-blooded killer, so I decided to wing it and hope Sullivan would show up soon. "I think I left a ring in our suite," I said. "Would you mind if I took a look?"

"Tamarra and I cleaned that room yesterday. There wasn't a ring."

"Could I look anyway? I know right where I left it."

Hyacinth glared at me. "There was no ring. What do you really want?"

Clearly subterfuge wasn't working, so I tried a little honesty. "To ask a couple of questions. Do you have a minute?"

"You got a badge? Because if you don't, I'm through talking to you."

Despite her fierce demeanor, I didn't back down. "Who made the pudding Dontae ate the night he died?"

Her eyes flashed to my face, and her expression turned to stone. "What on earth are you talking about? What pudding?"

"Rice pudding. Did you make it?"

Hyacinth looked at me as if I'd sprouted a second head. "I may have. What about it? Don't tell me it's a crime to serve dessert to my guests."

"It is if the dessert contained poison."

Her eyes narrowed a little further. "I didn't poison nobody's food."

"Well, somebody did."

She put down her dust rag and turned toward me slowly. "Are you crazy, girl? What you doin', accusin' me of murder?"

This was not exactly the way I'd planned on our conversation going, but I knew it would be a big mistake to show fear now. "Should I be?"

"Hell no! I didn't do anything wrong. You have a lot of nerve poking your nose into things that aren't any of your concern."

"But it is my concern," I argued. "Dontae was killed while I was sleeping right upstairs. I could have eaten that pudding myself."

"I doubt that. It was only for the folks in the annex."

"For everyone, or just for Dontae?"

Hyacinth just stared at me, so I tried a different tack. "It must have been quite a shock to find out that Willie may not have been the one who pulled the trigger that night at the warehouse. How angry were you when you realized that they'd let Willie take the fall for something he didn't do?"

Hyacinth moved to the table, sprayed and dusted with deliberation. Maybe she thought I'd grow tired of waiting for her to answer me. She was wrong.

"I know Monroe was there," I said. "I know that Pastor Rod was waiting outside in the car. That leaves Dontae, Grey, Cleveland, and your husband Willie inside, and all four of them were armed, isn't that right?"

She still didn't answer.

"Did someone other than Willie fire the shot that killed Tyrone? Which one let Willie die in prison?"

Hyacinth sprayed a chair and dusted it.

Okay, so she was more patient than I am. Point made. "Look, Hyacinth, it doesn't matter whether you talk to me or not, I'm still going to tell the police what I've learned. In fact, I've already left messages about it, and I'm meeting the detective on the case here. The story is going to come out. You can't stop it."

Hyacinth swore under her breath and tossed her dust rag onto the table. "Why are you doing this? What does any of this matter to you?"

"I'm a friend of Monroe's brother, and I'm not going to let him take the fall for something one of you did. If you didn't kill Dontae, why are you trying to protect a killer?"

"You don't understand," she said. "You don't understand anything."

"I understand that you're all afraid that Cleveland, Grey, and Pastor Rod are too old to go to jail for something they did a lifetime ago."

She sighed and sank onto one of the chairs. "Okay. Fine. You're right. Grey and Cleveland were in the warehouse with Dontae and Willie. That idiot Monroe set off an alarm, and Tyrone came to see what was going on."

"And Monroe called Willie by name."

She nodded. "Everything would have been fine if he hadn't done that. Willie and the others would have gotten away. But Tyrone was a friend. He knew them, and when Monroe used Willie's name, they knew it was all over."

"Willie must have believed that Tyrone would shoot him."

"Willie knew that Tyrone would turn them all in, but he couldn't have that."

That was the part I still didn't understand. "But why? I mean, the two of you were married and had a family. How could he just throw himself under the bus and spend the rest of his life in prison?"

"Wasn't like he had a choice about that, now was it? He was going to prison no matter what. But Dontae didn't have to go. He was married, too, and they had a brand-new baby. She left him shortly after the robbery, but by that time it was all decided. Cleveland's mother needed him. We didn't know what it was called back then, but we found out later she had Alzheimer's. She couldn't be left alone. And Grey? He's . . . fragile, in a way that I can't explain. You see how he is. Dressing up like a damn fool so he can teach those kids nobody else cares about. You can't put a man like that in a cell with some thug. Prison would have killed him. And besides, Willie felt responsible. The whole plan had been his idea in the first place, and he's the one who'd convinced the others to bring Monroe into it. And he thought he'd killed Tyrone."

"So he sacrificed himself?"

"They had him for the robbery. They could prove he was there. Had his gun, dropped in the confusion after the shooting. The bullets matched the one they found in Tyrone. Ratting out the others wouldn't have made any difference, I guess.

"By the time the police found Tyrone's body at the warehouse, Monroe had already disappeared. For a while we thought he might resurface, but we worried about what he'd tell the police if he did. In the end, him disappearing that way was the best thing for everybody."

"Didn't you feel betrayed and angry with Willie?"

Hyacinth snorted a soft laugh. "Oh, baby, you don't know the half of it. I didn't even speak to the man for nearly ten years. I wouldn't go see him in prison. Wouldn't let Pearl see him. Wouldn't have a damned thing to do with him. I thought that if he could just turn his back on me that way, I'd turn my back on him, too. Seemed fair."

I couldn't argue with that. "What about Lula Belle? How did she feel?"

Hyacinth actually laughed. "She was mad at everybody for a while, but she found herself a sugar daddy and moved on."

"She wasn't angry about what happened to her brother?"

"Have you met the woman, baby? Oh, sure, she was angry for a time, but it's been forty years. Besides, Lula Belle's only concerned about Lula Belle. As long as somebody is taking care of her, she's fine."

"So eventually you forgave Willie?"

"Pastor Rod helped me to understand. He said it was for me, not for him. All that anger . . . it wasn't doing me any good. I guess he was right. I did feel some better once I let it go."

I was really trying to believe her. Or maybe I was trying not to. Because if Hyacinth wasn't angry with Dontae, my whole theory fell apart. And that meant that I'd been focused on the wrong person. Hyacinth put both hands on her ample hips and glared at me. "Now I got a question for you. Do *you* feel better now that you've stirred up all this trouble and made us think about things we'd buried in the past?"

"You can't blame me for that. I'm not the one who stirred things up."

"No? Well, have it your way. But I think you've done enough. You're no longer welcome here, Mrs. Broussard. It's time for you to make yourself scarce."

I wanted to hang around and wait for Sullivan, but maybe that wasn't such a good idea after all. Hyacinth might not be a murderer, but she was still a force to be reckoned with. I decided to be smart and take her advice.

Thirty-three

❧

I left Hyacinth glowering after me and hurried back to the Mercedes I'd recklessly left parked on the street. I sat there for a few minutes, trying to make myself inconspicuous—as inconspicuous as a woman in a Mercedes could be in that neighborhood—and thinking about what Hyacinth had just told me, reconciling it with what I already knew. And I came to the obvious conclusion: if Hyacinth hadn't put the poison in Dontae's pudding, maybe Primrose had. Or Lula Belle.

They both had the means and the opportunity. And Pastor Rod had told me that Primrose was intensely protective of the people she loved. How far would she go to protect them? Hyacinth was fierce but Primrose was unsettled, and I found that far more frightening.

I thought about calling Gabriel to bring him up to speed, but there was still the awkwardness of our last morning here at the Love Nest between us, and I wasn't sure how to get past it. Deciding that avoidance was the most sensible course of action—at least for today—I looked around for a police presence, hoping to spot Sullivan somewhere.

No such luck.

I really had stirred the pot this time. If Hyacinth told the others about our conversation, the killer would probably get nervous. I wasn't brave enough or foolish enough to walk back inside and incur her wrath. Nor did I want to confront any of the others alone. Right now, I had a whole lot of nothing. Even if I was right, Sullivan couldn't do anything based on what I merely thought might have happened. I needed to find physical evidence that would actually help him make a case. Like maybe an empty bottle of poison with Primrose's fingerprints on it.

While I tried to figure out what to do, Primrose herself rounded the back of the inn and onto the driveway, carrying a bulging white trash bag. Immediately, I sank down in my seat and hoped she wouldn't spot me. Primrose walked slowly, hauling the garbage toward a hulking metal Dumpster a little way beyond the garage. It seemed to take her forever, but she finally got there. She put the trash bag down and paused for a moment to catch her breath. Then, with a guilty glance around, she lifted the lid a few inches with one hand and pushed the bag inside with the other.

I didn't know what was in that bag, but the furtive way she'd acted convinced me it contained something important. I stayed where I was until she went back inside the inn, then I got out of the car and moved stealthily up the driveway. My heart was pounding, and my senses were ultra-alert. Every sound felt ominous, every shadow threatening.

Was garbage considered private property? Or did it become public property once it was thrown into the trash receptacle? I was pretty sure it was safe for me to check, but could I base such an important decision on reruns of *Monk*? It was a risk, but I didn't have time to do the research.

My own breath sounded like thunder in my ears. I skirted along the fence, past the locked gate to the garden, and finally reached the Dumpster. Working as quietly as possible, I lifted its giant metal lid. The hinges groaned and squealed, and my heart worked like a jackhammer inside my chest.

Once I had the lid open, I stood on tiptoe to look inside. The bag Primrose had just tossed lay among at least ten other identical bags, several of which had split open. Wet garbage, coffee grounds, fruit peelings, and eggshells covered almost everything in sight, making it impossible to tell which bag had been added most recently.

I frowned at the mess in front of me for way too long. I was out in the open, exposed to anyone who might glance out one of the inn's windows. Like, oh say, the killer. Watching me look for evidence.

I needed to do something. Fast!

Holding my breath, I stepped up onto a piece of metal and leaned into the container, snatching the first bag my hand brushed against. I clutched it as if it contained the Hope Diamond, and scurried from the Dumpster, heading for the garage several feet away.

The bag chunked against my leg as I walked, and the sound of tin cans and glass banging together sounded so loud to me I was sure someone would come to see what all the noise was. Finally, as I leaned against the garage's rear exterior wall, out of the inn's line of vision, I put the bag on the ground.

And stared at it.

Now what?

Wet coffee grounds dripped from the side of the bag like grains of damp sand. As a particularly large blob plopped onto the ground, I realized that maybe I hadn't thoroughly thought through this move. I couldn't hide out in the garden and paw through the rubbish without being caught. I couldn't very well haul the trash bag all the way back to my car. And what if this wasn't even the right bag? Running back and forth between the Dumpster and the garage half a dozen times hauling trash to and fro just wasn't going to work.

I was standing there chewing a thumbnail and considering my options when I heard the scuff of shoe leather on pavement and my heart stopped beating completely. An instant later, my pulse exploded, making the previous jackhammer rhythm seem cool, calm, and collected in comparison.

A shadow fell across my hiding place. Frantic, I looked around for someplace to hide, but there was literally nowhere for me to go. A crumbling fence enclosed two sides of the area where I now cowered behind the garage, and the garage itself backed onto the third. That left only the direction the noise was coming from.

The shadow grew longer, and then I found myself looking up at a doughboy from World War I, his wool service coat buttoned up to the neck, his riding-style breeches bloused at the hip and laced below the knee. He wore a wool cap and leather boots—and he seemed almost surprised to see me crouching there with my back against the garage.

"Mrs. Broussard? What are you doing? I thought you and your husband had checked out of the Love Nest."

I laughed, embarrassed by my reaction, and stood slowly. I brushed dirt and coffee grounds from my hands onto the seat of my jeans. "We did. I . . . uh . . . left something in our room."

Grey Washington—or whoever he was this afternoon—ran a look over me and then moved on down to the trash bag. "And you think you'll find it in there?"

Another nervous laugh bubbled up to my lips. "Funny story—" I moved away from the trash bag as if distance might keep me safe. "Primrose thought it was garbage, but it was actually some important work papers."

"Why didn't you just ask her for it?"

That was a good question. "I got here too late," I improvised. "She'd already thrown it out."

I don't think Grey believed me. Imagine. It was such a great story. "Did you find . . . whatever it was?"

I glanced down at my empty hands and shook my head. "Not yet. But I haven't had a chance to look in the bag yet." Maybe I'd get lucky and find some generic documents I could claim as my own.

Grey tilted his head and looked again at the trash bag. "Do you need some help?"

"No. Thanks. You're all dressed up. I wouldn't want you to ruin your uniform." I kept my tone chatty and friendly as I bent over the bag. The smell of something rotten wafted up to greet me, and I barely contained my gag reflex. "Are you on your way to the library?"

Grey glanced down at his uniform as if he'd forgotten he was wearing it. "Yes. At least I was."

"Well, then, don't let me keep you."

"Mrs. Broussard—" His voice sounded strange, and a look of regret tugged at his face. "I really wish you hadn't come back."

And for the first time I started getting a bad feeling about being out there alone with him.

"Oh?" I chirped. "Why?" I was still trying for friendly and chatty, but I'm pretty sure I sounded like a wind-up toy. If ever there was an inappropriate moment for my cell phone to ring, this was it. So, naturally, that's exactly what it did.

Grey's eyes narrowed, his hand moved, and before I could blink I was looking down the barrel of a handgun. It was the only thing about him that wasn't in costume, though I'm pretty sure it was vintage. I guessed it to have been a popular model of handgun back in the seventies. The kind of gun someone might use if he wanted to steal a hot load of eight-track players.

Sweat rolled down my spine. "Grey?"

"Take out your phone," he ordered.

I did what he said, keeping one hand in the air and using two fingers to pull the phone from my pocket. I tried to glance at the screen, but Grey yanked the phone from my hand and smashed it beneath his boot before I could see who was calling.

My spirits sank.

"What are you really doing here, Mrs. Broussard?"

The gun and his display of temper convinced me this wasn't a good time to come clean about my true identity, so I just shrugged, as if I wasn't bothered by the gun he'd pulled on me or how he'd destroyed my cell phone. "I told you. I'm looking for something my husband and I left behind when we checked out."

"I don't believe you. What are you really looking for?"

The way I saw it, I had two choices: tell the truth, or lie through my teeth. Lying didn't seem to be working all that well, but I wasn't convinced the truth would serve me any better. How would he react if I told him I was looking for proof that Primrose had killed Dontae? Especially since I was now sure that evidence didn't exist?

There was a third option: *Run!* But I put my chances of outrunning a bullet right at *no way in hell*.

I wondered if Grey was using new ammunition or old, and if it would make any difference if he decided to pull the trigger. If that was the gun he'd used during the Letterman Industries robbery, there was a chance he didn't have any ammunition at all. But that wasn't a risk I was willing to take.

He was waiting for an answer, so I decided to try my luck with option number two: the truth. "I was looking for proof that Primrose put the poison in Dontae's food."

"You thought Primrose killed him?" He seemed honestly surprised.

"I did," I said, mentally adding, *right up until you pulled out that gun.* "I'm confused. Why did you do it? Was it because you found out that Dontae killed Tyrone in the robbery?"

His brows knit in confusion. "Dontae? You think—" He let out a sharp laugh. And that's when I realized that once again I'd been on the wrong trail. The light dawned as if storm clouds had parted inside my head. "Dontae didn't kill Tyrone, did he? You did. But why did you kill Dontae now? Why was he a threat to you after all this time?"

"I just wanted to keep things the way they were," he said. His hand trembled, which meant that he was either emotional or nervous. Either way, I didn't think it was a good sign. "There was no reason to dig up the past. Everything was copacetic."

Thirty years living in a bed-and-breakfast? No wife? No family? That didn't sound copacetic to me, but nobody had asked my opinion. "But Dontae wasn't responsible for digging up the past," I pointed out. "So why kill him?"

"Because he was scared," Grey said. His voice was filled with disgust. "Oh, he put up a good act, but that was Dontae for you. When things got hairy, he panicked. The very minute Monroe came back, Dontae started imagining cops everywhere. He was even dreaming about going to jail, expecting the worst just like he always did. He came to me one night after Monroe showed up, whining about what he thought might happen. I tried to convince him that everything would be all right, but he wouldn't listen."

Well, I did. I listened intently to every word that came out of Grey's mouth. But I was also trying to figure out a way to save myself. I still couldn't see a way to slip past him to freedom, and I couldn't see anything I could use as a weapon either. I decided my only chance was to attract attention so I could get help. Until I could figure out how to do that, I needed to keep Grey talking. If he was thinking about answers to my questions, maybe he wouldn't be thinking about pulling the trigger.

"Why was Dontae worried about what Monroe would do?" I asked.

Grey dipped his head slightly. "I told you, he always ran scared. A man that size . . . you'd think he could hold his own, but he was afraid of his own shadow. Monroe opened his yap at the warehouse, and Dontae went ballistic. If he hadn't gone crazy like that, I never would have shot Tyrone."

His eyes looked a little wild, and the gun shook in his hand. "I did what I had to do in that warehouse. If I hadn't shot Tyrone, one of us woulda been dead. I protected the rest of 'em. That's the way it's always been."

Yeah. Right up until the moment you poisoned your friend. "I don't understand. Why kill Dontae instead of, say, Monroe? I thought Dontae was your friend."

"I just told you!" Grey shouted. "You're like everyone else. You're not *listening*." He swiped sweat from his eyes and readjusted his aim. "Dontae went crazy after Monroe showed up. Oh, sure. I could have gotten rid of Monroe. That was my plan at first, but Dontae was nuts by then. If I'd taken Monroe out of the way, Dontae would have turned me in. After everything we'd been through together, he got scared and *turned* on me."

"I am listening," I assured him as calmly as I could. "I'm just trying to understand. Why poison? Why didn't you just shoot him?"

Grey's gaze flickered down to the gun. "I never would have gotten the drop on him."

"So you put something in his food?"

"I told you. I did what I had to do."

If you say so. "Where did you get the poison?"

He looked at me as if I'd lost my mind. "What does it matter? It was lying around in the garage. Something Hyacinth used to kill bugs or something." His gun hand shook a little harder. He waved the pistol around in front of my face, threatening me. "Look, Mrs. Broussard, you're a nice lady. I don't want to hurt you. But I don't have any choice. You understand."

Um . . . not really. "But you do have a choice, Grey. Why don't you just put the gun down? Then we can figure out what to do next."

"No ma'am. You're just trying to trick me."

"No, I'm trying to save us both."

He choked out a laugh. "You can't save me."

He might be right, but I needed him to hold on to hope. Otherwise, he'd figure he had nothing to lose and I'd be leaving the Love Nest in a body bag.

"It's never too late," I said. I kept my voice low and soothing, but inside I was screeching like a banshee, trying to send a subliminal message across the miles to Sullivan—*Check your voice mail!*—and kicking myself for not letting Gabriel, or anyone else, know that I was coming back to the Love Nest.

I tried again to keep Grey talking. "Why don't you tell me exactly what happened with Dontae that night? Maybe there are extenuating circumstances. You said that you were trying to stop him from hurting the others, isn't that right?"

Grey removed his cap and tucked it beneath his arm, then wiped away a band of sweat that had formed under the hot wool. "I'm not a child, Mrs. Broussard. I know the law. I understand my position."

"Well then, try to understand mine." Confessing the truth was a huge risk, but I had to do something. Letting a crazy man with a gun think he was boxed in with no options wasn't working for me. "I'm working with the police, investigating Monroe Magee's reappearance after all these years and helping with the investigation into Dontae's murder."

Okay, so it wasn't *entirely* true, but it was close enough. Grey's gun hand dropped a fraction of an inch, and uncertainty flickered across his face. But that only lasted a second before he tightened his bead on me. "You *lied* to us?"

I gaped at him in disbelief. "You shot one man and poisoned another," I reminded him. "I don't think you can claim the moral high ground here. I'm a friend of Monroe's brother. He asked me to make sure the man who wrote to him really was his brother."

For the second time in thirty seconds, Grey's aim wobbled a little. "You know Old Dog Leg?"

I grasped at the hope that I'd found something that might help me. "He's a good friend. Do you know him?"

The cap slipped from under Grey's arm and fell to the ground, but he didn't seem to notice. "He was one of the best horn blowers around. That man could really jam."

"He still can," I said.

Grey ran a sleeve across his forehead. He seemed nervous, which worried me. A nervous man with a loaded gun could mean real trouble for the person in the gun's crosshairs.

"Tell me what happened the night Dontae died," I urged again.

Grey mopped his forehead again and loosened the button on his collar. "I told you. Dontae said—I—" He broke off and made a funny noise. "I—" Sweat poured off his face, and he put his free hand up to his chest.

"Grey? Are you all right?"

He staggered a little and slumped against the wall of the garage. "I think I—" His eyes grew wider, wilder, as if he couldn't believe what was happening.

"I think I'm having a heart attack!" he said, and then he collapsed to the ground.

Thirty-four

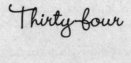

Grey hit the ground like a sack of potatoes, and all I could do was stare down at him. Was he *kidding* me? A heart attack?

My brain churned slowly while I tried to process what had just happened. Grey. Heart. Gun. Panic!

It seemed to take forever for my thoughts to begin connecting. When they finally did, I vaulted toward Grey, kicked the gun out of reach, and then hunkered down beside him to check for a pulse.

Nothing.

I grabbed him by the shoulders and shook him. "Grey? Can you hear me? Are you okay?"

Nada.

I put my ear by his nose and mouth and tried to pick up the sound of his breathing. If any air was getting in or out, I sure couldn't hear it.

"Help! Somebody! I need help over here!"

I'd had some CPR training. Once. A long time ago. Trying

to recall the instructions for saving a person's life was like trying to find a toothpick in a pile of sludge. Time seemed to crawl, but I knew my perspective was off. How long had he been lying there? Too long? Could I save him?

Should I?

The man was a confessed murderer. He'd poisoned a friend, and if his heart hadn't dropped him, he probably would have shot me. But I couldn't just let him die. My conscience wouldn't let me. Logical or not, I had to do everything I could to save him.

A wisp of memory floated to the surface. Something about making sure his airways were clear and unobstructed. I did my best to position his head the way I thought it should be, but I still couldn't hear him breathing.

I shouted for help again as I tried to remember how to position my hands on his chest. The heel of my hand in the middle of his chest. Was that right?

"Somebody," I shouted, "call 911! We need an ambulance now!"

How many breaths? How many compressions? My mind was a blank. Would I hurt him if I did this wrong? Would he die if I didn't?

I put one hand over the other and pushed. His chest compressed, and I felt a distinct *pop* beneath my hand. I stopped pushing, and his chest snapped back into position. Had I pressed too hard, or not hard enough?

Frantic to save him, I shoved aside the self-doubt and threw myself into the task. Ten compressions. Twenty. I did thirty for good measure and then pinched his nose and covered his mouth with my own.

I blew into his lungs hard enough to make his chest rise. Once. Twice. As I quieted my mind, the lessons I'd learned crystallized. Thirty compressions. Two rescue breaths. I focused my energy on counting and breathing over and over again. My arms and lungs ached, and I prayed alternately that Grey would wake up and that he wouldn't throw up in my mouth when he did.

After what felt like forever, I heard sirens, then footsteps pounding up the driveway. Someone pulled me away from Grey, and someone else took over the CPR.

"Are you all right, ma'am?"

I looked into the concerned brown eyes of a young Hispanic woman in uniform. "Is he alive?"

"I don't know, ma'am. Someone's working on him now. Can you tell me what happened?"

I shook my head and felt my limbs begin to shake. "I think he had a heart attack."

"Your name, ma'am?"

"Rita. Lucero." My legs buckled, and tears filled my eyes. "Is he going to be all right?"

"We're doing our best, ma'am. Do you know his name?"

"Grey Washington." My throat hurt, and my mouth felt like someone had filled it with ash. I wondered where his gun had gone, and I wondered what was going to happen to him now. He'd admitted to killing Dontae, and I honestly think he would have killed me, but for some reason I couldn't understand I still hated the thought of him going to prison.

I heard voices and I turned, catching sight of Hyacinth, Primrose, and Lula Belle huddled together near the garage. They looked terrified, and my heart twisted for them.

Heavy footsteps sounded somewhere behind me, and then Sullivan was there, pulling me close in his strong arms. "Rita! Are you okay?"

I choked back a sob and collapsed against him, relishing the safety of being with him. I tried to nod, but it took some effort to get my head moving. "He did it," I croaked. "Grey killed Dontae. He was going to shoot me. His gun is somewhere around here."

"I tried calling when I got your message," he said. "The call went straight to voice mail."

"My phone's around here somewhere, too. In a million pieces."

He pressed me away from him and looked me over carefully. His eyes were strong and gentle at the same time. "Why didn't you wait for me?"

"I didn't think I had time."

"You could have been killed."

I managed a weak smile. "Yeah, I got that."

He brushed a lock of hair from my forehead, his fingers lingering for a fraction of a second. And then he covered my mouth with his and kissed me thoroughly. I responded with great enthusiasm, and it was a few minutes before either of us spoke again.

"I should have known you'd do more than ask a few questions," he said when we came up for air.

"Yeah," I said. Thanks to his unique brand of CPR, I felt a little stronger now. "You should have." I tried to stand on my own, but my legs felt like rubber. "Do you think I could sit down somewhere? Otherwise, you may need to call the paramedics for me, too."

Sullivan actually looked a little sheepish. "Of course. I want them to check you out anyway."

It wasn't until we turned to walk down the driveway that I caught the shocked expression on Hyacinth's face and the scandalized look on Primrose's. Apparently, they had objections to a new bride kissing a man who wasn't her husband. Lula Belle, on the other hand, looked impressed. She even gave me a discreet thumbs-up as Sullivan and I passed.

I guess we shameless hussies have to stick together.

Thirty-five

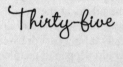

Sullivan followed me home and stuck around for a while that evening to make sure I was really okay. I spent Thursday morning at work and most of the afternoon at the police station answering questions and giving my official statement about my encounter with Grey. On Friday, I spent several hours locked up with Miss Frankie, Thaddeus, and a real estate agent.

After some debate, Miss Frankie had decided to sell a lot and small office building located on Poydras, but both Thaddeus and the real estate agent had warned us that the transaction could take a while. Selling the property would ultimately provide a fix for Zydeco, but the next few months might still be touch-and-go. Miss Frankie was still adamantly opposed to making the changes Ox had suggested at the bakery, but I hadn't had a chance to tell him that yet. Or maybe I'd just neglected to take the chance. To paraphrase Scarlett O'Hara a little, tomorrow was bound to be a better day.

By the time the meeting ended, I was ready for life to get

back to normal so I drove straight to the Dizzy Duke. I still didn't know how to clear the air with Gabriel, but the Magee brothers would be performing together for the first time in forty years, and I wasn't going to let a little awkwardness keep me away.

Grey had survived his heart attack, but he was still in pretty rough shape. The prognosis for recovery was good, but I was concerned about the others at the Love Nest. Every one of them had been involved in the robbery and murder in some way, either by actively taking part or by covering it up later. I wondered what would happen to them now.

I'm a big believer in the concept of facing up to the consequences of our choices, but I wasn't sure that hauling the whole senior citizen gang to prison was the right solution in this case. Maybe it was a good thing that I wasn't the one who had to make the decision. I'm not sure I could have done it.

Just thinking about what was going to happen to all those old people had given me a stress headache, so when I walked into the Duke I made a beeline for the bar. I claimed an empty bar stool, snagged a bowl of peanuts to munch on, and waited for Gabriel to notice me. I'd been avoiding him for days, but I didn't have Dontae's murder and the search for Monroe to distract me any longer. It was time to put on my big-girl panties and clear the air.

It took him about thirty seconds. He tossed a coaster onto the bar in front of me and treated me to a Sexy Cajun smile that made me think we would be okay. "I was beginning to wonder if you were going to show up."

"I was in a meeting and it ran a little late, but I wouldn't miss this for the world."

He searched my face for a moment. "You're okay?"

"Yeah. Thanks. Look, I'm sorry about what happened the other night. I didn't lie to you. I just—" I broke off, uncertain how to finish that sentence. I took a deep breath and tried again. "Thanks for caring. I don't always handle it well, but I do appreciate it."

"Good to know." He leaned across the bar and kissed me quickly.

I relaxed into him, savoring the sensation. He moved away sooner than I'd have liked. I hid my disappointment and asked, "Does this mean we're okay?"

"Oh, we're not finished with this conversation," he said. "But this isn't the time or the place for all the things I plan to say."

I didn't know what he meant by that, but I didn't want to worry about anything tonight so I filed his cryptic warning away for later and tried to relax. Behind me, the band was just finishing its first set of the night. After a short break, Old Dog Leg and Monroe would be taking the stage and the Magee brothers would be performing together for the first time in forty years. "How are the brothers doing? Have you seen them?"

Gabriel nodded toward a table near the stage. "They're over there. Monroe's a little nervous, I think. Dog Leg's cool. They've been here most of the afternoon, running through their set and catching up between songs."

I craned to see the two old men. Dog Leg looked happy, and that was enough for me. "So what do you think? Will Monroe stick around this time?"

Gabriel lifted one shoulder. "He won't have much choice if he goes to jail."

"I don't think that's going to happen," I said. "I heard from Sullivan this afternoon. The district attorney isn't going to prosecute. The statute of limitations ran out long ago on the armed robbery charges, and there's no evidence to build a case against any of the gang on the murder charges."

Gabriel looked surprised. "Even with Grey's confession?"

I nodded. "He's recanting already, and even with my testimony the case isn't strong enough to get a conviction on Tyrone's murder."

Gabriel rubbed his chin thoughtfully. "Then I guess there's not much for Monroe here except his brother. But to hear him talk there's nothing for him anywhere else. His wife died a few years back, and his kids are scattered around the country. Busy with their own lives. I think he'll give it a try here. Maybe now that the truth is out, he'll be able to patch things up with the rest of the gang."

"Those old folks really wormed their way into your heart, didn't they?" I teased.

"Not all of them," Gabriel said. "But I have to admit I'm really going to miss seeing Lula Belle."

I laughed. "Should I be jealous?"

"Well, she did try to warn you."

"Yes she did." I heard Old Dog Leg laugh, and I turned in time to see Monroe grin. It did my heart good to see them together and that Monroe really would give sticking around a fair shake. When I turned back to Gabriel, he'd grown serious again.

"And what about the professor?"

"Sullivan told me that Grey's condition has been upgraded to stable. He'll remain under a doctor's care for a while, and the district attorney is going to ask the judge to be lenient when it comes to sentencing in light of his advanced age and his health issues."

Gabriel's expression went from Sexy Cajun to Volcanic Eruption in a blink. "Lenient? Are you kidding me? The guy is certifiable. He shot Tyrone, he poisoned Dontae, and he would have killed you if he hadn't keeled over."

My independent streak reared its ugly head, but I shoved it down again. Everything he said was true, and I couldn't blame him for being concerned. "He's also eighty-two years old. I don't think prison with a bunch of gangbangers and meth heads is the answer for him."

"I don't see why not. It would give him a steady supply of underprivileged youth to perform for."

"They're not talking about letting him go free," I said. "They're going to ask that he spend the rest of his life under a doctor's care."

"If by *doctor* you mean *psychiatrist*, that might be okay. The man's dangerous, Rita. He shouldn't just be allowed to walk away after what he did."

I held up both hands in surrender. "Again, I don't disagree. I just don't think it makes sense to throw a sick old man into the general prison population. I hope they can find a compromise that works for everyone."

"Yeah. Okay. Whatever." The music stopped, and Gabriel pushed away from the bar.

I reached for his hand before he could get away. "Thanks for caring, Gabriel. I mean that." Neither of us moved for a few seconds until another group of patrons entered the bar, Gabriel pulled his hand away. "Duty calls. They'll be starting their set soon. What can I get you?"

How about one of your incredible margaritas?" I said, reaching for my wallet.

"On the house," Gabriel said, patting the bar in front of him a couple of times. "Call it a divorce present."

A smile spread across my face. "Let's not get a divorce," I said. "Let's go straight for an annulment."

He laughed and his tension evaporated. "Ouch, that hurts. My ego may never be the same."

"You were a pain in the butt as a husband," I said. "But it was kind of fun, wasn't it?"

"Yeah. Right up to the part where you almost died. No man should lose his wife before the marriage is even consummated. It's not right."

"Ah! I see where your priorities lie."

He waved me off. "Go. Sit with your crew. I'll send your drink over." He jerked his chin toward several tables pushed together near the dance floor, where I saw that the Zydeco staff had all congregated.

Grinning from ear to ear, I made my way across the bar. I grabbed an empty chair from a nearby table and carried it with me the rest of the way. Isabeau greeted me with a little wave, and Ox gave me a manly nod. Sparkle rolled her eyes in my direction and looked away slowly, and Estelle shouted, "Rita's here y'all!" in case someone hadn't noticed.

Dwight scooted over a bit to make room for me, and I wedged my chair between his and Edie's.

I thought I spotted dark circles under her eyes, but she greeted me with a smile, so maybe it was just a trick of the light.

"How did your meeting with Miss Frankie and her attorney go?" she asked.

"It went well," I said. "Now we just have to cross our fingers and hope for a quick sale."

"How likely is that to happen?"

"No idea. It could take a while, but at least we're doing something to improve the situation . . . right?"

She shrugged.

I pressed on. "Just don't give up on me, okay? You can't leave Zydeco."

She turned her head slowly. This time I was sure about the shadows beneath her eyes. Was she ill or just tired? "You don't need me, Rita. You don't even really like me. You only put up with me because of Philippe."

I stared at her with my mouth wide open. "Is that what you really think?"

She stared back. "Are you trying to claim that we're friends?"

I wouldn't have said *friends*, but we'd been friendly—sort of.

Okay, she was right. Philippe had *liked* her; I'd *tolerated* her, usually in an annoyed manner because of the thing she had for Philippe way back when. He hadn't shared her feelings, but that didn't change the fact that she'd had them.

But as the folks at the Love Nest would say, that was all water under the bridge. And that's what I told her.

She ducked her head, probably embarrassed to find out that I'd known how she felt all along. "Nothing happened between us, you know."

"I know. That's why you're still at Zydeco." I grinned.

Her porcelain-doll lips quirked ever so slightly, but her eyes were still glazed with worry. The cocktail waitress interrupted us to bring my margarita, and I took a sip. Sweetly sour. Icy cold. A perfect rim of salt. Gabriel was so much more than just a pretty face.

"What if we can't pull Zydeco out of this hole?" Edie asked, jarring me from my private margarita moment.

"We will," I assured her.

"But what if we can't?"

"We *will*," I said again. "Miss Frankie's property will sell just in time. We'll get the money we need just in time. We'll get the customers we need to stay afloat between now and then, and we'll be fine."

Edie's lips twitched again. "I think you're being naïve."

The band took the stage again, and the lead singer, an aging guy with a long gray ponytail and a Fu Manchu moustache that would have put Fu himself to shame, introduced Old Dog Leg and his brother Monroe.

We fell silent and listened to them play. Despite all the years I spent with Philippe, it wasn't until I'd moved here to New Orleans that I'd really begun to learn about jazz, and though I couldn't name the first two numbers they played, at least the tunes sounded familiar. I counted that as a personal milestone—proof that I was acclimating to life in the Big Easy.

As they started the third song, Edie nudged me with her elbow and leaned close to shout in my ear. "I don't know if I can wait."

I dragged my attention away from the music and frowned at her. "Why not?"

"It's a bad time," she shouted. But the music was too loud, and her voice faded in and out. ". . . need a stable income . . . can't be without benefits right now . . . it's going to be rough . . ."

I cupped a hand around my ear to indicate that I hadn't understood, and then tried again to plead for patience. "Stick with me, Edie. Please. If we succeed, we succeed as a team. If we fail, at least we go down fighting."

She shook her head and said something back to me, but the music swallowed her words again.

I shook my head again and mouthed, "Later."

But she seemed determined to make me understand. "I wish . . . don't have time."

That got my attention. "Why? What do you need? Tell me and I'll find a way to get it for you."

She sighed with frustration and put both hands to her mouth. Just as the music died away, she bellowed, "I'm *pregnant*!"

People sitting a couple of tables away burst into spontaneous applause. The reaction at Zydeco's table was a bit more delayed. Dwight swore. Ox tipped back his head and laughed. Isabeau bounded out of her seat and wrapped Edie in an enthusiastic hug, and Estelle called over a cocktail waitress so she could order a round for the table.

Sparkle and I remained quiet. I was trying to figure out what I'd do with nine months of Edie fueled by emotions and hormone surges. Sparkle was apparently pondering something more concrete.

"Who's the father?" she asked when everyone settled down again.

Good question. I never would have asked that—at least not now, at the Duke, with everyone listening in. I hadn't even been aware that Edie was dating anyone. But that didn't stop me from holding my breath while I waited for the answer.

Edie waved away the question. "Nobody you know."

"Are you going to keep it?" Sparkle asked.

Edie frowned at her. "Yeah. I am. Do you have a problem with that?"

Sparkle actually smiled. "Naw. I love kids."

"The point is," Edie said, turning back to me, "I need things to be stable in my life right now. I have to know I can pay my rent and that I'm not going to lose my health insurance. I kind of need it right now."

I gulped another mouthful of margarita and sent her my very best smile. "You can pay your rent, and you'll have insurance. I promise." And then I put my arm around her shoulders and said, "You're going to be okay, Edie. We'll make sure of it." I looked at the others for backup, and bless their hearts, every person at the table gave it.

Edie grabbed a wad of napkins from the center of the table and pressed them to her eyes, and beneath my arm her shoulders began to shake.

I didn't know what else to say, so I told her what I'd want someone to tell me under the same circumstances. It's all I could do.

"It's going to be okay," I said again. "You're going to be okay. We'll look out for you and for the baby. We're family at Zydeco, and that's what family does."

Edie pulled the napkins away from her eyes and sniffed

loudly. She gulped hard, then gave a little laugh that might have been relief and threw her arms around my neck.

I could feel hot tears on my shoulder as I looked around the table at my staff. They were watching me carefully, listening to every word I said and filing away the promises I'd just made for future reference. They'd hold me to them and keep my feet on the ground. I could see it in their faces. But that's also what family does.

I had no idea how I was going to keep the promises I'd just made, but as I looked into the eyes of my friends, I knew I'd find a way.

The important thing was I wouldn't have to do it alone.

Recipes

Blueberry Sour Cream Coffee Cake

Yields one 9-inch Bundt cake

This is a delicious if admittedly less-than-healthy coffee cake. It's been a family favorite for years. Adjust the bake time to a bit longer if you're using frozen berries.

1 cup butter, softened
2 cups white sugar
2 eggs
1 cup sour cream
1 teaspoon vanilla extract
1 ½ cups plus 2 tablespoons all-purpose flour
1 teaspoon baking powder
¼ teaspoon salt
1 cup fresh or frozen blueberries
½ cup brown sugar

1 teaspoon ground cinnamon
½ cup chopped pecans
1 tablespoon confectioners' sugar for dusting

Preheat the oven to 350°F (175°C). Grease and flour a 9-inch Bundt pan.

In a large bowl, cream together the butter and sugar until light and fluffy. Beat in the eggs one at a time, then stir in the sour cream and vanilla. In a separate bowl, combine the flour, baking powder, and salt; stir the flour mixture into the wet ingredients until just blended. Fold in the blueberries.

Spoon half of the batter into the prepared pan. In a small bowl, stir together the brown sugar, cinnamon, and pecans. Sprinkle half of this mixture over the batter in the pan. Spoon the remaining batter over the pecan mixture, and then sprinkle the remaining pecan mixture over the top. Use a knife or thin spatula to swirl the pecan-sugar layer into the cake.

Bake for 55 to 60 minutes in the preheated oven, or until a knife inserted into the crown of the cake comes out clean. Cool in the pan on a wire rack. Invert the cake pan onto a serving plate, and tap firmly to remove the cake from the pan. Dust with confectioners' sugar just before serving.

* * *

White Chocolate Raspberry Cake

FOR THE CAKE

> ³/₄ cup butter, softened
> 2 ¼ cups sugar
> 4 eggs
> 1 cup white chocolate chips, melted and cooled
> 1 teaspoon vanilla extract
> 3 cups flour
> 1 teaspoon baking powder
> ½ teaspoon baking soda
> 1 cup buttermilk

FOR THE FILLING

> 2 cups fresh or frozen raspberries
> ³/₄ cup water
> ½ cup sugar
> 3 tablespoons cornstarch

FOR THE FROSTING

> 1 8-ounce package cream cheese (or Neufchatel cheese),
>   softened
> 1 cup white chocolate chips, melted and cooled (or substi-
>   tute vanilla chips)
> 1 12-ounce container of refrigerated whipped topping,
>   such as Cool Whip (or 1 ½ cups very stiffly whipped
>   cream)
> Fresh raspberries for garnish

FOR THE CAKE

Preheat the oven to 350°F (175°C). Grease and flour two round 9-inch cake pans.

In a large bowl, cream together the butter and sugar until fluffy. Add the eggs one at a time, mixing well after each addition. Beat in the melted chocolate and vanilla. In a separate bowl, combine the flour, baking powder, and baking soda.

Add the flour mixture to the butter mixture, one third at a time, alternating with some of the buttermilk after each addition. Stir until well combined.

Divide the batter evenly between the cake pans.

Bake in the preheated oven for 28 to 32 minutes until a toothpick inserted in the center of the cakes comes out clean. Cool 10 minutes in the pan, then turn the cakes out onto a wire rack to finish cooling.

FOR THE FILLING

In a small saucepan, bring the raspberries and water to a boil. Reduce heat and simmer for 5 minutes. Using a fine sieve, strain the raspberry mixture into a bowl. With a fork, press down on the berries to release their juice and pulp; discard the seeds and any remaining solids. In the same saucepan, combine the sugar and the cornstarch, and stir in the raspberry puree until smooth. Bring the mixture to a boil, then cook and stir for 2 minutes until thick. When cool, spread the filling on top of one of the cake layers.

FOR THE FROSTING

In a large bowl, beat the cream cheese until fluffy, stir in the melted chocolate chips, and then fold in the whipped topping.

Spread about a third of the frosting on the raspberry-filling-covered cake layer, then stack the second layer on top. Frost the top and sides of the cake, and garnish with fresh raspberries. Store in the refrigerator.

* * *

Cilantro Almond Chicken Salad

Serves 8 to 10

This recipe is adapted from the Village Tea Room, in New Paltz, New York. You can make it with any cooked chicken (rotisserie, roast, and maybe even canned if you're short on time), but for the best tasting and, if you are preparing the chicken yourself, the least heat-producing version in your summertime kitchen, use freshly poached chicken breasts. Skin-on, bone-in breasts produce meat with more flavor, and you can use the poaching liquid later for soups and sauces if you want.

FOR THE CHICKEN

> 4 large chicken breast halves, with skin and bone (about 1 pound each)
> ⅓ cup kosher salt
> 1 small carrot
> ½ onion
> ½ celery rib
> 4 parsley sprigs
> 2 to 3 quarts water

FOR THE DRESSING

> 2 cups slivered blanched almonds (about 6 ounces)
> 3 garlic cloves
> ½ to 1 fresh hot jalapeño, coarsely chopped, including
>   seeds
> ¾ cup mayonnaise
> ½ cup sour cream
> ½ cup fresh lime juice, or to taste
> 1 tablespoon kosher salt, or to taste
> 3 cups chopped cilantro

ACCOMPANIMENTS

> Mixed greens; roasted yellow, orange, or red bell peppers

POACH THE CHICKEN:

Coat the chicken with the kosher salt and let it sit in a large bowl at room temperature for about 20 minutes. Turn once or twice during the standing time.

Rinse the salt from the chicken, and put chicken breasts in a deep pot with the vegetables and the parsley. Add enough water to cover. Over medium-high heat, bring the pot just to a boil and skim the froth.

Reduce heat to a bare simmer (the water should "tremble," but you don't want big bubbles erupting on the surface) and poach the chicken, uncovered, for about 25 minutes, or until its internal temperature reads 160°F on an instant-read thermometer.

Remove the pot from the heat and let the breasts stand, uncovered, for about 20 minutes. Transfer the chicken to a large bowl and let it cool. If desired, reserve the broth; discard the vegetables and let the broth cool before chilling.

When the chicken is cool enough to handle, shred the meat; discard the skin and bones. This should yield about 8 cups of meat.

WHILE THE CHICKEN COOLS, MAKE THE DRESSING:

Preheat the oven to 350°F (175°C) with rack set in the middle. Place the almonds in a single layer on a four-sided sheet pan and roast until golden and fragrantly toasty, 10 to 15 minutes. Cool.

Drop the garlic into a food processor and finely chop. Stop the processor and add the desired amount of jalapeño, and the mayonnaise, sour cream, lime juice, and kosher salt. Blend until smooth.

Add the cooled almonds and pulse in the processor until the almonds are chopped. Add the cilantro and pulse until just incorporated.

Season with additional salt and lime juice to taste.

ASSEMBLE THE SALAD:

In a large bowl, toss the chicken with the dressing. If the salad appears dry, use some of the reserved broth to moisten. Serve with the mixed greens and roasted peppers.

The salad will keep, properly chilled, for 5 days. Bring it to room temperature before serving.

The leftover broth will keep, properly chilled, for 3 days or frozen for 3 months.

A heartless murder for Valentine's Day.

FROM

JENN MCKINLAY

Buttercream Bump Off

A Cupcake Bakery Mystery

Melanie Cooper and Angie DeLaura's Fairy Tale Cupcakes bakery is gearing up for Valentine's Day. Unfortunately someone has iced Baxter Malloy on his first date with Mel's mother. Now she's a suspect, and Mel and Angie need to find time between frosting Kiss Me Cupcakes to dig into Malloy's shady past and discover who served him his just desserts.

PRAISE FOR *SPRINKLE WITH MURDER*

"A tender cozy full of warm and likable characters . . . Readers will look forward to more of McKinlay's tasty concoctions."   —*Publishers Weekly* (starred review)

"A delicious new series!"
    —Krista Davis, author of the Domestic Diva Mysteries

INCLUDES SCRUMPTIOUS RECIPES!

facebook.com/TheCrimeSceneBooks
penguin.com
jennmckinlay.com

M980T0911